ONE MORE DEAD MAN

Colter cautiously raised himself to his hands and knees and peered at the battered, bloody face lying on the Paris cobblestones.

The agent was sprawled on his side. Blood ran from his mouth and nostrils, forming dark worms. There was a smear of blood beneath his right ear as well, caked now. The agent wasn't moving at all.

Feeling suddenly cold, Colter felt for a pulse, knowing he would find none. His own head still throbbed with pain and he gingerly touched his skull behind the ear, finding a knot the size of an egg.

Something had to be done, but he couldn't clear his mind. All he could do just then was sit there shivering, his arms folded, his head bowed. Death had come back. His old friend, old adversary . . . his constant companion.

THE COLTER CONSPIRACY

BY KEN CROWDER

ZEBRA BOOKS
KENSINGTON PUBLISHING CORP.

ZEBRA BOOKS

are published by

Kensington Publishing Corp.
475 Park Avenue South
New York, N.Y. 10016

First Printing: November 1984

Printed in the United States of America

ONE

The clanging of the iron bell brought Vesely's head up, and he lay staring at the darkness of the barracks, trying to convince himself that he was alive. It seemed a futile exercise and he gave it up, lying back briefly to listen to the grumbled curses, the coughing, the squeak of the beds as men groped for their boots, their greatcoats in the pre-dawn cold.

The barracks lights flickered on and Vesely squinted up at the bare bulbs strung along the center of the roof. Each had its own misty halo. The bell had stopped clanging and now the outer door burst open and the warders entered the barracks, stamping the snow from their feet.

"Come on, come on. It's five o'clock. Everyone get up. Don't lie there like the dead. There's work to do—on your feet, that's right."

Stepan Vesely swung his feet to the floor and

sat rubbing his head as the warders walked past, shaking men awake. Bulgakov's feet dangled into Vesely's line of vision, and the poet looked up with a smile.

"Good morning, Artem."

"Good morning, Stepan."

The bunk squeaked and shifted as Bulgakov climbed down, gray and shrunken, eyes too bright. He had on his fur hat, felt boots and sweater that he slept in every night. His gray-flecked mustache stuck out wildly.

"God, it's cold," Bulgakov complained as he did each morning.

Vesely got down on hands and knees to fish for his boots under the bunk. Reaching under his straw-filled mattress, he removed the red and yellow muffler Anna had knitted for him and wrapped it around his throat. Bulgakov, sitting gloomily on Vesely's bed, carefully wound his hands in rags before buttoning up his greatcoat and standing.

"What a sorry sight we are," Bulgakov said, looking up and down the aisle. There was a brief scuffle over a stolen pack of cigarettes. It was Kerensky who had done it. He had no one at home to send him things and he was a nicotine fiend. The warders broke up the awkward wrestling match with a few solid kicks and everyone finished dressing.

Then they filed out into the black clarity of the morning. Five a.m. and the stars were brilliant against a black velvet sky. The men moved into formation, stamping their feet and clapping their hands together against the cold, which was unbearable when one stood still. Vesely had his muffler wrapped around his neck and face to the eyes. He breathed in slowly. Last week there had been three cases of frozen lungs.

The warder, Podgorny, moved past them with a flashlight, counting heads. Across the yard steam rose from the mess hall, the sour smell of gruel reaching out to tighten empty bellies. They knew what the meal would be. It had been the same each morning for three months. Cabbage leaves and fish. Sometimes there was a little barley thrown in. Terrible stuff. Yet there was never enough to eat. A man was always hungry. As repulsive as the meals were you looked forward to them hours ahead of time. While you ate you lived. The body was nourished and you continued. Men had been killed over a bowl of gruel in this camp.

Vesely hunched his shoulders and stamped his feet with the rest of them as the warder finished his counting. Then they queued up behind Barracks Two to wait for the mess hall to open.

Vesely looked up to the stars once more then gradually lowered his vision to the wooden tower, the black strands of barbed wire strung atop the fences and around the towers. The wire had ice on it and it gleamed in the starlight. It was quite beautiful in its way, Vesely thought. Farther down one could see the prison graveyard.

The mess hall doors opened and the prisoners shuffled forward quickly, in perfect order. If they weren't just on time Barracks Four would invariably crowd in ahead of them.

They sat at long benches in silence. Gruel was passed from hand to hand and following it chunks of bread, good bread, dark bread without so much as a weevil in it. Vesely held his spoon in one hand and his bread in the other and he ate, thinking of nothing else but the food, the last bit of barley stuck to the side of the bowl, the last crust of bread.

To survive you had to eat. Some of them gave up. They just didn't eat and then they were gone one morning. Vesely was too strong to give in that way.

It was dawn when they emerged and reformed into groups. The warders came and asked if anyone had to go to sick call. You had to be falling down sick to see the medic. It was a formality, that was all.

"Comrade warder," Bulgakov said, "I am sick."

"Again?"

"It is no joke to me, sir. It's my lungs. . . ."

"And last week it was your heart. The doctor's too busy to see malingerers. Step back in line."

Bulgakov tried to argue, but the warder turned his back and walked off. Now the work bosses came out of their mess hall and took over from the warders. The prisoners were marched slowly toward the front gate. Six greatcoated guards armed with AK-47s flanked Vesely's group as they trudged across the muddy, snow-stained yard toward the high electrified gate.

"Are you all right?"

Bulgakov had begun coughing heavily and

Vesely looked at his friend with concern.

"I'm all right. My lungs, that's all. They burn."

They waited as the gate was opened, Bulgakov leaning on Vesely's arm. The sun was in their eyes now—huge, misshapen, orange as it gleamed across the snowfields beyond the gate.

"All right! Forward now, keep it closed up," the head guard shouted, and they started forward like automatons, their breath rising in a great cloud to hover over them as they slogged through the deeper snow outside the compound.

It was a six-mile walk to the work site, which the official papers in the camp commandant's office designated a "Socialist Community Development." There was nothing there now but heaped rubble, snowdrifts, barbed wire, and tree stumps.

The wind off the Barents Sea gusted across the countryside, lifting clouds of lighter snow, shaking the sparse windrow of trees ahead of them. Bulgakov fell into a heavy spasm of coughing. He stumbled and then had to stop. Vesely took hold of him again and held him while his body trembled with the force of his coughs.

"Are you all right?" Vesely asked.

Bulgakov looked up into the compassionate bearded face of the poet and smiled. What answer could a man give when the blood kept coming out of his lungs? He nodded.

"All right. Yes. Thank you."

"If I talk to the work boss perhaps they'll send you back."

"No, no. Don't do that. It will only mean

trouble. I'll be all right."

"Bulgakov! Vesely!"

The work foreman, who was one of them, a prisoner, stood hands on hips, glaring at them impatiently.

"Get over here. What the hell's the matter with you? Get your hands wrapped around these tools."

"Right away, comrade foreman," Vesely answered.

"Filthy bastard," Bulgakov cursed under his breath.

"He's only a man," Vesely said.

A man who lorded it over his comrades, bullied them for an extra portion of gruel, an extra blanket, a pair of felt mittens. They all despised him, but any one of them would have eagerly jumped at the opportunity to take his place.

Bulgakov picked up his shovel, wiping the ice from the handle, and looked around to see which way they were shoveling the snow today. Vesely followed suit.

They worked slowly, a forlorn file of men seemingly made of rags. Yet within them was spirit and intelligence, sinew and need. They had not yet managed to extinguish all of that. Stepan Vesely worked without thinking about it. His mind was far distant, lost in its work. He composed stanzas as he shoveled. Composed, discarded, and reconstructed lines of poetry. He had nearly all of a book in his mind now, after all of this time. It was too dangerous to write anything down. They could make something out of nothing so easily.

When he could not compose any longer, when his mind was exhausted with the effort, he thought of Anna. Of Anna so bright and so young, beautiful. So like her mother. She at least was well. Anna the headstrong, the impetuous, the lovely, lovely thing. . . .

It was nine in the morning when Vesely lifted his head. The approaching motor had caught his attention. Now, below him on the road that led to the camp from the city of Khabarovo, he saw the gray Volga sedan jouncing along through the snow that had drifted across the highway during the night.

All the prisoners watched the car for a few minutes until it rounded the bend and went out of sight behind the barren chestnut trees and the foreman began yelling again.

"Get to work, you lazy bastards! Do you think the state sent you here for your health! Do you think this is a vacation!"

Vesely smiled, threw back his head, and took a deep breath, looking at the clouds that drifted in now from the north. They were scalloped, wind-torn and blurry. They fused and then separated . . . blurring again. Vesely had been developing cataracts on his right eye. It was inevitable. The body ages. Yet he hated to think of losing his sight.

He shook his head and got back to work, not halting again until lunchtime, when a horse-drawn cart from the camp arrived with their meal. One-quarter pound of black bread each and a pint of tea, the same as it had been every day for two years.

Vesely waited patiently for his ration served up by that little runt Senka who had gotten his soft job by turning in Prokov for lifting a woolen cap from the warders' office. Then he went with Bulgakov to their regular eating place. A low brick wall, which another construction crew had begun and then abandoned for lack of mortar, jutted up out of the snow. Behind it was a section of poured concrete slab. It was warmer there only because the wall cut off the prevailing wind from the Barents.

Bulgakov had arrived first. He was sagged against the slab, appearing boneless inside his shabby coat. His tin cup rested beside him, his bread was on his lap untouched.

"Are you ill?" Vesely asked and Bulgakov's eyes turned toward him with something akin to fear. "What is it?" the poet asked, hunching down beside his friend. Bulgakov's rag-wound hands reached out and gripped Vesely's coat, pulling the poet to him.

"They've come for me, Vesely."

"Who's come for you? What do you mean, Artem?"

"In the automobile. The one we saw drive past toward the camp. It was them—oh, God!" he buried his face in his hands. "I can't go through that again. I know that I can't." Bulgakov gripped Vesely's coat front again. His mouth hung open soundlessly for a minute. There was sheer terror in · his eyes. The wind toyed with his huge mustache and sparse dark hair.

"I don't think it was anyone for you," Vesely said calmly. He gently pried Bulgakov's fingers from his lapels. "No, certainly not. You've got yourself excited over nothing. You must try to relax."

"It's them," Bulgakov moaned. "I know it is. It's all over for me this time." He brightened suddenly, got to hands and knees, looking from side to side like a frightened beast. "Vesely, I've got to talk to you."

"Yes, all right." Vesely put his tin cup aside. His stomach was growling ferociously.

"You are my friend, aren't you?"

"Of course," Vesely said.

Bulgakov's eyes glittered strangely as he studied Vesely's face. "Yes," he relaxed visibly. "You are my friend. Listen, please. I'm going to leave something here. If it's not them then I'll recover it tomorrow when we come to work. If they . . . well, if I can't get back then it's for you to see to. It's seven years of my life, Vesely. Seven years of work. If they take me away, you must see that it survives."

"Artem!" Vesely laughed, but he was feeling uneasy. "I am sure nothing is going to happen to you. Besides. I wouldn't know what to do with it. I don't think you are sure yourself what to do with it."

"No." Bulgakov looked as bleak and wintry as the tundra. "I don't. Seven years of a man . . . what does that mean to them?" He took a deep breath and then grinned. He lifted one shoulder in a partial shrug and then, reaching into an inside

13

pocket, he removed the zinc box. He held it in his hand for a long minute, staring at it, his thoughts lost to Vesely, who could only read the anguish in the man's eyes.

"It will be here, Stepan," Bulgakov told him. Looking anxiously at the poet to be sure he understood, Bulgakov placed the small, flat zinc box between the ends of two badly fitted bricks. He poked it in farther still with a broken stick and then proceeded to tamp dirt in behind it. Vesely watched him silently. The man sucked the breath in between his teeth as he worked. His head bobbed. One would have thought Bulgakov was performing a ritual.

He spun suddenly on Vesely. "You can't see it?"

"No, Artem."

"No one could find it there!"

"No one. I am sure of it."

"Good." Bulgakov sagged back and breathed deeply. He flung the stick away and picked up his tea. It was not far from being frozen. He smiled weakly and drank it anyway as the foreman's voice sounded shrilly, calling them back to work.

The gray Volga sedan swept through the gates of the labor camp, the helmeted guards saluting as it did so. "Over there," Volkovoy said, jabbing a stubby finger toward the commandant's hut.

"Yes, comrade colonel," the driver answered. He steered the badly sprung automobile through the slush toward the building where the camp commandant in his best gray uniform stood, hands clasped behind his back, watching their approach.

When the car had swayed to a stop, the driver leaped out and opened the rear door for the colonel, Aleksandr Volkovoy, a porcine, browless man stuffed like a sausage into his fur-collared overcoat. The driver stood at stiff attention, careful as always not to meet Volkovoy's eyes. The name derives from the word of wolf, and there was something always lurking in the depths of those dark, tiny eyes that suited such a name, something feral, vulpine, and evil.

Volkovoy grunted and swung his stubby legs out of the car, rose, and strode across the mud and slush to meet Major Sergei Yevgeny, commandant of the Khabarovo Labor Camp.

"Come inside, please, colonel," Yevgeny said. His mind hectically sorted the events of the past few months, scanned his service record and searched for loose ends. He did not like having the KGB around at any time, in any form. In the person of Colonel Volkovoy he found it menacing and intimidating. Yevgeny was shaking like a miscreant schoolboy when he sat at his office desk, leaning forward servilely, intently, to face Volkovoy.

"How may I be of service?" Yevgeny managed to say brightly. His throat however, was constricted, his mouth dry, his heart pounding rapidly. Volkovoy didn't answer, and Yevgeny felt terror surge through him. Those bright little eyes fixed on his, and his face went pale.

Volkovoy sighed, and, puffing with the slight

exertion, the KGB colonel opened his fancy coat and removed a long yellow envelope, which he glanced at before handing to the camp commandant.

"Custody papers," Volkovoy wheezed, and Yevgeny relaxed. "I'm taking one of your prisoners with me."

Yevgeny, who was scanning the papers, nodded and said, "Artem Bulgakov, yes, colonel."

Volkovoy again failed to respond. He sat staring at Yevgeny, seeing the anxiety in his eyes, the flush of fear on his cheeks, the unsteady hands. What petty larceny has he been up to now? Volkovoy wondered. The last time it was selling millet on the black market. Volkovoy, who had spent most of his adult life across the table from those who were guilty or simply panicky, easily read the signs. He had no interest in Yevgeny's misdemeanors, however; not at this time. It was Bulgakov who interested him. Intensely interested the KGB colonel.

"I shall have Bulgakov brought in immediately," the major said, rising to cross the room and call out to his orderly. "Would the colonel find a glass of vodka agreeable? In this weather . . ."

Volkovoy would find it quite agreeable. The colonel remained in his chair, watching Yevgeny pour the vodka, which was Starka, an excellent brand, undoubtedly the proceeds of the major's black market ventures.

"Colonel?"

Volkovoy took the proffered vodka and drank

it down in a swallow, gesturing for more, feeling the flush creep over his face, the room grow warmer. He removed a silver cigarette case from his coat and extracted a German cigarette, lighting it without offering one to the commandant. Then, with his fingers interlaced, the cigarette dangling from his rather thick lips, he waited.

Yevgeny spent an uneasy hour across the desk from the KGB colonel until they heard the scraping of feet on the porch, the door screeching open, the slow pained footsteps.

"Major?" The orderly nodded toward the man he had in tow.

"All right, Shukov. Artem Bulgakov?"

"Yes, commandant."

"Come in, please."

"Yes, commandant."

Bulgakov looked around uncertainly and then came forward into the room, his treasured fur hat in his hands. The commandant looked almost relieved to see him—something Bulgakov could not understand. The other man he understood perfectly, and he shuddered, his stomach going cold.

The KGB man's head never turned. He sat in the chair waiting until Bulgakov had inched his way across the room to stand beside the major's desk, dripping water onto the floor, before he even looked at the prisoner.

Bulgakov sighed with resignation and futility. He had known it all along, he had felt it all morning. Hadn't he told Vesely that they were coming for him?

"You remember me?" Volkovoy asked. There seemed to be amusement dancing in his eyes, and Bulgakov cursed him for it.

"Of course, comrade colonel," the prisoner responded. As if one forgot that sort of meeting. Volkovoy's lips had spread into a mocking, flaccid smile.

"Good," the KGB colonel said. He inspected Bulgakov, noticing the sunken, sallow cheeks, the haunted eyes, the stooped posture of a man much older than the scientist's forty-three years. "You and I are going to take a trip together, Comrade Bulgakov," the colonel told him.

"Yes?" Bulgakov felt all hope drain out of him.

"Yes. You don't want to stay in this terrible place, do you?"

"No," Bulgakov answered, although he wanted to scream, "Yes, leave me here! Just don't make me go with you again!"

"No," Volkovoy agreed amiably. "This is no place for a man such as yourself. We are going to go back to Moscow together, Bulgakov. I am sure you would prefer to be in Moscow, wouldn't you?"

"Yes, comrade colonel," Bulgakov replied, his eyes cast down. For just a moment his heart fluttered with hope. Volkovoy sounded nearly sincere, maybe they had decided that a mistake had been made. Certainly they never could have meant for that fool magistrate to sentence him to a hard labor camp. That was it—it was a mistake, and now they would turn him loose again with an apology.

He thought briefly of Moscow, of Marina and little Katrin, but did not let himself dwell on them. By now they would be living in disgrace somewhere. They certainly no longer had the private apartment on Cherepkovo that had delighted Marina so. She had only to go out the back door to take Katrin to the park . . . Volkovoy's eyes were hard and cold, shining chips of obsidian, and they brought Bulgakov back sharply to reality.

"Have you signed the papers, major?"

"Yes, colonel," the commandant replied, coming to his feet as Volkovoy did.

"Fine. Get this man some clothing, will you? I'm not riding with his stink all the way to the depot."

Bulgakov was taken out then. He was given a shower in the mess hall kitchen and issued new clothes. The shoes didn't fit, but they had no holes in them. They even shined, dully. He was allowed to shave; then he was taken out to the waiting Volga, flung into the front seat beside the driver as Colonel Volkovoy eased into the back, and in minutes they were out of the camp, whirring down the Khabarovo road, his feet warm, his body scrubbed clean, his heart empty.

He glanced once in the rear view mirror and met those tiny, gleaming eyes of Volkovoy, then he turned his head quickly away to stare out at the passing snowfields all the way to Khabarovo.

It was dark with sleet falling three days later when the train pulled into Moscow's Yaroslavi

Terminal and Bulgakov was led from the compartment. On the platform, the guard Volkovoy had procured in Khabarovo—a lean, clean-shaven army captain who had said nothing in three days of rail travel except, "I need to go to the bathroom"—was augmented by two KGB men in long gray coats, hats tugged low. They stood beneath the station awning, watching the colonel approach.

Bulgakov was not handcuffed—what was the point in it?—and he briefly, in blind panic, considered trying to make an escape. Unarmed, wasted by his months of labor, he wouldn't have a chance. Maybe it would be best, he thought, if he were just to throw himself under the wheels of the locomotive. But the locomotive was at rest. One couldn't even expect any consideration when he wanted to kill himself. You would die when the party willed it, not before.

If a man could make it into the depot proper, however, if a man could lose himself in the crowd . . . he had to surrender the futile hope as the captain hooked an arm around his at the elbow.

Bulgakov was bundled into a waiting automobile, and with a lurch the car swung out of the parking lot and onto Shchelkovo Highway, the windshield wipers flapping noisily, the sleet silver in the glare of the headlights, slanting down.

Bulgakov sat back and closed his eyes. He knew where he was going. Still, it was with something akin to horror that, half an hour later, he realized that the automobile was swinging down the long concrete ramp to the underground parking lot beneath the drab, gray stone building. He must have given a jerk because the army officer beside him said, "Easy, old man." Then he seemed to smile. Perhaps it was a genuine smile, well-meant, perhaps not. You never knew. Nothing was real in this world inhabited by Volkovoy and his creatures.

There was always a reason for a smile, a kind word, a warm drink. And often these were followed by a kick on the kidneys, the skull-shattering thump of a heavy truncheon. Bulgakov knew all of this. He was, after all, a man of some experience by now.

"Oh, God," he murmured, burying his face in his hands as the automobile braked to a stop in the dank, empty chamber beneath the KGB headquarters building.

It was then that Volkovoy turned and placed his hand on Bulgakov's knee, his stubby, powerful fingers digging at the nerves there. Bulgakov nearly vomited, he found it that repulsive. Volkovoy was smiling now as well, and there was no need to guess about the sincerity of his expression.

"Home again, eh, Artem Bulgakov. Nothing to say? You will talk, my friend. This time." He turned to the army captain. "He cost me a lot, this one. But now he's come back home to give me another chance, isn't that right, Comrade Bulgakov?"

Bulgakov didn't answer. He couldn't. He was petrified. His heart was hammering against his throat. Volkovoy smiled; the captain smiled. Everyone smiled, and it hurt, damn them, it hurt.

Without remembering being taken from the car, Bulgakov found himself and his escort walking down a long, white, lighted corridor. Doors without handles flanked the windowless hall. Their heels rang on the white tile.

Coming to a T in the corridor, they turned right and stopped before an elevator door. Volkovoy pushed a button and stood rocking on his heels. Bulgakov's leg felt warm and damp and he realized he had wet himself.

The elevator doors parted and the scientist was ushered into the antiseptic compartment behind them. The doors closed and they began to descend. There was a faint electrical whirring somewhere. Bulgakov stood staring at the floor, smelling the pine-scented cleaner they had used. There was a small maroon-colored spot on the stainless steel runners beneath the door they had missed. The elevator jerked to a stop and the doors opened again. Bulgakov was escorted out and down a flight of red-painted concrete stairs. They turned right sharply and entered an open doorway.

Bulgakov saw the white, windowless walls, the iron bed with the crisp linen and a brown blanket. There was a writing desk in the corner and above it a light bulb protected with steel mesh.

"Home again, eh Comrade Bulgakov."

"Yes. Is my case . . . ?"

"It is under review. That's all I can tell you at this time. I'm sure there is nothing at all to worry about, eh?"

"I hope I haven't . . . I hope it is all right. I would be glad to answer any questions at all," Bulgakov said anxiously.

"I know you will—at the proper time. For now I want you to get some rest."

The others had gone and for a mad moment Bulgakov thought of flinging himself at the KGB man, tearing out his lying dirty throat. Volkovoy stood watching him, fingertips pressed together, as if reading his thoughts.

"There was something else?"

"No." Bulgakov shook his head. He thought about asking for his family but realized that would be the worst thing he could do. "No, there is nothing."

He stood staring at the floor, adopting the submissive posture he had learned in the prison camp. He heard the iron door clang shut and he did not even look up. There was nothing to see, nothing to be learned that he did not already know deep in his heart. Bulgakov sagged onto the bed and sat staring at his feet.

"Damn you all to hell!" he screamed suddenly, but that brought on the coughing again and his body was racked with it. There was much blood this time and he wiped it away with his sleeve before lying back on the bed to stare at the white ceiling, to listen to the humming of an electrical generator nearby.

Colonel Volkovoy walked back toward his own small office, which was on the second floor next to the OGPU nerve center. Dozens of telex monitors whined and chattered away as radio intercept and the masses of diplomatic intelligence dispatches reached terminus.

Volkovoy walked to the end of the hall, paused for a drink of water, and found his key for the door. He went inside to the neon luminescence of the cold gray outer office.

"Good afternoon, comrade colonel," the dull-looking young man with a bald head and wildly distorting thick-lensed glasses said from behind his metal desk.

"Good afternoon, Grin. Anything important come in while I was away?"

"Nothing urgent," Volkovoy's secretary answered. "The most important messages are on your desk."

"All right." Volkovoy ran a hand across his thinning hair. "There's a new visitor. In room thirty-three."

"Yes, comrade colonel." The secretary scribbled something down on a pad. "His name please?"

"Artem Bulgakov."

"Yes, comrade colonel," Grin replied. "Will that be all?"

"That's everything. You know what needs to be done."

"Yes, Comrade Volkovoy," the secretary said. Volkovoy nodded and went into his private office. Grin would see to food and drugs, scheduling conferences, entering Bulgakov on the roster as "in charge."

Volkovoy flicked on the electric lights and

closed the door behind him. He hung up his fur-collared coat and turned on the little electric heater behind his desk. Then he sat down to go through his reports. Nothing of any importance seemed to have happened.

Nothing of the importance of Bulgakov. The scientist had cheated Volkovoy once before. He had gotten off soft and been shunted off to Khabarovo by that fool magistrate. What had that accomplished? Nothing whatsoever. This time it would be different. There would be time to work on Bulgakov. No one yet knew he was in charge and it would be a good while before they did.

By the time it was discovered Volkovoy would have the full dossier on Artem Bulgakov, his report verified, filed, complete. After that no one would be able to say anything about his methods.

It was early still, but Volkovoy decided that a small celebration would be in order. He opened the bottom desk drawer, removed the vodka bottle, and filled his coffee mug.

"You do not cheat me this time, Bulgakov, I promise you," was Volkovoy's toast. He drank the vodka down and sat smiling, warm and pleased.

The secretary in the outer office gave Volkovoy a minute or two to get settled in. Then, turning to face the door, he picked up his telephone, punched 99 for an outside line, and waited while the relays clicked loudly before he dialed the Moscow number.

There was a very long pause before the call was

answered. "Yes?" a rather haughty voice said at the other end.

"Give me cultural affairs, please," the secretary said, his eyes, huge behind the thick lenses of his glasses, flickering to Volkovoy's closed door.

"You have not dialed properly," the voice at the other end of the line said. "Please hang up."

"I need Bolshoi tickets," Grin persisted. "For the Belgrade delegation."

"One moment."

The wait was interminable. The secretary sat drumming his fingers on his desktop. He watched the office door, but the colonel was quiet. Likely he had opened the bottle again and fallen asleep in front of that heater. One day he would roast himself.

Finally the voice came on the telephone line. A new voice, one utterly calm, deep, with odd accents. It was nearly inhuman, that voice, and the secretary had often wondered about the man who owned it.

"Belgrade?"

"Yes," the secretary answered. "Artem Bulgakov, sir. Colonel Volkovoy has brought him back from Khabarovo. Just now."

"Very good. I'll send someone," the voice said without inflection.

The secretary immediately hung up and got back to work, typing Bulgakov's card, informing the kitchen that there was a new guest in Room 33.

*　　*　　*

Remizov was thirty-three years of age. He had been a naval pilot with the Pacific Fleet Air Force. Having lost an eye and shattering his left leg in a bad carrier landing during a storm at sea, he had been transferred to naval intelligence. One day new orders had come. Report to the office on Mazilovo Avenue in civilian clothing. Speak to the man in Apartment 15.

With those terse instructions came a promotion to lieutenant-colonel, three thousand gold krugerrands, and a playing card. A jack of diamonds with one corner snipped neatly off. Remizov, sensing trouble, had tried to return the gold immediately. His commanding officer had turned a deaf ear to Remizov and advised him to clean out his desk.

With trepidation Remizov had taken a navy automobile to Mazilovo, dismissed the driver, and gone up. That had been five years ago, and still Remizov went each morning to the apartment and reported to the man who worked there, lived there, perhaps would die there, behind the leather-covered, littered desk.

The man Remizov reported to had an odd voice, one which seemed toneless, nearly dead, as if a machine were speaking. He was a chain smoker, apparently abstained from alcohol, and seemed never to leave the building in which he had his office. His name was Fyodor. If he had another name or an official title, they were unknown to Remizov, who knew only that Fyodor had ears everywhere, that whatever he needed done was done promptly.

Remizov rapped at the door and went in, dragging his left leg, his good eye searching the room, which was nearly in darkness, the heavy drapes closed, the tall corner lamp turned down.

"Sir?"

It was a time before Fyodor looked up at his aide. When he did his mouth twitched, possibly with a faint smile. His high forehead gleamed dully in the poor light. His eyes were hidden in shadow.

"Do you know Bulgakov?"

"Artem Bulgakov? Of course, sir," Remizov said. "I recall his case well."

"Volkovoy has him. I wish you to take care of it for me."

"Yes, sir," the colonel responded. That was as much instruction as he usually received. Fyodor knew just how competent the ex-naval officer was, knew that intricate programs frequently stumbled over themselves.

Remizov hesitated only a fraction of a moment, then turned away, Fyodor's eyes on him. The colonel heard Fyodor mutter coldly, "The stupid bastard," as the door closed. It was the most emotion he had ever heard his superior express, and the sound of that inflectionless expletive was enough to send a shiver up the spine of the tough intelligence officer.

They came before Bulgakov had fallen asleep. It might have been only minutes since Volkovoy had left, or hours. Time had no meaning in the whiteness of the cell.

The door banged open and they stood there, purposeful and quite calm. There were three of them, only black figures before the light, and Bulgakov heard a voice he only dimly recognized as being his own ask hoarsely, "What do you want?"

"Comrade Bulgakov?"

"What do you want. You know my name, tell me—what is it you want? Did Volkovoy send you? Does he wish to interrogate me? Can't you speak?"

He sat up rigidly, his body suddenly cold with sweat. They stepped toward him, blocking out the light. Hands slipped under his arms and he was lifted helplessly in their grasp.

"What is it you want?" he asked desperately. "Where are we going now?"

There was no answer again, nothing but the hands propelling him forward, the close press of their bodies. He was taken out of his cell and into the corridor. Ahead of them was the elevator. Up above there were three floors; below there was only the basement where . . . God, don't let them take me down, he thought frantically. Not again, please.

They squeezed into the elevator, the dark men standing shoulder to shoulder with the scientist. The elevator stank. It was a time before Bulgakov could identify the smell, realize it emanated from his own body. The stink of fear. Sweat, bile, loosened sphincter muscles.

The third man pushed the button marked "B"

and the elevator dropped to the lowest level. The doors opened again and Bulgakov was looking down a gray, seemingly endless tunnel.

"Straight ahead, comrade," the tallest man said, and Bulgakov's knees buckled. He collapsed and they jerked him upright again, moving ahead, out of the elevator.

The corridor was dark, lighted only at long intervals by bulbs of minuscule wattage. Unpainted iron doors fronted the hallway, which was cold, terribly cold. Behind the doors were invisible souls. Bulgakov could sense pain and fear now, like an animal penned before the slaughter.

"There's been a mistake. I'm certain of this," he said, twisting around to look up into his guards' faces. "Please check with Comrade Volkovoy. I beg you!" Then he began to sob again and his words came out as small unintelligible sounds. His knees would not support him and he discovered that he was being dragged along by the dark men. "There's been a mistake . . ." he tried to say, but his throat was incapable of speech.

He was turned sharply to the left and taken past a steel door guarded by a man who sat on a three-legged stool reading a magazine. There was a room beyond, a cold, deathly cold room.

"Strip, please, comrade," a voice said, and Bulgakov attempted it shakily. He fumbled with his shirt buttons, seeing the flat aluminum table before him, the glassed medical cabinets on the walls, the specimen jars, the many-tentacled electrical apparatus. The smell of ether and alcohol was nauseating. There was another, fainter, deeper smell that filled Bulgakov's nostrils and tightened his stomach. They were helping him undress now, making sounds of disgust at the way he had fouled his clothes.

"Up here, please," they instructed him, but again they had to lift him bodily and place him on the aluminum table. It was cold against shoulders, buttocks, thighs.

"You must check with Comrade Volkovoy! Damn you all, I tell you there has been a terrible mistake!"

They didn't even seem to hear him. He fell into another coughing fit. He had to turn his head to clear the blood. He could see the dark figures bent over him, see the white light beyond. They smeared petroleum jelly on and then expertly clipped the electrodes to nipples, eyelids, genitals.

Bulgakov lay unmoving, unable to move, his heart hammering like an express train racing through a provincial station. The light above him flickered and the pain surged through his body.

Bulgakov's head rolled from side to side, his strapped-down limbs strained against their leather bonds. The electricity coursed through him. His brain went fiery red and then black. He felt a flat stick being jammed between his teeth so that he could not shred his tongue as the agony tormented his muscles to spastic excesses. Veins bulged, his eyes popped from his head. A small voice far away in his skull's depths cried out over and over again.

He wished for one thing—an end to pain. *I will tell you anything*, he said with his eyes, but the dark men were not capable of reading his eyes.

The pain diminished and then came back with a jolt. Bulgakov's chest felt as if it would cave in. He glanced down to assure himself they had not opened him up and set fire to his entrails. He tried to speak, gagged on the stick, and sagged back, letting the stillness conquer his consciousness. The last thing he felt was a rubber-gloved hand being placed on his forehead, a rubber-sheathed thumb lifting his eyelid.

"What happened there? What game is he playing?"

"He's not playing. God." The eyes in the attendant's face were as wide as saucers. "Dead," he said in a whisper.

The first man shoved him aside. "Are you crazy? He can't be dead! Not from that. That was nothing, do you hear me? It wasn't my fault! God, he is dead. Get the doctor. Run!"

It didn't do any good. They rolled in the resuscitator and began working feverishly over the body. The doctor, a small man in a brown suit who had seen many cases like this one, could only shrug.

"You've killed him."

"Do something!"

"Do what? Do I look like a sorcerer? You've killed him, and that's all, it's over for him." He lifted the green sheet and draped it over the dead body, crossing the room to wash his hands with strong green soap.

"He can't be dead," the attendant said numbly, and the doctor only shook his head and went out.

"Bastard," the second attendant muttered. "Die on me, you little swine!" He raised a fist as if to smash the corpse in the face, but he lowered it again slowly. "This is the first time this ever happened to me. I swear it! You can believe it or not. They'll take that into consideration, won't they?"

"With Volkovoy who knows. Which one of us tells him?" There was a long silence between the two men. they almost wished they were lying on the slab. Volkovoy could be very vengeful. After a minute they pulled themselves together and went out, turning toward the elevator.

In fact Volkovoy said nothing. He just sat there staring at the two men. It was worse than if he had ranted and threatened to kill them with his bare hands. He just shook his head heavily, as with a great sadness. Only that. When the two attendants went out they knew that it was all over. They'd be lucky if they didn't get hard labor themselves. They barely noticed the young, slender secretary with the thick-lensed glasses as he passed them.

Grin tapped at the door and opened it.

"Comrade colonel?"

Volkovoy's red eyes lifted to the doorway where the secretary stood, leaning slightly forward, his hand on the doorknob.

"What is it?" Volkovoy asked, taking another deep drink of the vodka before him.

"Colonel Remizov is here, sir."

Volkovoy stared bleakly at the man. He turned his glass in his hand, swallowed the last of the vodka in a gulp, and nodded to the secretary.

"Show him in."

Remizov walked across the carpeted room, his stiff leg dragging. He settled into a gilt, red-velvet-cushioned chair and sat, watching Volkovoy with his good eye. The KGB colonel filled his glass again and drank it down without apology. Then he leaned back, his round figure slumped and sagging, his small red eyes empty, and Remizov knew.

"I've come about Artem Bulgakov, colonel," Remizov said. "He wants him."

Volkovoy knew full well who *he* was and he sighed deeply, closing his eyes. It was over, damnit! Over. He had had a full if not spectacular career. Now he had tried to achieve the spectacular and had fallen on his face.

"Bulgakov is dead," the KGB man said, reaching for the vodka bottle yet again. Remizov only nodded, taking a cigarette from an inside pocket, lighting it as Colonel Volkovoy's bloated figure sagged more deeply into his chair.

"You knew this man was ill," Remizov said quietly. "A year in an *osoblager* couldn't have helped. According to his medical records he had heart trouble and incipient tuberculosis."

"I thought it expedient . . ." Volkovoy began, but Remizov's eye flashed and the KGB man fell silent. Volkovoy's head was ringing. His high blood pressure, he thought. He took another deep drink of vodka.

"You can force a confession from a man, Volkovoy, but how in the world did you expect to force a scientist to write out involved computations under stress and pain!"

"Once he had agreed . . ." Volkovoy just lifted his hands and let them fall, slapping against his heavy thighs. Remizov asked politely:

"May I use your telephone, comrade colonel?" Without waiting for an answer, Remizov took the black telephone and dialed a Moscow number as Volkovoy's unfocused red eyes stared into the distances. "Cultural affairs," Remizov said quietly. Volkovoy lifted his bottle, saw that it was empty, and let it drop.

"Hello," Remizov said, his eye flickering to the man across the desk from him.

"Hello," Fyodor's toneless voice responded. "There is trouble." It wasn't a question.

There was trouble or Remizov wouldn't have called. Remizov looked again at the KGB colonel and answered, "Yes, that is correct. Some trouble with the arrangements. The guest of honor did not arrive."

"Dead."

"So it seems." There was a long silence and then Fyodor said:

"Finish up then the best you can. Please make sure that nothing is missing."

"Yes. Yes, I will. Could I have Tyurin to assist me?"

"I'll send him over. Is that all?"

"That is all for now, yes."

Then, without saying goodbye, Fyodor broke the connection. What he thought, Remizov did not know. He knew what his superior would do, however; so did Volkovoy, who sat exactly as he

35

had, staring at nothing.

Remizov got to his feet and walked to the door to call out to the secretary, "Would you come in, please?"

"Yes, of course," Grin said, pushing away the sandwich he had been eating. "What is it?" He glanced once at Volkovoy, who sat behind his desk inert and swollen.

"Artem Bulgakov—all of his papers, please."

"There was nothing much yet, only his schedule and admission form."

"No interviews?"

"There haven't been any yet, no."

"Then there won't be. Nothing was delivered here? No papers?"

"You can't suspect . . ." Volkovoy said, lurching to his feet. Remizov ignored him.

"There has been nothing at all," Grin said apologetically.

"Will you look through his private file?"

"Of course," Grin said. He got to it as Remizov stood over Volkovoy, rocking on the balls of his feet.

"I am not a *traitor!*" the KGB man said angrily. Again Remizov failed to answer.

Half an hour's search failed to discover anything whatever. By that time Tyurin, Remizov's affable, red-faced assistant, had arrived.

"And what have we here?" he asked cheerily. "Bad luck for the KGB."

"Very bad," Remizov, who was used to Tyurin's rather breezy personality, answered.

"So sorry," Tyurin said with mock sympathy.

36

"Colonel Volkovoy is involved?"

"Yes. Do you have your full kit?"

"In the car."

"Why don't you stop this nonsense," Volkovoy said. "I told you that I haven't anything of Bulgakov's. There hasn't been time."

"There was time to kill him," Remizov said and Tyurin lifted a surprised eyebrow.

"Artem Bulgakov?"

"Yes. We are going to go to Volkovoy's apartment and have a look around, Grin. Your supervisor is going with us. I do not think he will be back this afternoon."

"My old lady's at home," Volkovoy snarled. "No sense bothering her. There's nothing, nothing!"

Remizov glanced at his watch and then at Tyurin. "Ready? If you will lead the way, Colonel Volkovoy."

Fyodor sat in the near-darkness of his office, massaging his weary eyes, eyes which grew daily more sensitive to light. His peripheral vision was going too, as the doctors had said it would. There was occasional pain, occasional temporary blindness.

None of that bothered Fyodor. The only thing that bothered him was failure. Any failure. He had always been that way, for as long as he could remember. He had to be first at games. There was no excuse for losing.

There was still no excuse. Volkovoy, the fool,

had ruined everything, but Fyodor should have foreseen something like this. It was failure; he was responsible.

Maybe there was something in Volkovoy's apartment, maybe the little pig had been preparing a trade with the West. Other men, bigger men, had been caught doing that. Somehow Fyodor did not think that Volkovoy was capable of that. If there was anything in the apartment, Remizov would find it.

Fyodor lit a cigarette and held it before him in clenched hands, watching the smoke twist and spiral through the darkness beyond. There were people to be notified, people who would not take it well that Artem Bulgakov was dead, and foolishly dead—Fyodor's superiors did not believe in excuses for failure either. With a sigh he picked up the telephone and dialed.

TWO

Osip Gamilev emerged from the Gum Department Store and stood blinking into the sunlight. Gum was not officially open for another hour, but for the Minister of Internal Affairs there were no set hours. Tatyana had wanted that fox stole very much. Now she would have it. She would be very appreciative tonight, the minister thought with great pleasure. He would have her strip before he let her wear it. She would like the touch of fur against the smoothness of her flesh. . . .

The minister glanced at his bodyguards and nodded. Together they set out across the slick avenue toward the Kremlin. The sleet of the night before had melted and refrozen, glazing the brick boulevard with ice, and Gamilev picked his way carefully, clutching the department store box.

The tour buses were already pulling up as Gamilev approached the high Kremlin walls, and his mouth tightened. He turned toward Spassky Gate, glancing toward the bulk of St. Basil's Cathedral and the Minin and Pozharsky Monument with the unseeing eye of one to whom they had become a daily prospect.

As had the dark-haired, gaunt girl in black sweater and knee-length gray skirt who sat cross-legged beside the path leading to Spassky Gate.

She had been there every day for months, in all kinds of weather. She bothered no one, never attempted to accost the minister or make a display of herself. She simply sat there, sometimes reading a book, speaking only three words as the minister crossed toward the gate.

"Free Stepan Vesely."

She did not even look up at Gamilev on this cold, bright morning, and the minister sighed. The bodyguards scowled at the young woman, but that was the extent of their menace. When the girl had first appeared there, Gamilev had had her identified and investigated.

Her name: Anna Vesely, daughter of the reactionary poet. Age twenty-two, a student at the University of Moscow. An artist.

She was a pretty thing, with wide, dark eyes, high cheekbones, full lips, small round ears. Her figure, from what Gamilev could deduce, was slender, athletic beneath her shapeless clothes. He could, of course, have had the girl barred from the Kremlin grounds or had her officially reprimanded. He had done neither. Nor had he changed his own routine to avoid the intent, pale face, the dark eyes of the girl.

Gamilev had continued doggedly to adhere to routine, at first to show Anna Vesely that he could not be intimidated. Later he had come to accept her as a part of his routine. He actually looked forward to seeing the pretty young woman standing or sitting on the bench beside the walkway, to hearing her pleasant contralto voice say:

"Free Stepan Vesely."

Osip Gamilev's face gave no indication of any of his thoughts. There was no reaction whatsoever to the girl's words. He simply swept past her, flanked by his two bulky bodyguards, and entered the Kremlin through Spassky Gate to make his way toward the Council of Ministers.

Anna Vesely waited until the minister was out of sight, then she carefully marked her place in her book, and rose, dusting off her skirt. With a last long look at the high Kremlin walls, the gilt and crimson, the onion-shaped cupolas, the long lines of tourists, she walked to the street and caught her Number Four bus, dropping ten kopeks into the change box.

She sat through a stupefyingly boring lecture on revolutionary symbols in the nature studies of Van Gogh and then went home early, cutting her afternoon conferences, which were all political studies anyway.

The Number Four Bus took her back to the Social Artists Hostel on Enthusiasts Highway, across from Izmailovo Park, where children even on this bitterly cold day flew brightly colored kites.

The electricity was out again, she discovered as

41

soon as she entered the foyer, which was dark and cold. Comrade Voloshin, who was the women's registrar, was working behind the counter by the light of a candle. She did not even glance up as Anna Vesely trudged past and started for the staircase, eyeing the inoperative elevators.

It was four floors up, and Anna had to stop on the third landing, her head bowed, pressed to the narrow, bluish wall, as she gasped for breath, her legs trembling. She had been feeling weak lately.

"Anna?"

She lifted her head and looked around to find Tanya Akhmatova and a friend, books in arms. They looked solicitously at Anna, who smiled.

"Hello."

"You're all right?" Tanya asked.

"Just a little faint," Anna Vesely answered.

"You should sit down and rest."

"They promised to have the elevators fixed by tomorrow."

"Yes," Anna said, "last time it was four weeks, Tanya Akhmatova, or am I wrong?"

"You are not wrong," Tanya laughed. "Be careful if you're dizzy. Do you want us to walk you to your flat?"

"No. Thank you, but no. I'm fine now."

Anna smiled again, and Tanya and her friend went down the stairs, glancing back once. Sighing, Anna Vesely climbed the last flight of stairs and went to her apartment, which she shared with two other women. Neither was home, she discovered gratefully, and, throwing her books onto the faded plush sofa, she sat on the floor, leaning her head back against the deep cushion of the couch.

She closed her eyes and tried to empty her mind, but the spinning colored dots confused her efforts and she rose, walking to the window, which she threw open. Leaning out, she watched the children in the park, the traffic buzzing up Enthusiasts Highway toward the Moscow Ring Road.

"Hello!" The voice was young, male, and too cheerful. Anna turned with a sigh.

"Hello, Boris."

"Ah, then you do remember me," Boris Buynovsky said, entering the room. His dark curly hair was brushed forward over an intelligent brow. Arched, heavy eyebrows sheltered speculative blue eyes. His nose was slightly long, his mouth eternally pursed. It was, he had been told, an amiable face.

"Where were you, Anna? I looked everywhere."

"I was here, obviously." Anna crossed the room wearily and Boris stepped to her, his arms encircling her waist.

"You are ill," he said with concern.

"Only weak."

"The hunger strike," Boris said indulgently. "You have lost weight everywhere." His hand cupped her breast and he laughed. Anna shrugged him off and turned toward the little nook where, against the house rules, she kept a hot plate.

"Would you like tea, Boris?" she asked. From the drawer at hand she took a box of cigarettes, lighting one, blowing out a plume of smoke.

43

"Are you allowed tea?" Boris asked with mock seriousness. Anna turned away in irritation, searching for the tea. She paused and knotted her dark hair at the back of her head before opening the tea cannister. She measured it out and turned the hot plate on under a battered copper kettle.

Boris watched every move she made, liking the sleekness of her, the feline grace. The gray skirt she wore tautened across her rear as she bent to recover the spoon that had clattered to the floor.

Beautiful, beautiful—and she was driving Boris Buynovsky mad.

"Why don't you marry me," he said, as if the notion were a casual one that had just now popped into his head. Anna glanced at him but did not reply. "You ought to eat," Boris said in a different tone of voice. "Hunger strikes are remarkable for their ineffectiveness."

"You understand nothing," Anna said, turning. Two spots of color had blossomed on her pale cheeks, Boris noted. "It is for my father!"

"It does him no good, Anna, and it harms your health."

"You do not understand."

"I understand counterrevolutionary behavior well enough," Boris said, stretching his legs out beneath the table, crossing them at the ankles, clasping his hands behind his neck.

"Is that what this is?" Anna asked. She had turned her back and was pouring the hot water into the samovar. "That's right, though, you're very good at your political classes, aren't you?"

"At least I have a chance of graduating, Anna,"

44

Boris said seriously. "That is what I mean precisely—you're ruining your life over this. Your father was expelled from the Union of Soviet writers. Glavlit purged his works. Nothing you can do will change that."

"I don't care about that now. Now I only want him home, somewhere where he can live decently, out of that filthy camp. I went there, if you recall, Boris. I know what I'm talking about. They wouldn't let me in the camp, but I saw the prisoners in rags, their bodies hunched and frail. . . ."

"Shades of Solzhenitsyn," Boris said.

"You admit his existence, then."

"He wrote of another time," Boris shrugged. "It has nothing to do with us."

"Tell that to my father." Anna sat at the table and poured tea while Boris sat looking more and more somber. Anna really was going to get herself in trouble, he thought. "He isn't allowed to write me letters," she persisted. "His eyes are very bad. He needs an operation for cataracts. He's old, Boris, and not so strong. If they cannot honor him, they at least should not torment him."

"He confessed," Boris offered, stirring sugar into his tea.

"Confessed," Anna said with bitterness. "Yes, he was guilty of everything." She threw up her hands in despair. "Guilty of writing poetry of absolutely no political worth. I can't talk to you about him—drink your tea,"

"I want to talk to you about it," Boris said.

"You understand nothing."

"All right. Then we can study—or make love, while you still have the strength for it."

"You may have your tea and then leave," she said briskly. "I am going to engage in counter-revolutionary activity, and I'm sure you wouldn't want to witness it."

"What are you talking about now?" he asked a little shakily. "What are you up to, Anna Vesely?"

"Nothing so terrible. I am only going to write a letter to Comrade Gamilev," she explained.

"Anna—you have written him every day for nine months! You annoy him on his way to the Kremlin. You will push this madness too far. Please," he reached across the table and took her slim white hand, "be reasonable. It can do no good. Nothing can."

The report was on Osip Gamilev's desk the next morning. Written concisely, it detailed the last days of Artem Bulgakov. A copy had been sent to the military, who had been vitally interested in Bulgakov, and one to International Affairs.

Bulgakov's project, Gamilev recalled hazily, had been laser guidance. A sophisticated short-wave modulation was involved, a breakthrough that would have allowed ballistic missiles to reach their targets with something under .001 error factor.

Something, however, had gone wrong with Bulgakov's mind. An unhappy love affair, the death of a daughter, perhaps misplaced humanitarian impulses. At any rate, Bulgakov had refused to submit his final report, claiming that his work had been a failure. A laboratory assistant had informed the authorities that this was certainly untrue, and Bulgakov had been interviewed and then arrested.

The KGB had had a try at him, though they had been commanded to keep the velvet gloves on. No one in authority wanted a man as valuable as Bulgakov damaged. Bulgakov had failed to respond to the KGB interrogations and had ultimately been sentenced to thirty years in a labor camp where everyone confidently expected Bulgakov to change his mind and confess. He hadn't done so, although his health had begun to collapse.

Apparently Colonel Volkovoy of the KGB, who had resented the orders limiting his interrogation procedure during Bulgakov's initial confinement, had decided to have another try at it. If it had worked and Volkovoy had recovered the missing scientific documents, Gamilev considered, the colonel would have been amply rewarded. But he had failed. Bulgakov was dead.

All of Bulgakov's confiscated files were again being pored over, but there was little hope that anything would be found at this late date. Gamilev tilted back in his chair and swiveled toward his window, looking out across the Alexander Gardens. Rubbing his chin thoughtfully, he turned the Bulgakov incident this way and that, trying to decide how it affected his own ministry.

It was at that moment that the telephone rang,

and Gamilev, picking it up, heard that odd, toneless voice. The voice of the man who had written the report on his desk.

"Fyodor?"

"Yes, comrade minister."

"What's to be done?"

"Colonel Volkovoy is under detention."

"I assumed as much." Gamilev was considering more than the arrest of an overzealous KGB officer, however. Bulgakov was internationally known and word of his death would leak out inevitably, embarrassing the nation. That must not be allowed; or if it had to be allowed, the impact must be softened.

"What do we do, Fyodor, to explain this folly?"

"There are, I consider, only two possibilities, comrade minister," Fyodor said. "One, Comrade Bulgakov died of ill health while at the farm. Ill health or accident. Two, we admit that Bulgakov was brought back to Moscow by elements of the KGB, tortured, and killed."

"Then we must use the first explanation, Fyodor."

"Yes, Comrade Gamilev, I quite agree. Bulgakov's death cannot be hidden—it is best that he died far from the seat of power."

"It will, of course, reflect rather badly on the 'farms.'"

"A man can die anywhere, at any time, comrade minister. We can present this quite convincingly, I'm sure. There is, if I may point it out, one ancillary complication concerning the Khabarovo Farm, however."

"Ah, yes." Gamilev tilted back farther yet in his chair. He had forgotten about that. "Our other notorious resident."

"Yes, comrade minister. Stepan Vesely is also in ill health. He also has an international reputation of some substance. If we release the information that Comrade Bulgakov died at the Khabarovo Farm, it would not do at all to have Stepan Vesely die there as well. The reactionary elements would be waving Stalin's Gulag in our face."

"You are right, of course," Gamilev said musingly. Fyodor was never caught off balance. Another operative would never have considered this aspect of things let alone mentioned it to the authority who *should* have thought of it. "What is the matter with Stepan Vesely, Fyodor?"

"His eyes are bad, sir. And his lungs, as everyone's are there. His general condition is not good because of natural aging processes and severe weather, poor nutrition. I doubt very much, comrade minister, if our poet will survive this winter's labor at Khabarovo."

"It is that bad?"

"So my informants say, sir."

"I see." Gamilev sighed and picked at a loose thread on his coat cuff. "And then the first thing we have is the Western press and their horror stories." He frowned, silently mulling. "I will have him transferred to the south," he decided suddenly. "Perhaps we can release a bulletin simultaneous with the information concerning Bulgakov's unfortunate death—what do you suggest for the cause, Fyodor?"

"I had considered a tractor accident, sir."

"Excellent. It must be convincing."

"We have done this before, sir. It will be. We can include a photograph of a wrecked tractor with a surrogate Bulgakov beside it."

"Excellent. Proceed with that plan then, Fyodor. I'll take care of our poet."

"Yes." Fyodor hesitated. "Comrade minister—you seem almost pleased about Stepan Vesely."

"I am a lover of poetry," Gamilev said, hanging up. Then he sat smiling, fingers interlaced. He was thinking not of Stepan Vesely, but of the girl who accosted him each morning, who cluttered his mail box with petitions. Then, shaking off his reflective mood, the minister got back to work.

"What are you doing?" Boris Buynovsky stared in amazement at the apartment, which was turned upside down as Anna Vesely, nearly hysterical, it seemed, had turned out drawers, flung papers across the room and was now throwing books into crates or the trash as she chose.

"What are you doing?" Boris asked again. It was pandemonium in the tiny apartment. Anna's cheeks were fiery. He thought at first that she was drunk.

"Boris!" She came to him, leaped up and threw her arms around his neck, kissing him full on the mouth. "And you said it could do no good!"

"What could do no good, Anna? What?" he asked, not failing to take advantage of her mood by kissing her neck, holding her finely molded body to his.

"The hunger strike, the letters, the petitions!" She pushed away and spun in a circle. "Father is free! Do you hear me, my father is free. We're leaving for Batumi—do you know where that is?"

"Of course. In the south," Boris answered, still stunned, "by the Black Sea, but . . ."

"He's already left Khabarovo. All I have to do is finish packing—I feel like throwing away all of this junk. Take what you want, take it all. I'm going to Batumi to meet my father. We're going to have our own cottage and a patch of ground to garden. He's free, Boris, free!"

THREE

The pilot banked and swung in low over the pine-fringed lake. There was ten inches of snow on the roof of the trading post on the eastern shore, but the weather reports had been accurate. There was no ice on Flagstaff Lake.

The pilot, who wore a faded Philadelphia Phillies baseball hat beneath his headphones, gave Cassidy the thumbs-up, pulled back on the wheel and circled the lake, bringing the Cherokee aircraft in on a westerly course, feathering back the throttles as the small, pontoon-equipped aircraft coasted over the tips of the snow-clad pines and drifted toward the startlingly blue surface of the Maine lake.

Cassidy sat tensely erect as the twin engine aircraft skimmed over the mirror of the lake. He was not even aware of the pontoons touching down. The landing was as smooth as silk. Glancing at the pilot, he saw the man grin. Cassidy wiped his palms on the knees of his light gray suit pants, and pushed his horn-rimmed glasses up the bridge of his nose as the Cherokee coasted toward the pier before the trading post.

Ten minutes later Cassidy was out on the log pier, the icy wind tugging at his clothing, slipping icy probing fingers up his pants legs. He waited shivering until the pilot had handed him his suitcase before turning toward the trading post, seeing a stocky man with an axe on his shoulder watching his approach.

"What can we do for you?" the woodchopper asked.

"I need to go to Dulhaney," Cassidy told him.

"Dulhaney. Nothing there," the other responded in his nasal Maine accent, "and no way to get there. County don't maintain that road anymore."

"On the map . . ."

"That is something a fellow ought not to put too much trust in, my friend. Maps are always out of whack somewhere or another."

Cassidy groaned inwardly. The operation had looked so simple on the map. Hitch a ride to Flagstaff Lake and follow the logging road, which showed as a dotted line on the map. Now he would have to circle all the way back to Lewiston.

"Course, if a man had a snowmobile, he could likely just cruise on over the hump there. It's done," the man with the axe said.

"You have a snowmobile?" Cassidy asked through clenched teeth. His knees were knocking together with the chill off the lake.

"Damn right I have one. Up here you just have got to have a snowmobile. This time of year . . ."

"Have you got one to loan?" Cassidy said with exasperation.

"To loan, I don't know," the man replied, rubbing an ear.

"Look," Cassidy wanted to know, "can we go inside and talk about it?"

"Inside? It's a business proposition then," the man said, his Yankee twang deepening as he considered the lamb standing before him.

"It's business," Cassidy said. "I have to get to Dulhaney one way or the other."

"Come along inside then, my friend," he said, and he smiled contentedly. Cassidy followed him up onto the split log porch and into a high-ceilinged trading post where a moth-eaten moosehead peered down morosely from the wall. An iron stove glowed in the corner and Cassidy gravitated that way.

"Are you maybe interested in a mackinaw?" the storekeeper asked. "It's hard weather for the way you're dressed."

"I left my coat at the airport in Portland," Cassidy said. He removed his glasses, which were steaming up rather badly. "I need to get to Dulhaney," he said again, slowly, as if speaking to a deaf man. "If you can rent me a snowmobile, find someone to drive me there, I'd be very much obliged."

"It's necessary then, good and necessary." The storekeeper's eyes were positively glittering by now.

"It is necessary, yes. I would be willing to pay you or someone else a reasonable fee, pay for the gas and oil," Cassidy told him.

They settled on a hundred dollars for the ride over and back. The storekeeper apologized for the price. "But, I stand to lose some trade, you understand."

Cassidy understood well enough. Looking inside, the thought of going back into the weather prompted him to pay another eighty dollars for a mackinaw that he could have purchased in Washington for thirty.

He followed the storekeeper out to a leaning, weathered shed made of unbarked logs and waited patiently while the man searched for his red can of gasoline and filled the tank of the sleek little two-seat snowmobile. At least he was out of the wind in the shed, he reflected,

Minutes later he wasn't. Cassidy was put into the back seat, and the storekeeper, tugging down a set of tinted goggles, took off at a terrifying rate of speed through the pine and birch forest, dodging tree stumps and half-hidden rocks like some circus daredevil as plumes of snow flew up behind them, and the engine roared like an oil-fed banshee. They covered the five miles to the village of Dulhaney in just over ten minutes.

The storekeeper shut off the engine at last, and Cassidy, whose muscles were still vibrating, looked around to see a small, quiet, snow-clad town.

"I'll be waitin' at the inn there until nine, Mr.

Cassidy," his driver told him. "After that, you'll have to find another way back."

"It wouldn't bother me a bit to find another way back," Cassidy said sourly. He stood up, awkward in his new mackinaw, chilled to the bone, and stepped out of the snowmobile.

"Nine o'clock," the driver repeated, wagging a finger at Cassidy, and, having said that, he tramped off toward a log inn where two chimneys sent twin columns of smoke into the crystal-blue sky.

Cassidy stood shivering, looking slightly ridiculous, he supposed, with that yellow and red coat over his gray suit. The village was a scattering of log cabins and a handful of older clapboard houses sprinkled among the tall, snow-heavy pines. An icy creek twisted through the trees, making its way southward.

Taking his bearings, Cassidy started off up the muddy road toward the big red barn, where there was supposed to be a lane leading off to the right.

He trudged throug the ankle-deep mud, his feet cold, his shoes in danger of being sucked off his feet at each step. The wind shrieked through the trees and a pine cone dropped painfully onto the top of his head. A bucketful of snow followed, and he abandoned the trees to walk beside the road.

A Ford pickup truck on huge, chain-clad tires roared past Cassidy, spraying him with mud and slush, and he breathed a curse. Outside of that he saw no one until he reached the barn, which was dilapidated, leaning with age, as every other building in this part of the world seemed to be.

He had trouble finding the lane until he realized that it was under the snow. He struck off along the line of a wire fence that seemed to parallel the byway. The fifty-foot pines lining the lane swayed in unison, creaking and moaning in the wind. It grew colder yet, and there was mud beneath the snow again. He was thoroughly uncomfortable and in an altogether foul mood when he finally came upon the ancient clapboard house at the end of the lane.

It might once have been painted green—or perhaps that was just moss—but now the house was weathered to a damp gray. Cassidy could see holes in the window screens, patches of shingles missing on the steeply pitched roof. Icicles hung from the eaves, which were decorated with rotting gingerbread. A thin curlicue of smoke rose from an iron stovepipe.

Cassidy's head turned as he heard the sound of approaching feet. The old man hobbled forward, his gnarled hand clenching his cane. He smiled toothlessly and waved a greeting.

"Hello," Cassidy said. There was no response, and so he repeated it more loudly. The old man appeared to be partially deaf. He cocked his head toward Cassidy like an intent, faithful dog. "Hello, Mr. Koltsov!"

"Yes, yes," the old man said cheerfully. "Koltsov. Hello."

"I'm looking for Michael."

"In the jail again?" the old man asked, and Cassidy shook his head.

"No. No one's in jail. I'm looking for Michael Koltsov. Is he here, sir?"

"I don't know," the man said in some confusion. "The old woman would know." He switched his cane to his other hand before leveling a gnarled finger at the house. "Why don't you ask the old woman?"

"Yes, I will," Cassidy shouted. "Thank you, Mr. Koltsov."

The old man bobbed his head as Cassidy walked toward the ramshackle house. He was still watching, his head still bobbing, when Cassidy looked back from the porch.

"Come in!" a voice called before Cassidy could knock, and he did so, having a little trouble with the swollen door. Inside all was dry, overly warm, quiet. Turkish rugs worn down to the backing covered the hardwood floors. A cuckoo clock, the bird half in, half out, hung on the wall beside a dark watercolor rendition of a larch grove. The walls had been cream and were now badly weather-stained. The furniture was old, an overstuffed sofa and chair, a rocker with a painted flower design in the corner. A glass-fronted bookcase with volumes all awry stood next to an ancient gas heater.

"Back here," the voice called again, and Cassidy followed it, removing his mackinaw as he went, tracking mud and water across the floor.

He eventually found her in a small, neat kitchen near the back of the house. There was a chicken boiling on an ancient Hotpoint stove, and the clacking of knitting needles as the old woman worked on an unidentifiable object of bright orange and rust brown.

She herself was over eighty, her thin face lined and sunken, her eyes bright behind gold-rimmed spectacles. Bright and merry—the years had left her with a sense of humor and that humor seemed to deepen as she turned her eyes on Cassidy.

"I heard you shouting at my brother," she said, her voice a little shaky, her accent still heavy despite thirty years in the United States. "He doesn't hear so well at times, and then there are times when he hears but does not understand. There are also times when he understands perfectly but pretends not to hear, if you see what I mean?" She laughed dryly and shook her head.

"I'm sorry to bother you, Miss Koltsov, but I need to find your great-nephew."

"Mikhail?" She pursed her lips in surprise.

"Yes. It is important that I find him."

"Is that so?" She put her knitting aside and rose to look at her stewing chicken. Cassidy put out a hand to help her but she was already on her feet, apparently quite spry and still strong. "Why is it that you wish to find him? You are from the lumber mill, perhaps?"

"No."

"I had hoped things would be starting up again there." She tasted the broth with a large steel spoon, shaking her head. "They say it is going to start up again, but no one knows when."

"I'm sorry. I'm not from the mill."

"No. I see that now," she said, resuming her seat.

"But it is important. . . ."

"He is not in trouble."

"No. Not at all. There's no need to shield him, Miss Koltsov. I don't know what sort of trouble he may have been in. I am merely representing a group of people who would like to offer Michael employment."

"Is that so? I see." There was a shrewdness in those eyes as they measured Cassidy. "Mikhail will be happy to see you then. Or so I would think. He hasn't worked for a long while. It bothers him, I think."

"Michael is . . ."

She took a moment before she made up her mind. Then she told Cassidy, "Mikhail is at a place they call Lakewatch. It is there, on the lake—the little lake, that is, not the big one." She shook her head nervously and clicked her tongue as she dropped a stitch.

"What is this Lakewatch? A resort of some kind."

"A place where the men go. I don't know what you would call it. If he is there he is fishing. He fishes much, does my Mikhail. There is too much time on his hands, I think."

"Fine. Thank you. I'll go on down and see if I can't locate him then."

"He'll be fishing," the old woman repeated. Then she was lost in her knitting, in her thoughts again, or at least she appeared to be. Only Cassidy, as he started out the door, glanced back and caught a look of unambiguous alertness in her eyes.

"You old faker," he thought. Then he waved a hand and went out, grinning. Pulling on his mackinaw again, he stepped out onto the porch of the old house. The wind had picked up considerably in the last hour. It had been chilly before, but now the wind was positively cutting. The great dark ranks of pines swayed heavily in unison. Clouds scudded in from the north, shadowing the hills.

The old man was standing in the middle of the snow-covered yard as if he were trying to remember something, perhaps something lost in the years. Cassidy lifted a hand in farewell and the old man simply gaped. Cassidy turned and went back down the lane toward the village,

The first person he met was a boy of ten, who eyed Cassidy suspiciously, but warmed at the sight of a dollar bill. For that amount the kid steered him toward the lake—the little lake, not the big one—and told him how to find the Lake-watch.

It was a mile's walk, and Cassidy looked mournfully to the gray skies and hunched in his mackinaw. Then he walked on, cursing the department, Maine, and all of creation indiscriminately.

The lake suddenly appeared through the trees. Steel gray, touched with whitecaps, it seemed to form a rough crescent. A dozen buildings fronted it, huddled together as if for protection from the winds that whipped across the water. There were dozens of small, swaying boats tied up at a wooden pier, and at the end of the pier, a single man was fishing, his hat tugged low over his eyes, his coat collar turned up.

Cassidy started that way, hearing the jukebox music blaring forth from the Lakewatch, which seemed to be a tavern of some kind. Three Jeeps, a Toyota, and a battered red pickup were parked at random before the place.

A woman inside the bar shrieked with delight as Cassidy walked past and tramped down the pier, which smelled strongly of rot and creosote and swayed underfoot enough to undermine any sense of security.

The man at the end of the pier never turned around. He seemed unaware of Cassidy's approach, but he knew Cassidy was there. He had to know. His pretense was as sham as the old woman's seeming inattention.

Cassidy stopped behind the man and watched the red bobber float on the iron-gray lake surface. Still the fisherman did not turn, and Cassidy was left with a view of the back of a faded red and black plaid jacket, of dark hair curling over the collar, of an incredibly stained felt hat studded with multicolored, bright fishing lures.

"Michael Colter?"

"That's right."

"I'd like to talk to you. Can we go somewhere?"

"Sorry, I'm busy," Colter answered.

"I'm serious, Colter."

"Yes, sir. So am I."

"It really is important that I talk to you," Cassidy persisted. "I assure you it is to your advantage to listen to what I have to say."

"And any time now, you'll tell me what it's about," Colter replied. His voice was soft, yet a tension, almost electrical, danced through it. Cassidy felt slightly unnerved by the voice and by Colter's reception.

"It's something better discussed in different surroundings," Cassidy said. Colter didn't answer, and he added, "It's about a job, you see."

"A job?" Now Colter did turn his face. He was still young—thirty-one years old—had the dark, handsome features of a matinee idol marred by a white scar over his right eyebrow, and a nose that had been patched well, but not well enough to conceal the old break. His eyes were very pale. Blue or gray, Cassidy couldn't decide which. Just now they were also red-rimmed and weary appearing. "What sort of job?" Colter asked, his eyes measuring Cassidy, revealing the same sort of amusement Cassidy had seen in Colter's great-aunt's appraisal.

"If we could find someplace more private, Mr. Colter, I would feel more comfortable."

"This is private. What was your name?"

"Cassidy."

"From the lumber mill?"

"No."

"I didn't think so. Are you cold, Cassidy?" he asked.

"Damned cold!"

Colter grinned. "Why didn't you say so?" He stood, reeling in his line. "We can talk in the Lake-watch. It's so damned noisy and crowded it's the last word in privacy. What sort of job did you say?"

"For the government, actually," Cassidy said, and he saw Colter stiffen.

"No, thanks. None of that," he said. He had his line in now, and, picking up his tackle box, he repeated it. "None of that."

"You don't even know what it is," Cassidy objected.

"I don't want to know."

"We can at least talk about it."

Colter stood, looking down at Cassidy. He shrugged, grinned again, and replied, "Sure, if you're buying."

"I'm buying if it's inside," Cassidy said frankly, and together they turned toward the Lakewatch. Colter stored his gear in the ancient red pickup and then led the way into the smoke and din of the Lakewatch. A plump blonde was dancing frenetically to some electronic music. Six or seven men stood at the bar drinking beer from deep mugs. No one bothered to glance at them.

"In the loft," Colter said, and Cassidy followed him up a narrow flight of stairs to an area that contained five unoccupied round tables.

Cassidy shed his mackinaw, watching as Colter tossed his own coat on the chair beside him. He was a strong-looking man. Six feet tall, not overly broad, but with the catlike movements of a man sure of himself and his strength. His hands were very large, his forearms small, but above the elbows, and especially in the shoulders, there was heavy muscular development. His neck looked strong. A tuft of dark hair curled up over his T-shirt.

"Seen everything?" Colter asked. Cassidy started to reply, but his answer was interrupted by a barmaid in a starched white blouse and skimpy black skirt who appeared with two bottles of beer, two mugs and two shot glasses filled with bourbon. She also had a bright smile for Colter.

"Hello, Mike."

"How are you, Mary?" Colter asked.

"Fine as can be," she responded pertly. "If you see George, would you do me a favor, send him around."

"He's out hunting, Mary."

"Sure . . ." she frowned. "He's always off hunting. One day soon he's gonna come home and find I'm doing the same." Then she winked and walked away, the tray in one hand, her backside swinging.

"Nice kid," Colter said, downing the bourbon. "What's this about, Cassidy?"

"As I told you," Cassidy began, clearing his throat, "it is a government project, one for which you have been highly recommended. It is a short-duration position, I'm afraid, but one which would pay you very well indeed for your time."

"Yes? How much are we talking about exactly?" Colter asked, sipping his beer.

Cassidy slipped his billfold from his inside coat pocket and slid a yellow certified check across the table. Colter nearly choked as he saw the five zeroes lined up across the paper.

"Two hundred thousand dollars? Do you have some identification on you, Cassidy? If so, I'd like to see it. I'm beginning to suspect you're an escapee from the county asylum."

Cassidy dipped into his wallet again and passed the plastic-coated green card across the table. Colter held it up between two fingers and shrugged.

"Looks like you're the real thing." He handed the card back to Cassidy, who tucked it away.

"Yes. And so, believe me, is the check."

"Oh, I believe you. The thing is, you've come to the wrong man, my friend."

"I don't think so . . ."

Cassidy fell silent as the barmaid reappeared with two more bottles of beer, two more shot glasses of bourbon. Cassidy, who hadn't touched either of his drinks, took a hasty swallow of the beer.

"You'll have to do better than that to keep up with this maniac," the barmaid said. Then she picked up Colter's empties, smiled, and swished away again.

Cassidy leaned forward intently. His voice was low and intent. "Look now, Colter, I've come a long way to make you a very serious proposal involving a lot of money. The trouble is, you don't seem to be taking it very seriously."

"I am taking it seriously, friend," Colter said. "The only thing is, as I said, you've come a long way to find the wrong man. What is this, anyway? Are we going to attack Fidel or something like that? I gave all of that up a very long time ago, and you should know it if you've searched my background. I gave it up because I didn't like that line of work anymore. It left me just a little lonely, Mr. Cassidy. I had to make new friends all the time, you see. The old ones kept getting themselves buried.

"Besides, you've got something very heavy in mind. Two hundred thousand is too much wages for a foot soldier, which is all I am when you come down to it. This stinks, my friend." He drank his whisky down and reached for the second beer.

"You were a special type of soldier, Colter. Special Forces and then . . ."

"I remember it all, Cassidy. You don't have to brief me on my career."

"All right." Cassidy drank a little beer, studying the pale-eyed man across the table from him. "If you're interested, this isn't any sort of guerrilla action, assassin's mission, hopefully no blood involved at all, if that sets your mind at ease."

"Very little."

Colter reached for Cassidy's untouched whisky. "You don't want this, do you?" Without waiting for an answer, he drank it down and Cassidy found himself wondering what sort of demons were living with Michael Colter.

Michael Colter. Born Mikhail Koltsov. Six years of war and then, after a field promotion to captain following conspicuous gallantry, he became a deserter. He returned home under guard, had his sentence reviewed and then commuted to a dishonorable discharge. He drifted for a year, taking a dozen widely disparate jobs, all manual labor, then matriculated at Princeton University, where he was a loner, a sporadic scholar, one semester in danger of flunking out, the next achieving the dean's list. Three years of that and he got up from his desk in the middle of a lecture on Elizabethan dramatists, packed a suitcase, and came to Maine to live with his great-uncle and aunt.

Since that time Colter had held no steady job, had devoted himself to the bottle and little else. Cassidy had believed all along that a man with Colter's inconsistent record wasn't the man for this job, but he had been overruled. The boss had once been Colter's commanding officer.

"I don't care what you see on the surface," the general had said. "Underneath there is Mike Colter and I want him for this mission. He fits it like a glove. He's nerveless, clever. Once he starts on something, he doesn't quit."

"Yes, sir." Cassidy and the other agency man had looked at each other and shrugged mentally. It was General Waverly's project, and if he wanted Colter it appeared he would get him. Assuming Colter wanted to come. He didn't.

"What do you do with yourself, Colter?" Cassidy asked.

"Do?" Colter grinned and raised a glass. "This is it, Cassidy."

"It's not much, is it? Not much to hook a life on."

"No. Have you found something like that, Cassidy? Something for me to hook a life on?"

"Different people lean different ways."

"Right. I leaned into the bottle. I like it there."

"What happened with your last job?" Cassidy asked.

"Which one was that? I don't recall it," Colter said, and his mood was darkening.

"Never mind. Does this all go back to Asia? This problem?"

"What problem. Damn you, I haven't got a problem. I'm perfectly happy. It's you who has the problem, Cassidy, you and your damned agency. You and the rest of the world."

"You quit school and came home."

"Sure." Colter shrugged. He had cooled down some. "You don't start up again easily after six years of hell. The faculty, the students, hell, everyone—all of them were like something on another planet. I came home."

"And what do you do now?"

"I go fishing!" Colter slammed his glass down, shaking the table. "By God, I go fishing. Why shouldn't I?"

"No reason."

"No. None at all. If I want to go fishing, I go." The barmaid made another circuit, sweeping away the empty glasses, leaving fresh drinks. "That's all, Cassidy. I just go fishing."

"And keep on fishing."

"That's right."

"Living off the old folks."

"Damn you," Colter said, and his voice was very low, issuing from deep within his throat. His hands were knotted into fists and his eyes warned Cassidy. "Don't say that."

"All right." Cassidy was silent for a time, listening to the distant music, watching his man, sipping at his beer. "You could help them, you know. You could help the old folks out."

"By accepting this lousy job of yours."

"Sure. Haven't you done enough fishing, Colter?"

"Maybe." Colter's head came up, his eyes focusing sharply, "But I've damned sure done enough killing, and you haven't got enough money to pay me for that kind of work. Go find yourself another sucker."

"I told you this isn't that kind of work!" Cassidy said intently. He leaned forward, looking into those pale eyes. "It is not a warrior's pay."

"Then what? Or can't you tell me?"

"Not in detail," Cassidy answered, removing his glasses to clean them. "But I can tell you a little. You're of Russian extraction, aren't you?"

"Ukrainian."

"I'm sorry—I'd forgotten there's a difference."

"There's not much anymore. Only to the old people."

"You are fluent in the language?"

"Fluent?" Colter's eyebrows drew together. He nodded. "Sure. That's all Aunt Katrinka speaks unless there are strangers around. Yes, I'm fluent." Colter seemed to withdraw a little, not liking the drift of the conversation. "Look, why don't you tell me what this is, or forget it."

"What it is, Colter, is a sick old man who wants to leave the country where he's now living. But he can't. They won't let him."

"What country?"

"That I can't tell you," Cassidy said, and Colter just stared at him in disbelief before throwing back his head and laughing loud and long. It was a rich laugh, deep and booming, and Cassidy could only stare at him in astonishment.

"You can't tell me?" Colter said, wiping a tear from his cheek.

"No."

"Let me see if I can guess then," Colter said, still chuckling as he spoke. "Is it a large country? One east of here, maybe? One where I might speak the language fluently? One where they shoot foreigners who come in playing games like you and the other desk-bound maniacs in D.C. have come up with?"

"I really can't confirm anything like that just now," Cassidy replied. His ears, Colter noticed, were flaming.

"No. I supposed you couldn't, and you don't have to—not for me, Mr. Cassidy." Colter reached across, picked up the certified check and tore it into little pieces.

"You're far too hasty, Colter."

"Am I? Don't come back soon. What do you think I am? Crazy? What kind of fool idea is this, I wonder. All I see in it is death for some poor bastard hard up enough to let himself be hypnotized by a string of zeroes. Is that the way it was supposed to work with me? Poor dumb Mike Colter, down on his luck, let's give him the dirty end of the stick and see what happens."

"It's not like that at all," Cassidy said. "The

71

project can be accomplished, no matter what you think. A workable plan has been devised. . . ."

"Good. All you need then is the donkey. You're looking in the wrong place, Cassidy." Colter stood, finishing his drink, and snatched up his coat. "Good luck. To you and the poor dumb bastard who takes you up on this."

With that Colter turned and walked toward the stairs, zipping up his jacket, leaving Cassidy to stare at the confetti Colter had made of the check.

Colter was still chuckling to himself when he walked through the Lakewatch, waving to Al Simms, the local auto mechanic, and Beatrice, his girlfriend, who seemed to be semipermanently attached to him as they swayed together on the sawdust-littered dance floor.

Outside it was getting damned cold. The sun was going down. The lake was gilt and burnt orange, shimmering in the sundown light. The dark ranks of pines crowded up to the lake's edge.

Cassidy had followed Colter out and he caught up with him on the porch. "If you change your mind . . ." He gave Colter a card, which he pocketed without a glance. "Colter . . ." Cassidy tried again, but Michael Colter was walking away from him already, down the split-log steps and across the snowy yard to the parking area. He climbed into his battered, ancient pickup truck, started it with a roar, and drove out of there, his rear tire throwing up mud and slush.

Cassidy just looked after him until the truck was gone. He looked at the bits of yellow paper in his hand and let them fall to the ground where the wind scattered them. Then, sighing, he put on his mackinaw again and started back toward the heart of the town, hoping against hope that the snowmobile operator was still at the inn. He was in no mood to walk back to Flagstaff Lake.

Colter drove down the muddy Lakewatch trail with the foot-feed to the floorboard, spinning onto the Ridge Road and then dipping down through the wooded hollow that bordered the road on the west. He fishtailed across the snow-covered meadow, and, grinding the gears as he dropped into low, he crested the rutted timber road that overlooked the lake.

There he shut off the motor and got out, staring out over the darkening woodlands. To the south he could see the dull glimmer of Flagstaff lake and the few early lights from Eustis, the nearest town beyond Flagstaff.

The dying sun lit the serrated tips of the pines and the wind, which had been building all afternoon, began to die. Bulky cumulus clouds were drifting in from Canada. Colter sat down on the running board of his pickup and watched night fall, watched the world go empty.

If you looked long enough in this light, it seemed the trees around you were ancient temples. It seemed that someone was laughing far away, down in the valley, melodiously laughing as she brushed her long, silky hair.

Colter got up and climbed into the pickup, reaching across to the glove box for the pint of Jack Daniels. It was half gone already, and Colter finished the other half as he sat watching the last dusky rays of sunlight be swallowed up by the conquering night.

He flipped the bottle out of the window and ground the starter until the pickup roared to life again. Turning on his headlights, he started off down the timber road, bouncing over rocks and ruts and stumps until he reached Canridge, two miles distant.

Canridge was five houses set at long intervals along a narrow, tree-lined road. It had no reason for existing that Colter knew of; perhaps that was what called him to it.

The porch lights were on at the Elk Lodge, and he wheeled in, seeing a man in a sheepskin coat, his arm around a slender woman in dark ski pants and chinchilla coat. Henry Huggins and Marlene.

"Hey, Henry!" Colter yelled out the window, and Huggins, glancing back, lifted a hand in greeting.

"Better get yourself inside, Mike. You're getting behind!"

"I don't get behind 'em, pal. You ought to know that!"

Huggins and Marlene laughed at that and went on their way, hurrying toward the Elk Lodge as Colter switched off his engine. The truck gasped a little, as if pained.

Colter turned on the dome light and peered at himself in the rearview mirror. Flattening his curly hair, he squinted and shook his head. The lines were getting a little deeper around the eyes and there was some puffiness beneath them. There was one good solution—he turned off the light.

He slid from the truck and tramped toward the Elk Lodge. It was hot and noisy inside. The band—Ed Freeman's son, the Baxter kid, and a drummer from New Hampshire—played just a little too loudly, finding most of the notes with their amplified guitars.

Colter waited for an opening and then planted himself solidly on a red vinyl bar stool, lifting a finger. The bartender was Soapy Sharpe, and he brought Colter a beer and a shooter of bourbon without being asked.

"How's things, Mike?"

"Terrific," Colter said with a shrug. Soapy was already away, chatting up a woman Colter didn't know, one laced into a red jumpsuit of some kind so tightly that it looked like torture. Soapy evidently had high hopes.

Colter turned back to his drinks and stared at them for a while, feeling something close to nausea. There was a cure for that too, he thought, and he downed the whisky. Then he turned around on his stool, beer in hand, to watch the dancers, most of whom looked red and sweaty, too old for that kind of nonsense.

It seemed that half of the county's population of two hundred people must have been crowded into the lodge by midnight. Colter found himself dancing with a blonde who said she knew him. He couldn't place her or the sweet smell of her jungle gardenia perfume. She was a head shorter than Colter, with amazing mammary development that she showed thoroughly above the low-cut gold dress she was wearing.

Colter must have been staring at them. "Do you like it, big boy?" she asked.

"Sure. Fine. Everything's fine," Colter muttered. His feet were hot and very heavy. The woman jiggled a lot as she danced, so that her voice was shaky.

"Let's go over to Nova Scotia. Just the three of us," she was saying. Colter bent his head nearer to hear her and she kissed his ear. The band was loud now, very loud. The walls seemed to rattle. Someone had given the kids some liquor and permission to turn up their amplifiers. Joe Gilly had joined them with his saxaphone. It didn't sound like they were all playing the same song.

"So, do we do it, honey?"

"Do what?" Colter asked. Things were suddenly very hazy.

"Nova Scotia," she said.

"Can't go to Nova Scotia," he said, stumbling more than a little over that name. "No way to get to Nova Scotia."

"Duke's got a boat at Belfast," the blonde shouted into his ear. Her face was flushed. Red beneath the powder white. A strand of yellow hair hung across her left cheek. She smelled very nice. Her hand kept groping Colter's haunch. "Did you hear me? Duke's got a ketch at Belfast."

"Who's Duke!" Colter shouted back. The damned music was getting out of hand. His head was pounding in time to the drums.

"My husband!" the blonde yelled. "You know old Duke. They always called him that on account

76

of he looked like John Wayne, you know. His real name's . . ." Colter missed hearing Duke's real name as the band reached a crescendo. The blonde was giggling helplessly. "Isn't that something! What a name to tag someone with, but if you knew his mother." There was some more that Colter didn't catch. "Out in the car," she seemed to be saying.

"Duke's in the car?"

"No—say, don't you like women? Don't you pay any attention to me when I talk to you."

"I thought you said Duke was in the car."

"Hell, no. Say, what's the matter with you?"

"I need a drink," Colter said. He stopped dancing. All around him people were gyrating, panting, shouting. "Damn, look at that line-up at the bar."

"I got a bottle."

"Let's have at it," Colter said.

"It's in the car, beautiful. In the car. I told you that. Weren't you listening?"

Colter turned toward the door, the blonde heavy on his arm as he elbowed through the bouncing throng. Her hip was rubbing against his. Jungle gardenia wafted up into his nostrils. An ill-advised drum solo was being batted out by the pimply kid from New Hampshire. It looked like there was a fight starting up back in the restaurant. Colter pushed on through into the night.

The cold air hit him like a hammer. He staggered as he took a deep breath, nearly fell stepping down to the ground, and knocked an ankle painfully on something he couldn't see.

"Are you okay, honey?" The blonde was half holding him up. Someone walking by laughed and Colter grumbled a slurred curse.

"Let's get that bottle."

"Sure, baby. It's the Caddy. Over there." The voice came from a long ways away. It was a minute before he realized that it was Duke's wife, that he was still hanging on to her, that she meant the yellow car in front of them.

"You gonna make it, honey? God, you're heavy."

"I'll make it. Open the damn door."

It was cold in the Cadillac as he slid in, smelling leather and wax and more jasmine. Duke's wife started the engine, the heater blowing cold air frantically as the blonde thrust something at him.

It was the bottle. He didn't bother to look at the label. Colter took a deep swallow. Fire bubbled up into his nostrils. He threw his head back and stared at nothing. The heater was starting to warm up. His feet were warm.

"It's an empty place where they keep killing people," Colter said, his voice elided and hoarse. The whisky was burning a hole in his stomach. He had to fight to keep the last swallow down.

"Sure, honey, I know."

"I can't put it any plainer."

"It's all right. It doesn't matter tonight," Duke's wife said. Her voice was muffled and it was a minute before he realized that it was because her face was on his lap.

The heater was blasting hot air at them now. The lodge looked oddly tilted as if it were about to be sucked under the waves. But there were no waves, only cresting ranks of pines, deep green, menacing. Colter shook his head, but it wouldn't clear. He reached across and took the blonde by the shoulder.

"Let's get the hell out of here," he said. "This is no damned good a place."

"No." She kissed him, her tongue rough as it forced its way between his lips. "I'll take you someplace."

She scooted over and dropped the big car into gear. They barreled out of the Lodge parking lot and slid onto the road. She drove very fast, losing the big Cadillac on one icy corner, banging it into a sapling with the loss of a parking lamp and a deal of paint. The car bogged down in the snow on the shoulder.

Colter got out and stood looking at the fender. The woman was beside him, and they stood there, their teeth chattering. Neither of them could figure out what to do. He thought someone came along and towed them out of the snow.

"Almost there," she said, and he realized they were back in the car, back on the road, driving as fast as hell.

"Where are we going?" Colter asked.

"Down there." She jabbed a finger at the window. Down below them was only darkness. The road snaked along the side of the hill. Colter had no idea where they were. "There's a cabin down there, belongs to a friend of Duke's."

"Where's Duke?" Colter asked. *Nova Scotia*? Why did that stick in his mind?

"He's gone home, honey. We had us a knockdown brawl. That's where I got this shiner. The son of a bitch pasted me one and he went home." The car slid through another corner, the back end banging into the bank on Colter's side. She got it straightened out again and sped on.

Colter squinted at her, trying to make out the shiner that Duke had given her. All he could see was heavy blue mascara and some kind of glittery eyeliner all illuminated eerily by the greenish glow of the instrument panel.

Colter must have nodded off, because when she hit that last rut he came alert, not knowing where he was, whom he was with. The pint bottle was still in his hand, and so he tried it again as she braked what was left of the Caddy to a rough stop before a tiny, dark cabin and switched off the lights.

There was nothing to be seen anywhere. The world had gone dark. The stars had hidden themselves away in the dark fleece of the clouds.

"Nice, huh?" she said, and her voice sounded ten years younger. "Sitting in the dark. It makes you feel small, though. Awful small."

"Sure. Real small." Colter took another drink. If I get much smaller, he thought, they'll never find me again.

The dome light flashed on, blinding Colter. "Come on, honey," Duke's wife said. "Let's get on inside."

He clambered out of the Cadillac, banging his

head on the roof and was led across the muddy yard. The blonde fished for her key in a flashy metallic purse and Colter stood staring bleakly at the darkness, finishing the whisky. He reared back and threw the empty bottle at the Cadillac. He must have missed, there was no following crash.

He heard the cabin door creak open and Duke's wife said, "Come on now, honey."

Inside it was neat, chilly, redolent of fried bacon. Very rustic and masculine. Knotty pine paneling. There was a braided rug on the floor, a leather-covered sofa and a stone fireplace with wood neatly stacked beside it. Duke was a hell of a guy; his wife was a hell of a gal.

Colter decided he was cold and staggered toward the fireplace. He spent five minutes searching his pockets for matches, watching the world tilt and spin, the fireplace yawn at him.

"Well?"

Colter turned to find the blonde, arms uplifted, standing before him. She had shed everything but a pair of pale blue panties. As she lowered her arms her great breasts sagged a little, but it did nothing to make her undesirable.

"I'm ready for you, honey," she said to Colter. "I've been ready all night." She stepped to him, smiling. Her fingers worked down the buttons of his shirt and she tugged it up out of his waistband. She kissed him greedily, smelling of jasmine and bourbon and faintly of vinegar. Her teeth grated against Colter's and he felt a dim, distant response. He was, he decided, tired of sex.

81

Of this sort of sex. All grabbing and tearing. He indulged himself only to prove to himself that there was nothing wrong with him. Nothing torn away and left to rust somewhere else, somewhere far away where the jungle steamed and a young, slender, dark-eyed woman sang as she brushed her hair to a blue-black gloss.

The blonde was on her knees, undoing his pants, when Colter felt the cold blast of wind and turned to find the man standing in the doorway.

He thought at first that the alcohol had burrowed in and turned his thought processes to shambles, destroying his perception, fusing connections. Because John Wayne simply doesn't burst into a Maine cabin in the middle of the night with a Louisville Slugger in his hands. Not anymore, at any rate.

"Duke!" the woman shrilled and took off on hands and knees across the carpet to wriggle behind the couch, giving Colter a last fleeting glimpse of her blue-clad buttocks.

"You're gonna pay, boy," Duke said, moving in, and Colter felt his body reacting before he had time to think it out. Once long ago they had taken that body and drilled it and drilled it, teaching it to react to certain violent stimuli. The violent stimuli were nearly on top of him now, in the form of a baseball bat, a snarling John Wayne face, and a low, animal growl.

Colter went in low, feeling the bat club his left shoulder glancingly. His right forearm had already come up, however, and it slammed into Duke's windpipe with enough force to decapitate a smaller man.

Duke staggered back, clutching at his throat. He tried to throw a knee up into Colter's groin, but Colter crossed his thigh over, blocking it. Then with two stiffened fingers he drove out savagely, striking at the "V" where the ribs meet below the sternum, and the big man went slack, folding up as he reeled back. Duke tripped over the edge of the rug and went down hard, his head smashing into the pile of firewood while Colter, fists bunched, hovered over him.

"Get up. God damnit, get up!"

He realized then that it was over, that Duke wasn't going to get up for a while, and he stepped back unsteadily.

He glanced around and saw the white face with the shiner peering over the back of the sofa, heard the shrill cries, then turned, not bothering to pick up his shirt or coat, and staggered from the cabin.

"You've killed him!" the woman was screaming still as he banged the door shut, stumbled forward and down into the yard. A blue GMC pickup, still running, radiator boiling over, was parked in the yard behind the Cadillac and Colter walked toward it, moving in a zigzag course.

He fumbled with the door handle, reached up and grabbed the steering wheel, pulling himself in. He searched for low gear, found it, and went roaring out of the yard, the screaming of Duke's wife following him up the road.

It was black and still. Steam rose from the GMC's radiator. The truck sat hissing and gurgling and it was the only sound in the world.

Colter, shirtless, hatless, sat in the cab, staring at the bleak and empty house.

It was empty, but it shouldn't have been.

The light Katrinka always left on for him was out. There had been a note on the table, scrawled so poorly that Colter was minutes deciphering the few words Uncle Isaak had written.

Bad stroke, Mikhail. Took Katrinka with the ambulance.

Took Katrinka with the ambulance and Colter couldn't even follow. The GMC had had it. So had he. He opened the door and tried to puke outside. Most of it got out of the cab, but not all.

Then he sat there, looking at the empty house.

All the empty houses, all the dead virgins, all the burned temples. His head was reeling, and he pressed it against the steering wheel. It was hours later when he woke up, his teeth chattering, the stink of vomit all around him, the sheriff's flashlight in his face.

FOUR

Ray Hollingshead was the full-time barber and the part-time sheriff of Canridge. His barbershop, in fact, abutted the single cell and tiny office of the sheriff's facilities—some said that was the main reason Hollingshead had been elected. On this Saturday he would have rather been deer hunting, as he had planned before Colter had run amuck. He had tried very hard to hand Colter over to the state police, but they wouldn't have him. The district attorney couldn't be reached—no doubt the bastard was deer hunting.

"Here you are," Hollingshead said, placing the tray of food on the floor beside the bars of Colter's cell.

Colter looked up at the man. "I've got to get out of here, Hollingshead."

"I can't let you out. You know that. I explained the whole thing to you, Colter."

"My aunt—she's had a stroke. I have to see her."

"I'm sorry about that, you know I am, but I can't let you go without the district attorney's say-so, and no one can find the man."

"Get me a lawyer!"

"Have you got one?" At Colter's negative shake of his head, Hollingshead said, "I don't even know where to find one around here, Colter, do you? Used to be old Judge McWhorter took a case now and then, but he's passed on. If you know of someone, though, why you just tell me and I'll try to get him up here."

"Hollingshead, I've got to get out!"

Colter pressed his head to the bars. His eyes were flaming red, his head ached heavily. He wore his own torn Levis and a patched wool shirt that belonged to Hollingshead. "Let me go on down to the hospital in Stratton and I'll be back by nightfall. I swear it."

"Sorry, son. I can't do a thing until the DA and the JP get together. The charges against you aren't pretty, and I can't take a chance on you going fugitive on me. Attempted rape, assault with intent, grand theft auto—those are the big ones, not counting resisting arrest and driving while intoxicated. I can't let you out on your own recognizance. Those are felony charges, Colter."

"She might be dying!"

"I'm sorry. I'm very sorry." Hollingshead met Colter's gaze, shook his head and walked away, locking the outer door behind him.

Colter sagged back onto the wooden bed and

sat looking at the pool of shadows at his feet. Four hours later Hollingshead returned to find him in the same position.

Colter rose and walked to the cell door, handing a folded business card through to the sheriff. "Call these people for me, Hollingshead, will you?"

Hollingshead looked at the card and shrugged. "If you say so," he replied. He wondered who paid for the long-distance charges and decided to reverse the call. If someone in Washington DC wanted to talk to Colter badly enough, they'd accept the call.

It was midnight when the front door to the jailhouse opened and Hollingshead, still rumpled with sleep, came into the office, followed by District Attorney Hap Fears and Cassidy.

"That was quick," Colter said.

"I was in Portland. The sheriff called the home office and they relayed to me," Cassidy replied.

"When do I get out?"

"Now."

"On what terms?"

Cassidy looked offended. "You get out now," he repeated. "Is that right, Fears?"

"That's right. Open up, Hollingshead. I've got to get back up to the hunting camp."

"Don't I need some kind of release, Hap?" Hollingshead wanted to know. "When we had that fellow from North Carolina up here we had to have that paperwork all done properly, if you'll recall. Your office was giving us hell."

"Open up," Hap Fears said through tight lips.

"It's all right, Hollingshead. I'm authorizing it."

Hollingshead didn't like it much. Shaking his head, he opened the cell door, standing back as Colter stepped out. Cassidy handed him a coat.

"Thanks. I've got to get to Stratton."

"All right," Cassidy answered. "I've got a car outside, a pontoon plane at Flagstaff Lake."

In five minutes they were highballing down the road to the lake, in ten they were airborne. Colter sat staring out the window of the small plane, watching for the hazy lights of Stratton. Another car was waiting for them when they landed and they were whisked down the icy roads of the town, reaching the hospital within an hour of Colter's release.

It was just half an hour too late.

Isaak, looking small and bewildered, rose and came up to meet Mike. He clung to his great-nephew's shoulders, the tears running unashamedly from his clouded eyes.

"She kept asking for you, Mikhail. She asked for you at the last. What will I do now? What will I ever do without her? I have no one now, no place to go."

"It'll be all right, Uncle Isaak," Colter told him, knowing that there was nothing he could have said that was more fatuous. The old man had nothing now. He had depended on his sister totally. Without her he was confused and helpless. Colter patted his shoulder and smiled.

"Everything will be all right. I promise you."

"Yes. I will just sit down." He wiped at his eyes and Colter helped him to sit on the long wooden bench.

The doctor came up minutes later, pink and scrubbed and full of solemn condolences. Then they took Colter to the small room where Aunt Katrinka lay. She was very small beneath the bed-clothes. Tiny, withered, gone to her peace.

Colter said, "She was Russian Orthodox. If you can find a priest somewhere . . ."

The doctor seemed uninterested. "You'll have to stop by the business office, Mr. Colter. There is the matter of charges."

"Damn you," Colter hissed, "I know there is the matter of charges! There is always the matter of charges. Whatever happened to the Hippocratic oath, you insensitive bastard?"

The doctor went red and started to snap back a response, but something in Colter's eyes stopped him. He spun away and marched briskly down the hallway.

Colter wiped away the single tear that had broken free and stood a moment longer. "Sorry," he said. "Sorry I wasn't here, Aunt Katrinka." But then he never had been there at the right time—and they kept right on dying. Those he loved.

The nurse in the business office was tight-lipped, brusque, and efficient. She kept asking questions Colter had no answer to. Uncle Isaak stood leaning against the counter, his old eyes uncomprehending. Someone good had died. Why did they not take her and bury her? What was all of this?

"You had no insurance then?"

"No."

"But surely . . ." the nurse glanced up, tight-lipped, impatient, "will you fill out this supplementary form, then? All we ask is your place of employment, length of time . . ."

"I'm not employed," Colter said.

"You are on welfare, then?"

"No. I am not on welfare then. I am simply not employed."

"But some arrangements, sir, have to be made to take care of Miss Koltsov's charges."

Cassidy was at Colter's elbow. He asked the nurse, "What's the total?"

"May I inquire who you are?" the nurse asked in starched tones. her eyes were as hard as diamonds.

"I'm the man who's asking what the charges are," Cassidy shot back, and Colter began to like the government man just a little at that moment.

The nurse told him and Cassidy settled up. In cash, a novelty that dumbfounded the nurse. Colter was given a bill stamped "Received in Full," and he jammed it into his pants pocket.

"This doesn't buy me, Cassidy," he said angrily.

"Listen, Colter," Cassidy said with unexpected savagery, "why don't you just go to hell? The agency doesn't trade on sorrow and pain—I damn sure don't. But you think about this, my friend: What now?"

What now? Colter looked at the white-haired old man hobbling off to the stainless steel water cooler. A lost and small thing. What now?

Now there would be the funeral and its expenses. The only way to pay would be to sell the old house and the five acres it sat on—worth very little in this part of the country. Then Uncle Isaak could be taken off to an old folks' home of some kind while Colter . . . while Colter was brought up on an assortment of felony charges and locked up for ten years and up. None of that mess was Cassidy's doing; it was Colter's own fault, every bit of it, and his problem to solve. Except there was no way out. None at all.

"Mikhail?" The old man hobbled forward, leaning on his cane heavily. "Where do I go, Mikhail? What should I do now?" And Colter had nothing to tell him.

He turned back toward the desk, but Cassidy was gone. Colter spotted him, coat over his arm, walking down the long white corridor toward the elevator.

"Cassidy!"

The government man didn't even glance back. He kept walking, his rigid back expressing his anger. Colter sprinted after him, catching him as the elevator door opened and Cassidy was stepping in.

"All right, man. All right." Colter still had hold of his arm. "I'll do it, whatever it is."

"What do you want?" Cassidy asked stiffly.

"I want another check. You have it here in the morning. The same amount. Only make it out to Isaak Koltsov. Then you'll have to talk to the DA. Get them off my back if possible. Most of the charges are phony."

"Then?"

"Then nothing. That's all, Cassidy. Then it's

your turn—then you tell me exactly what it is *you* want."

They told him. In a Lexington Avenue hotel room in New York City. Cassidy was there, a bald man named Reese who never looked Colter in the eye, and a white-haired, impeccably groomed agency higher-up whose name was very pointedly not mentioned.

Outside the hotel room door two janitors shampooed the carpeting in the hallway. Each was wearing a Smith & Wesson .38 cradled in a shoulder holster beneath his green uniform jacket. Earlier a nameless hound dog of a man had swept the room with an electronic instrument designed to detect bugs. Colter's meals had been brought in. He had been given everything he had asked for but liquor.

Now he perched on a low bureau, watching the three men before him. Reese did most of the talking, rubbing his bald head nervously from time to time.

"Cassidy has told us that you have the target in focus," he began.

"What's that mean? He told me that there was someone you wanted to get out of a foreign country surreptitiously. He didn't say who or where."

"No." Reese cleared his throat. The white-haired man was trimming a cigar. "This is going to be a locked-door job, Colter."

"Meaning?"

"Meaning we, uh, think it is best that you yourself don't know the target area."

"You won't even tell me that it's Russia, then?" Colter asked with a thin smile. Reese paled.

"Uh, no," Reese answered, incredibly. He looked at the white-haired man, who was concentrating on lighting his cigar evenly, turning it carefully over the blue match flame. "We really aren't authorized to pin this down."

"All right," Colter answered amiably. "I don't know that, then." He stood up and walked to the window to look out at the smear of neon, the long streamers of automobile lights along the avenue. "But if I did know that," he said turning, "I'd be damned worried. They don't take kindly to internal interference, do they? And if it was discovered that an American was behind it, it would more than embarrass this government."

"They'll never trace you back to your source unless you confess," Cassidy said.

"It's that close a blanket?"

"It is."

"All right—who am I after?"

The white-haired man across the room shook his head almost imperceptibly and took a tentative puff on his cigar. Colter waited.

"We can't tell you that," Reese answered.

"A military man?"

"No."

"A politician?"

"Not that either."

Colter nodded, somewhat relieved. Either of those two types would be relatively well guarded.

"For purposes of security you will be traveling

blind, Colter," Reese went on. "That is, you will not have more information than you need until you need it."

"In other words, you're telling me nothing at home base. Nothing except that I'm going to the south of the Soviet Union to bring out a non-political citizen."

"Who said it was in the south?"

"There aren't many Ukrainians in the north," Colter replied. He smiled, but no one returned the expression.

"Get on with it," the white-haired man said. He appeared only bored.

"You're leaving tonight for Paris on TWA," Reese told him. "No weapons, no papers but a passport in your own name. You'll check into the Alexander Hotel on Victor Hugo—a room has been reserved in your name. . . ."

"First-class," Colter mused. The Alexander didn't come for peanuts.

". . . In your name. Your contact will approach you at exactly eight p.m. at your doorway."

"Paris time?" Colter asked with a gleam in his eye.

"Yes, of course," Reese said soberly. The man apparently did not understand humor. Not many did after a few years in the agency, Colter guessed. Reese snapped his briefcase shut and looked at Colter, blinking. "That is all I have." He glanced again at the white-haired man, who shook his head definitely.

"That's it?" Colter asked, not quite believing the interview was at an end. The white-haired man rose, picking up his hat and coat. Reese was halfway to the door.

"That is it," Reese replied shortly.

"You don't give a man much, do you?" Colter asked, but again he got no answer. He was getting used to that with this mob.

It was Cassidy who spoke then, adding the last words: "Good luck, Colter."

Good luck. And don't call us if there's any trouble. Don't bother trying an American embassy —there won't be one, not where you're going. Just get on that plane and fly off into the night. You'll find out the rest when you get—to wherever the hell it is you're going.

They didn't mistake Colter. They figured he had two hundred thousand reasons for doing what he was doing, and not a single reason more. Like patriotism. They didn't try to fly that flag in your face much anymore. You were a mercenary again. We're all mercenaries. That was the way they saw it, and they were probably right, all things considered.

Colter glanced at the TWA tickets they had left on the bedside table. Then he lay down, listening to the night sounds the city made.

Two hours later, dressed in a light brown herringbone coat, tan trousers, and a black silk shirt, Colter was in the air, leaving JFK behind as the 707 knifed through the cloud cover and entered the moon-bright night sky beyond.

He had a whisky sour—the company be damned—and settled back to watch the stewardess swish up and down the aisle until sleep closed his eyes.

It was raining when they touched down at Orly Airport in the early morning hours. Colter rushed toward the baggage counter with the rest of the herd, recovered his new valise, and walked to the street entrance where tour buses and taxis wedged in together against the yellow curb.

"M'sieur?" The taxi driver wore a torn leather jacket and a corduroy cap. He also had a lousy accent. "Taxi, m'sieur? Taxi?"

Colter followed him to the green Citroen cab and climbed into the back seat, keeping his valise with him. The cab lurched out into the traffic and accelerated, tires slapping against the wet pavement. The driver didn't say another word until they were bulleting down the Boulevard Pereire, the red and green lights of the still-flourishing bistros watery and misted. The night life of Paris, it seemed, never ended.

"You would like the Alexander?" the taxi driver asked.

"That's right." Colter guessed, "Oklahoma?"

The driver looked into the rearview mirror and grinned.

The Alexander Hotel is on Victor Hugo, within spitting distance of the Arc de Triomphe. Colter, climbing stiffly from the green cab, was ushered in by a doorman with an umbrella and a gloomy expression.

His reservation was in order, and Colter was led up to his room by a tiny bellhop. In the break-

96

fast room early risers—or late-nighters—sat at French period furniture drinking coffee and cognac beneath a ceiling of gathered fabric that formed a sunburst over the tasteful gray walls.

Room 202 had silk walls, deep white carpeting, full-length mirrors, and a massive canopied bed. The window looked out on the tree-lined Victor Hugo Avenue where gray mists swirled still. The Arc de Triomphe was subdued behind the rain.

Colter had no French money, and the bellboy sulked away leaving Mike to stand grinning, looking appreciatively at the beautifully appointed, high-ceilinged hotel room.

The company had splurged for him. Well, why not? The odds were it wouldn't last long. The odds, in fact, were very good that Michael Colter wouldn't be dragging his weary form across this shadowed earth much longer. Despite company assurances.

You don't go into the Soviet Union. You just don't. True, along its mammoth borders, there were plenty of places where it could be done, but that wasn't the trick. Getting in was easy, but once inside you were confined. In Russia you need cards to purchase food, to buy petrol, to get new shoes. There are local police, army personnel, and secret police on the lookout for any stranger, for any movement or activity out of the normal.

Colter pulled off his coat and sat on the bed. He wasn't kidding himself about this; let the company think what they wanted. He was fluent in the language, but there were changes in a language in thirty years—and it had been thirty years since Aunt Katrinka, who had taught him the language, had slipped across the Polish border with her brother and a tiny baby: Mikhail Koltsov, the son of a man who had been taken to an *osoblager*—a hard labor camp—and his bride of a year, who had died in labor.

The idioms of Katrinka's youth were not those of a modern Ukrainian. He would undoubtedly appear humorless—but then most Russians are. He would not understand certain references, the local politics. It's not so easy, despite the impression war films project, to pass for a native in a foreign land. In a closed society, it was damned near impossible. Everyone, everything was covered by records, orders, documents and procedure. Colter could only hope that someone, somewhere, knew what he was doing when he had planned this operation.

Colter kicked off his shoes and lay back on the bed, staring up at the tiny winged cherub flying across the faded blue background within a tiny round recess in the ceiling.

"You're going home," he told himself, closing his eyes. Home to a country he had never seen, had never wanted to see. To the country that had killed his father for wishing to speak his mind. Maybe it was tempting fate just a little too much. He had no real hope of coming out alive; but then he hadn't been doing much living back in Maine. Filling in a lot of hours, but there was very little living to it.

He sighed, closed his eyes, and fell into a deep sleep.

He had breakfast at noon, sat on the small white balcony watching the bustling Parisians, the whirl of traffic, the cloud-dappled blue skies. After lunch he took another nap.

At three Colter went out and strolled up the Victor Hugo to the Arc de Triomphe, watching the tourists from fifty nations taking pictures, smelling the scents of the bright, overflowing flower carts, the stink of traffic screeching and blaring its weaving way across the city, hearing the noisy humming of the crowds—and feeling light-years away from all of it.

He walked on down the Champs Elysees, watching the French girls and sweater-clad tourists with only a modicum of interest. Turning down Franklin Roosevelt, he approached the Seine, watching a coal barge muddle past amid darting sailboats and canoes. Lovers sat on the quay; fishermen tried their luck in the murky, oily waters. Old men with berets hobbled past carrying long loaves of bread, and here and there an artist had set up his easel to try to capture the age-old scene.

By five Colter was back in his room eating herring and sour cream followed by cherry tarts and black coffee.

At precisely eight o'clock he opened his hotel room door and found a tall, youthful, red-headed man standing there.

"Colter?"

"That's me. Come on in."

The redhead did, his eyes moving about the room, not suspiciously, but with simple curiosity.

"Nice digs."

"I'm traveling VIP."

"It won't last."

"No."

Red took off his raincoat and sat on an armless chair—a good imitation Louis XIV. He lighted a cigarette and leaned back, blowing smoke out his nose.

"I'm Alvin," he said at length. "I'll get you started on the first leg. There are a few things that we have to take care of. Is now a good time?"

"If it has to be."

"It does, I'm afraid," Alvin answered, smiling. He walked to the telephone and dialed, speaking a few rapid words in French. Hanging up, he said, "These people aren't entirely clean, Colter." Meaning their security rating was only fair. "So the less said, the better."

"I don't know anything myself," Colter cracked, and Alvin continued to smile. It was all a very merry game,

"You will soon enough, I guess. Probably you'll end up knowing a hell of a lot more than you want to know. That's always my situation." He stubbed out his cigarette and asked, "Is this your first infiltration?"

"Yes."

The first as a civilian. You didn't count the armed infiltrations where you blacked your face and hoped to God the moon stayed hidden as you crawled through a rotten-smelling jungle to find someone to kill.

It wasn't long before the help showed up. At the knock on the door, Alvin rose and let in two locals. One of them, a tobacco-scented wheezer in tweeds, walked around Colter twice before attacking him with a tape measure, scribbling down the measurements in a crabbed hand. The second man sat patiently on the bed, a wooden box on the floor beside him.

"By the way," Alvin said, "I'd leave off shaving for a while, if that hasn't already occurred to you."

"All right."

"You might want to ditch the mustache though."

"I'll keep it," Colter said, as the tailor ran a tape from groin to cuff, stood, nodding to Alvin, and was shown out, still scribbling in his note pad. The agent slipped him a wad of francs on the way out.

"All right," Alvin said. "How about this chair, Pierre?"

The Frenchman only shrugged. He was unpacking a huge old portrait camera from the wooden box, squinting and puffing as he worked.

"A few snapshots for the folks back home," Alvin said. He seemed to be enjoying himself thoroughly, and Colter thought things must be pretty dull at the Paris office.

The photographer erected a folding screen hung with a black cloth, positioning it behind the chair where Mike Colter sat. He switched the plates and took a picture.

"Don't smile, for God's sake," Alvin coached. Another flash and the photographer was through, accepting a handful of folded banknotes from Alvin as he packed up, still puffing, still squinting as if he had never seen his equipment before and found it menacingly enigmatic.

Alvin let the photographer out and closed the door behind him. Counting to ten slowly, he opened the door again and peered out into the hall, giving Colter the thumbs-up as he turned around, latching the door behind him.

"You trust them a lot," Colter observed.

"Only when they're broke," Alvin said. "I've got a message for you, Colter."

"Go ahead."

"Do you know a Cassidy in DC?" Colter nodded and Alvin went on. "The message was, 'Have live-in nurse for old man. Deposit made his account.' All right?"

Colter said that it was and Alvin smiled. "No answer for Washington?"

"No answer."

"All right. Let's get to the meat then, shall we?"

"I'd appreciate it."

"They're playing this one very close, Colter. All I've been told is this: Vienna tomorrow. Via hired car. I'll be driving you myself. You'll be traveling as an Austrian. Your passport will be ready in the morning."

"That's it?"

"Afraid so."

"One objection—I don't speak German. How

do I impersonate an Austrian?"

"No problem. We're crossing from Switzerland. The Swiss don't know what security means. The Austrians aren't much better. They don't even have a checkpoint on the Chur Road, and that's the one we're taking. Everything will go okay. Your name is Rudolf Keller. There's a reservation in your name—Keller's name, that is—at the Regina Hotel on Rooseveltplatz. The end." Alvin spread his hands.

"Who do I contact in Vienna?"

"Don't know, chum. I expect he'll find you. They sure are closing the doors behind you, aren't they?"

"Yes." Colter frowned. He didn't like this, but then no one had asked for his approval. He had taken their money and that was that. He only hoped they didn't close one too many doors behind him. "All right, if that's it, that's it." He had to trust the company or get out now. Get out and go back to what?

He asked Alvin: "What do we do with the rest of the evening? Dominoes?"

"In Paris?" Alvin shook his head heavily. "Let me go by my apartment and change and we'll see a little of the night life. Unless you're some sort of fanatic?"

"Not that sort," Colter said. "Sounds good."

Alvin's apartment was on the Rue Cambon across the street from the Hotel de Castille. They reached it in five minutes, Alvin ignoring the rain, driving like a Parisian taxi driver, squirting his little green Fiat Spyder between other cars, skidding around the slick corners, chatting all the time, waving his arm in the air.

He left Colter in the car while he ran upstairs to change his clothes. When he emerged half an hour later he was wearing a pale green sharkskin suit and a yellow cravat that set up an amazing contrast with his flame-red hair. He scooted into the Fiat, looking sheepish.

"Well, no sense in being drab."

Drab wasn't the word for the get-up he wore now, but Alvin's raiment paled before the costumes of the other street denizens. In the Caveau de la Huchette they wore feather boas and sequins. So did some of the women. A Dixieland band blared in the basement and the stairway leading down to it was crowded with warm bodies trying to cram themselves into what seemed to be a closet-sized area, a sort of voluntary Black Hole of Calcutta.

"You can't get drinks down there," Alvin shouted above the din produced by an imitation Al Hirt and his French Whipcords. "Follow me!"

Alvin led the way to a relatively quiet dining room upstairs where four or five people sat around tables the size of a saucer, drinking chartreuse and absinthe from thimble-sized glasses. It didn't look real promising to Colter. Alvin waved to a small, nicely molded brunette encased in a glittering blue dress. She had her hair sheared off into pointed wings on either side of her pale, oval face. Her crimson, pouting lips blew Alvin a kiss and mouthed a few words. Alvin gestured back and moved his lips in answer.

Colter, his eyes on the brunette, asked, "Over there, I take it?"

"No. That's for later," Alvin replied with a wink. He led Colter across the room. It wasn't possible to walk through it without nudging tables and bodies, but Alvin somehow found a table in the corner, where they sat in reasonable security, watching the painted, scented, primped, and somewhat absurd night crowd.

They had two drinks, which cost the equivalent of eight dollars apiece, and then muscled their way back through the mob into the night. Darkness had settled, the lights came on. The night people had emerged in striped shirts, berets, knee-length boots, leather jackets, leotards, fishnet stockings and plastic raincoats.

They wove their way up town and found another dive. An expensive dive, which Alvin called The Frog and which seemed to specialize in embarrassing the clientele. A huge, mustached greeter just inside the door kissed every woman who walked in, hugging them tightly, drawing a variety of reactions, from squeals to something approaching passion. If the customers didn't resist too strenuously, they were given a small bronze frog. A lanky blond woman with makeup so pale she seemed to have no features at all performed the same service for the men. It was a hell of a way to start a mononucleosis epidemic, but Colter supposed it was harmless enough.

"I just don't get it, that's all. Does it mean something?"

"Now you're trying to understand the French?"

Alvin laughed. "Come on."

Colter stepped up and got his kiss. It wasn't bad. A pair of dry lips pressed briefly to his, scented rice powder in his nostrils. Then a small bronze amphibian was pressed into his palm. There was also a moment to collect the cover charge; they weren't that eccentric.

It was crowded, very warm inside. Much tobacco smoke. But the liquor was good. Colter had downed two drinks when he found himself standing face to face with a blonde. Face to face wasn't exactly the right way of putting it. She was a good six inches taller than he was. Her heavily mascaraed eyes never even blinked as he put his hand on her slender arms and told her lies about the bass fishing in Maine.

"What is this, dancing?" Alvin asked. His tie was slightly askew.

"International relations," Colter answered.

"Let's go over there," Alvin said. "Nearer the door."

"Just getting to know her."

Alvin looked her up and down himself and shook his head. "You know her well enough. Christ, white zombies yet!"

"She's a good listener."

"I just saw a friend of mine," the redhead said, downing his drink, turning slightly away. He held his bronze frog in the same hand as his cocktail, giving the odd illusion that he was sucking the frog dry—and enjoying it immensely.

"Friend?" Colter asked.

"Not a friend, no. Someone in the business—on

106

the other side."

"Christ," Colter muttered. "Already? Good-bye, darlin'. I hope you find a nice man with a good blowtorch." The blonde didn't move, but one eye slowly dropped in a heavy wink. It was, Colter considered, a wonder her eyelashes didn't stick together, gummed up as they were with that black goo. . . .

"Which one is it?" Colter asked, as Alvin hustled him for the door, moving past the inflowing tourists who screeched and complained and laughed as the tireless host and hostess of The Frog continued to practice their commercial osculation.

"Over there," Alvin hissed. "By the big plaster frog in the corner."

There was an immense gilt-painted plaster frog on a pedestal near the bandstand, and lounging there was a man conservatively dressed in a brown suit, white shirt, and brown tie.

He was also wearing a pair of yellow-framed, tinted glasses. His hair was cut short, smoothed back on a symmetrical, narrow skull. His shoes were polished brown oxfords. He looked a very respectable human being with the exception of the yellow-framed glasses, which added a touch of the bizarre. Perhaps it was the man's cover. Otherwise, he would have been out of place in the Paris night scene, which ran to the baroque and the fatuous.

"Let's go," Alvin said, nudging Colter. "I don't want to spend the night with him."

Outside Alvin grabbed Colter's wrist and

dragged him to a waiting taxi. "His name's Krylov," Alvin said, peering out the back window as the driver demanded instructions. "Around the Eiffel Tower!"

The Frenchman muttered vague curses and swung the Peugeot sharply to the right, narrowly missing two girl cyclists who waved feminine fists at him.

"Who's Krylov?" Colter asked. Alvin was still looking out the back window of the taxi. Finally he turned, settling with a grin.

"He's embassy staff," said Alvin. "You don't have to worry, though. He's on me, not you."

"You sure of that, are you?"

"No." Alvin grinned again. "Not really, but I think so—he's got an interest in some of my work. Drop us here," he told the cabby, who stopped with a squeal of rubber and an exasperated expulsion of breath. Alvin paid the man, who accepted the fare and a generous tip with Gallic insouciance. Colter and Alvin hiked back toward where the agent's Fiat was parked, keeping to the shadows of the chestnut trees.

"Want to go home?" Alvin asked when they had reached his car and gotten in.

"What for?" Colter asked.

"I was afraid you were the nervous type."

"I think I'll hold up," Mike Colter said.

"Good." Alvin switched on the ignition and started the Fiat with a roar, and they were off again, flying down the narrow streets. "That man makes my life miserable," Alvin said. "Krylov, I

108

mean. Plays havoc with my love life too. No sensitivity, the Reds."

They wound down a hill that was composed of around a thousand switchbacks, Colter's stomach churning as Alvin swung the Fiat sharply through each corner; maybe he was demonstrating his driving ability or maybe it was the only way to get to the long purple building at the foot of the street.

They walked in without being kissed and stood at the bar. Colter didn't remember ordering, but they were drinking something yellow-brown and very potent, you could tell that by the way it paralyzed the tongue as it slid over it and scorched its way into your belly. The music was something obviously designed to destroy brain tissue. Everyone was loud and French, and across the broad stage where pink baby spotlights shined, nine perfect and pink nude dancers cavorted, singing a song that must have meant what Colter thought it did by the way they moved.

By the time Colter had finally managed to get ahold of some authentic bourbon, he had swallowed six of the little yellow powerhouses and his insides hurt. The French, he decided, did not know how to drink. He downed the whisky and stood aching, his insides in torment. They just plain hurt.

Not his stomach. It lay steady down in that vast alcohol-saturated pit, content and warm. But his insides hurt. All of him, clean through. He could see Alvin gazing off into space through the wreaths of smoke that hung blue, ever-changing in the air above their heads. There seemed to be an awful lot of smoke, and Colter finally realized that he was smoking a cigar. That was fine—he didn't smoke,'but it was fine. When your insides hurt, you do things.

He began talking about it, telling Alvin how it had been in Cambodia, how the American forces, frightened by some Senate committee that had been frightened by a bunch of people with placards, up and pulled out, leaving the villagers they had promised to protect alone and virtually unarmed against an encroaching army.

It was politics—it had been a very political war—and there had to be sacrifices to the gods of the election booths. There were plenty.

Small people. Women with shining hair who sang joyously like a tiny waterfall when you watched from your bed in the morning, and she padded around naked, hair long and gleaming, eyes happy.

They had no placards, however; and so they gave them over to the butchers who liked to chop people up with machetes or stick bamboo splinters in their eyes. They did that to all sorts of people, all sizes, all shapes. Poor, mutilated Cambodia.

Alvin had his chin on his hand, his elbow on the bar, his eyes fixed on Colter's. Colter had told him how the only satisfaction he had gotten was driving his fist into that damned colonel's face.

"You see, his orders said move back, and he did. He knew they didn't have a chance, knew that

110

as soon as we pulled out the entire village was going to go under, but his damned orders said move back . . . they court-martialed me. How the hell could that even matter? What's a court-martial compared to a massacre like that . . . ?"

He realized that Alvin wasn't listening, couldn't have heard him if he'd wanted to above the happy sounds: the laughter, the clinking of glasses, the electronic music. It was for the best, Colter decided. Silent speaking. Silent protests against the gods of futility.

Someone moved the bar and Colter's elbow slipped. It was a long time before he could upright himself. Someone had spilled his whisky too, damnit! But Alvin was there, that stupid, likable grin on his face. Maybe he was thinking about later—the girl who was for later on. The one back at . . . whatever stupid name the place had had.

The girls on the stage were gone. The pink lights had turned blue and Colter was staggering toward a door, Alvin linking arms with him.

"If anybody wants to fight, by God, they can have us!" Alvin said. Colter couldn't make sense out of that. And for a confused moment he thought he was at the Lakewatch and he wondered where the regulars were.

The door opened and a gust of cold wind clutched at them. They stumbled outside and stood together in the alley, feeling proud of themselves for no particular reason.

"You got it made here," Colter said. The alley, of cobbles with a thin layer of asphalt over it, insisted on rising up, writhing, slanting, trying to slide Colter off. "Sorry," he said, realizing that Alvin was all that held him up. The night was cold, dark, horribly empty. Then the flares went off in Colter's head, and there was a brief, shattering jolt of pain behind his right ear before Paris went colder, darker, emptier.

FIVE

When you wake up it always smells like vomit. It's the drinking, you see. When you wake up you're usually on something hard and damp. Your head will be pinwheeling with sparking images. Each time one of those little golden sparks flickers, a shaft of white pain cleaves your skull. That's called the after-benefit of drinking. A part of the continuum of fun.

But you can usually get to your hands and knees properly, and you don't usually have company. Colter did, and as he sagged back on his rump, holding his head, he stared at the still figure beside him, trying to understand this.

He looked up, squinting through the pain behind his eyes. Where in Christ's name was he?

Paris. Realization descended on him suddenly, and with it was the simultaneous knowledge that he was not merely suffering from alcohol, that the

113

man beside him was not sleeping it off.

"Jesus!" He stretched out a hand, got cautiously to hands and knees and peered at the battered, bloody face. "Alvin!"

The agent was sprawled on his side. Blood ran from his mouth and nostrils, forming dark worms. There was a smear of blood beneath his right ear as well, caked now. Alvin wasn't moving at all.

Feeling suddenly cold, Colter felt for a pulse, knowing he would find none. His head still throbbed with pain and he gingerly touched his skull behind his ear, finding a knot the size of an egg. Something had to be done, but he couldn't clear his thoughts enough to figure out what exactly. He sat there shivering, his arms folded, his head bowed. Death had come back. Old friend, old adversary, constant companion.

"The Paris office isn't so soft after all, is it, Alvin?" he whispered. No, not on this hard, cold night. There was a girl waiting somewhere for a later that would never come.

"Get out of here, you damned fool," Colter hissed at himself. The voice seemed to come from somewhere impossibly distant, through a velvety muffling tunnel. Still the message came through. "Get out!" This was no time to tangle with the Sûreté. The French police could be very tough. Being tagged now would put the brakes on the game the agency was trying to run. It would be over before it started.

"Well, get moving then," Colter snarled. He tried to get up and found his mind more willing than his body. His knee buckled and he banged it hard against the cobblestones, numbing his leg. He cursed and braced himself with his palms and started to rise again, and it was then that he saw them.

Broken, twisted, knocked into the deep shadows along the brick wall in front of him. A pair of tinted glasses with bright yellow rims. Colter sagged down again and sat staring at them.

"They're on me, not you," Alvin had said. Now Alvin lay dead in a Paris alley and Colter was up the creek. Where had Alvin been poking his nose, Colter wondered. Krylov had wanted him badly to do it this way. Alvin must have burned the Russians good . . . if it was Alvin they wanted dead. It had to have been—they couldn't have mistaken the two men even in the poor light of the alley. Sure, why kill Alvin if it was Colter they wanted to stop! Hell, maybe it amounted to the same thing. He was helpless without Alvin. Krylov had gotten his two birds.

Colter was angry and despondent at once. Alvin hadn't deserved that. They played hard games. You're in a war again, my friend. A new kind of war, but it's war. He had to do something—he was still sitting there, just sitting.

Colter's head hurt too much to sort things out. he only knew he had to *get out*. A distant siren brought his head up and he rolled Alvin over, rifling his pockets until he found the agent's car key. There were no other keys on the ring and Colter could not find a damned apartment key.

The siren was altogether too close. Likely it

wasn't interested in this dark and stinking alleyway at all, but Colter didn't want to wait to find out.

Using the wall to brace himself, he dragged himself erect. Then, bent over at the waist, he jog-trotted to the mouth of the alley and emerged onto the street, where he forced himself to slow, to stand straight, to appear as casual as possible considering his condition.

The Fiat, bless it, was still there, coated with dew. Colter unlocked the door with shaky fingers and settled into the leather-covered bucket seat.

The siren was closer, its whine boring through Colter's head. He choked the Fiat, ground the starter, pumped the gas pedal madly, tried again, and finally heard the motor catch, saw the tachometer needle jump to life, swinging into the red.

He didn't even look back as he jammed the car into low gear and sped up the street, his heart pounding wildly. In the rearview he caught a glimpse of a flashing blue light, of a Renault pulling into the forlorn little alley.

Colter slowed to a less conspicuous rate of speed and turned half a dozen corners, left and right at random, snaking through the narrow alleys, finally emerging on the Rue Lafayette where he pulled to the curb and sat staring through the windshield, his hands tightly clenching the steering wheel.

What now? They had gotten Alvin. The Russians, or someone, had taken him out for some reason Colter couldn't guess at, and in doing so they had effectively cut his throat. He needed Alvin's help to get out of Paris on schedule. He knew there was a rental car waiting for him, but he did not know where. He had neither French nor Swiss francs, and, most important, he had no passport. He was stuck, good and stuck, and there weren't many options open to him.

Colter made his decision suddenly, and he pulled out into the swarming traffic, horns blaring all around him. He had to get to Alvin's apartment before the police did, and that wouldn't take them long. He wished he had been thinking clearly enough to lift the dead man's identification, but he had missed that bet. If the police found anything in the apartment with Colter's name on it, they would be looking for him soon enough. Colter wanted to clean out that apartment before the police could.

It took him twenty minutes to find the Rue Cambon again. His head was still fuzzy from the liquor and he cursed strong drink. He fully expected to find the police in front of Alvin's apartment house when he got there. He pulled up half a block away and sat for a moment in the Fiat, glancing at the driver's registration, which had Alvin's true name on it.

Colter got out of the car and walked through the drizzle along the opposite side of the street, his shoulders hunched, hands thrust in his pockets. He saw no sign of the Sûreté or the local police, of anyone else outside the apartment building. He crossed the street and walked boldly in through the foyer, keeping his head turned away from the concierge who sat in a cubbyhole with a glass of tea before him, working a crossword puzzle.

There was a directory near the stairwell and Colter found Alvin's apartment number beside the name the car registration had provided. He started upstairs toward the third floor.

He had no trouble finding the apartment and no trouble getting in. Colter had been wondering how to silently force the door, but when he tried the handle, the door, unlocked, swung in.

Colter stepped inside quickly and found the light button on the wall. The electric light glared to life and Colter found himself surveying the savaged room. It looked like the aftermath of a mau mau attack. Alvin's mattress had been hacked to shreds, his furniture torn apart, his wallpaper removed, pictures taken down, carpet taken up. Molding had been removed from the ceiling. Alvin's clothes lay strewn about the room.

Colter swallowed hard and cursed. He wasn't likely to find anything helpful. Not now.

The sound of approaching footsteps stung him into motion. He slipped to the window, which opened onto an iron fire escape, and stepped out into the chilly night to stand peering through the gap between the drapery and the window frame.

The footsteps had stopped—at least Colter could hear them no longer. He waited, stilling his breath. There were more footsteps then. Heels clicked on the hardwood floor of the corridor outside the room. Receding. Colter frowned and stepped back into the room. Then he saw it lying on the floor just inside the door.

He crossed the room in four long strides and picked up the brown paper-wrapped package. Inside was an Austrian passport in the name of Rudolf Keller, and from the passport Michael Colter's own picture stared bleakly out at him.

"I'm glad to see you, you ugly bastard," Colter muttered.

He pocketed the passport and sat down on the corner chair, which had had the bottom ripped out of it. He stared at the ravaged apartment, rubbing his aching eyebrow with his index finger. What now? He had his passport but no money.

Then he tried his own hand at rifling Alvin's belongings. It had been done thoroughly already, but then they probably hadn't been looking for the same things Colter was.

They hadn't been looking for money, for instance. Colter found a bundle of notes thrown carelessly aside. All used five- and ten-franc notes, both Swiss and French. Colter sighed with relief and pocketed the money.

He found the gun under Alvin's bed. It was an S&W Model 59 automatic. 9mm, 14-shot magazine. It was fully loaded. Colter hesitated. Carrying a gun could get him into more trouble than it got him out of. But then there was someone in the game who was killing people. For the time being he elected to keep it and he shoved it behind his waistband.

Again he heard footsteps in the hallway. Plenty of them. Colter dashed for the window and made the fire escape just as three uniformed policemen entered the room. Colter was down the fire escape and out into the street within a minute, strolling past the black police Renault with its blue light blinking. He reached the Fiat, casually slid in, and drove away.

In twenty minutes he was out of Paris, driving east through a dense fog. There had been no point in trying to return to his own hotel, and nothing there he wanted badly enough to take the risk for.

Rudolf Keller settled back into the snug bucket seat of the Fiat and drove steadily through the night toward the Swiss border.

"Idiot!"

"Comrade Fetyukov . . ."

"Idiot!" Fetyukov repeated. He slammed his fist down on his desk, toppling a set of brass scales. "To murder the man!"

"You yourself said that he was becoming intolerable," Krylov said rather weakly. The man behind the desk scowled more deeply, his heavy jowls drawn down as if by great weights.

"This is the sort of work you wish to do now? Now you are an assassin, Krylov? Now you prowl the streets with your—what did you use? Oh, yes, the lead pipe. Now you strike down the American counterrevolutionaries?"

"Alvin was intruding, comrade," Krylov said with some force. He was tired of being abused by Fetyukov. What had he done that was so wrong? How many times had he heard his superior tell of the time he killed the West German agent in Berlin?

"There was," Fetyukov said very slowly, "nothing at all gained by this, Krylov. Where is the list? Where are the rosters!"

"We searched the apartment thoroughly," Krylov said. He stood with his hands behind his back, staring out the window at gray early morning Paris. He was wearing his spare glasses, the wire-rimmed ones. His head hurt from this all-night debriefing, from lack of food, from the alcohol of the night before.

"Yes?" Fetyukov prompted.

"We searched the apartment most thoroughly. . . ."

"And found nothing. The rosters therefore are not there, were not there. They are at Alvin's place of employment as they should be expected to be."

"Our informer . . ."

"Sit." Fetyukov stared at his man and rubbed his forehead as if he too had a headache. The stupidity of this Krylov was amazing. What had he hoped to accomplish? Did he have dreams of promotion—he could forget any such ambition now. "Let us go through this again, please."

"I had the American agent 'Alvin' under surveillance. . . ."

"Please. One minute." Fetyukov lifted the tiny tape recorder from his desk drawer to the top of the desk.

"You are going to report this?" Krylov asked hollowly.

"Is there another choice?" Fetyukov peered at the tape recorder in puzzlement, found the switches, conducted a short test, and then read in the date and time of the interview. Krylov was slowly paling, shrinking in his chair. He hadn't counted on this at all. What *had* he done? They would have to recall him from Paris now.

"Please begin again." The tape recorder turned silently.

"I was following the American agent 'Alvin,' who has been giving our section considerable trouble. I picked him up at his apartment house and followed him to the Alexander Hotel. He asked for the room of someone named Colter and went upstairs. I waited in the lobby."

"Who is Colter?"

"Colter . . ."

"Yes, who was it he went to see, Comrade Krylov?"

"At the time there was no way of ascertaining that."

"Go on then."

"Sometime later the two men came down together. I followed them back to 'Alvin's' apartment and watched from across the street. 'Alvin' changed his clothes and returned shortly. I followed the two men to a series of night clubs. 'Alvin' has been known to get drunk and stay out all night. He has one favorite woman he sometimes sleeps with on these occasions. He met her as well. I think a signal was passed for a later rendezvous. . . ."

"Do you suspect her of being an American agent?"

"No, however . . ."

"Please confine yourself to the relevant."

"Yes. While I was in the night club I called a search team. We have been wanting to go through 'Alvin's' apartment. This seemed a good time."

"To look for the rosters?"

"That's correct, yes. The two Americans proceeded to become drunk and wander around Paris. Once they seemed to have spotted me and tried to evade surveillance. I found them again rather easily. 'Alvin' is known to habituate certain Paris saloons. I simply had to search his regular . . ."

"After you found him, then what?"

"That was when . . . it seemed appropriate to eliminate 'Alvin.'"

"To what?"

"To, uh . . . eliminate 'Alvin.'"

"And so this was done."

"Yes."

"On your own authority or someone else's?"

"On my own authority, Comrade Fetyukov."

"Can you describe what happened?"

"I saw 'Alvin' and his friend enter an alley. I managed to slip out behind them. Neither was very alert. I hit the first man behind the ear with a pipe I had procured for that purpose."

"The man Colter."

"Yes. I assume it was Colter."

"You assume that?" There was an unintelligible grumble from Fetyukov, a dismayed, nearly pathetic sound. He was trying to keep emotion off the tape, but it overflowed that once. "You did not positively identify 'Alvin's' companion?"

123

"No." There was a very long pause.

"Then what happened?"

"I then hit the agent 'Alvin.' Three times. He grabbed at my face but I fought him off and was successful in knocking him down . . . where I, uh, finished eliminating him."

"I see. Is that where you lost your glasses?"

"Where I . . . ?"

"The police report mentions a pair of yellow-rimmed glasses. Our man in the detective bureau was certain of that. You have worn such a pair of glasses, have you not?"

"Yes. That must be where I lost my glasses."

"Which the police now have."

"If you say so, Comrade Fetyukov."

"What did you do then?"

"Then I went to meet with the search team. They hadn't found what we wanted."

"The rosters."

"Yes. The rosters. They had searched thoroughly and had taken a great many pictures, which they showed me. They also had a list of items they had uncovered that they thought might be relevant to this operation or some other."

"Is that all?"

"Very nearly. I can't think of much more."

"All right. Thank you."

Fetyukov switched off the little tape recorder and leaned back in his chair, pressing his pudgy fingers together. His jowls seemed to sag even farther. His bulldog face was in temporary repose.

"No one is going to like this, Comrade Krylov,"

he said, peering from beneath his heavy eyelids.

"No," Krylov answered.

"You see, you exceeded your authority, that is all there is to it. Alvin was not a target but an adversary. All we have done, I'm afraid is to make the next man even more wary."

"I had to . . . I felt . . ."

"With the rosters certain to be under tight security now," Fetyukov said, lifting his head to scratch his sagging throat. "I do not think you used good judgment at all." He shook his head heavily. "No, not at all." He picked up the pile of photographs, the typed list before him. "This is the apartment inventory?"

"Yes, Comrade Fetyukov."

"I see." Fetyukov scanned it. "Small bills, a handgun, a small amount of heroin presumably for the purpose of bribery. 'Alvin' did not use drugs, did he?"

"Not to my knowledge, sir."

Fetyukov was looking through the hastily printed photographs. "What a mess. What kind of search is this?"

"It seemed necessary. . . ."

"He would have been alerted if he had returned." The big man tossed the stack of photos down. "A mess from one end to the other. You let this man 'Alvin' get under your skin, Krylov. That was your mistake. This is a dispassionate business, and only the dispassionate survive long in it. 'Alvin' was beating you in a game. That did not matter so much. It was an unimportant game. It was no vast disgrace. This, comrade . . . this *is* a disgrace."

Krylov tried to swallow and found that his throat was too dry to allow it. The man behind the desk sat squaring the stack of photos, the list of items in 'Alvin's' apartment.

"You have made us visible, Krylov." Fetyukov lifted his great bulk from the chair and walked to the window himself to watch the gray, drizzling day. He stood, hands behind his back, rocking on the balls of his feet. "Diplomatic immunity will, of course, smother any criminal charges, but you have pointed a finger at our operation. The Paris police are friendly. All France is friendly to us. So long as we do not dirty our nest!" Fetyukov's voice rose to a bellow and he turned suddenly on Krylov, glaring at him, at this man who had drawn attention to Fetyukov's own section, snarling a perfectly smooth operation, breaking the eggs Fetyukov himself was careful to tiptoe around.

Fetyukov's eyes were accusing, enraged. But as Krylov watched, they softened to an emotion he did not at first comprehend. And then he did.

It was pity.

Fetyukov had turned back to the window. He was silent for long minutes. It was so still Krylov could hear the ticking of the brass-cased clock on the wall.

"What happened to Colter?"

The question was completely unexpected, and it was a while before Krylov could answer.

"I don't know, comrade."

"Why didn't he go to the police? He didn't,

you know."

"Perhaps he panicked."

"He left his luggage behind. I had his room looked into." His tone added: And without tearing the place apart.

"I don't know where he is. Is it important?" Krylov asked.

"I don't know." Fetyukov shrugged deeply and sighed. "Probably not, but one wonders about loose ends like that. The man should have reported the incident to the police, but he didn't. He fled, leaving behind his luggage. Presumably he took 'Alvin's' automobile, since that too is missing. I have no idea as to why, as to who he was—but I don't like it, Krylov, and I wish I knew where in hell the man was."

Colter arrived in Vienna after a night and a day of hard driving, exhausted, dirty, and bleary-eyed. He found the Regina Hotel on Roosevelt Platz across from the Votive Church, and checked in with what must have seemed an uncommon amount of trouble for an Austrian in Austria. Colter tried to pass off Rudolf Keller as a drunk; more likely the room clerk thought him simply a mental deficient.

Outside the Regina presented a grand old facade with high archways; inside it was warm and welcome, a grande dame coming gracefully to the end of her days. Crystal chandeliers hung in the high-ceilinged dining hall. Deep carpets protected the mahogany floors. There was a bewildering variety of furnishings belonging to no particular period, which somehow blended happily—and in Colter's room, a soft, broad bed.

Colter managed to kick his shoes off before falling onto it and sleeping like the dead for nine hours. When he awoke, the whiskered man in the leather jacket was sitting beside his bed, pistol in hand.

Colter started to move in an automatic response to a perceived threat and then halted himself abruptly as the pistol came up. It was his own.

"Colter."

"That's right," Mike Colter said, although the man's tone had really not been interrogatory. He knew well enough who Colter was.

"My name's Ben."

Who was next—Charlie? Colter smiled at the company logic. Alvin, Ben, Charlie or Carl . . . no, that might be taken as Karl and would throw the sequence off. Colter shook his head. He was still half asleep, his mind roaming those fuzzy tunnels.

"All right, Ben. What's up?"

Ben, who had a distantly British accent, told him: "You're leaving right now. Get up and let's move. Here's a little proof that I'm a friend." He tossed a passport to Colter. The passport was Czech, the name, Anton Dubček, the picture Colter's own.

"Give me the Austrian passport," Ben requested. Requested was too polite a term, actually. He still had the automatic and he had his finger on the trigger. Colter sat up, slipped the passport from his coat pocket and handed it to Ben, who nodded.

"Get dressed," the agent said.

"Where are we going?"

"I'll tell you when we get there. I don't want to hold a meeting here," Ben responded, scratching his whiskered chin with the back of his hand. He watched silently, sullenly, as Colter dressed. Then, handing the Smith & Wesson back to Colter, he inclined his head toward the door.

"Let's go."

Colter followed him out of the room and into the midnight corridor of the Regina. There was a grille-enclosed elevator almost across from the room, but Ben elected to use the stairs. Colter followed silently, his hand around the pistol he carried in his coat pocket.

In the street Ben turned toward a narrow alley. There was a battered Volkswagen bus parked there and Ben climbed in the driver's seat, Colter getting in opposite. Without speaking, Ben started the bus and it clattered down the alley and out onto the road. Within minutes they were flying down Ob Danau Strasse, which parallels the Danube canal. Lights from canal boats and moored pleasure craft gleamed on the murky waters. Streetlamps glimmered dully. The night was clear, the air fresh, damp.

Ben suddenly yanked the wheel to the left and pulled into a tiny space between two nondescript dark buildings. Colter felt his stomach tighten a little as Ben turned off the Volkswagen's lights.

"What is this?"

"Take it easy. I'm just waiting a minute here to see if anyone I know goes by."

They sat in silence for a while longer, Ben lighting a cigarette in the darkness of the bus.

"All right," he said around the smoke. "It seems clear."

He started the bus again, continued down the narrow alley, and turned toward the darkly flowing, broad Danube, the Volkswagen gaining speed, its engine chattering like a Singer sewing machine. The heater was warm, but Colter was wide awake, alert. He nearly trusted Ben, but that wasn't going to be enough from here on. His hand never strayed far from the automatic in his pocket.

They pulled off onto a narrow road named the Ganzestrasse in an old and rotting section of Vienna where the damp nights had taken their toll, effacing the once pleasantly painted facades of the old, half-timbered houses. The road was in disrepair, filled with refuse.

Ben turned right and now they were driving down a nameless lane fronted with warehouses and shacks. If anyone lived down here it wasn't easily determined. There were no lights but the sprinkling of stars when Ben drove into a garage, hopped out and closed the warped double doors, and said, "This is it, Anton."

Colter got out cautiously, trying to search the shadows of the musty garage. Ben was already moving across the building. He opened a creaking door, and, by the dim light admitted, Colter saw a rough flight of wooden stairs.

"Come on," Ben snarled.

Colter followed him up the stairs and through a second door. The room beyond that was furnished with a round dining table covered with a tattered cloth, four spindly chairs, a torn sofa, and a young woman who yawned as Colter entered. Her hair was stringy, yellow, unarranged. She wore only a silky, apricot-colored slip that clung to her body.

"Abend," she said in a slurred voice.

"Er ist ja ein Tshech und kann Deutsch nicht sprechen," Ben said to her.

"Es tut mir Leid," the girl answered sarcastically.

"Was gibst zu essen?" Ben demanded, and in fact there was something prepared to eat. Colter could smell fried sausage and potatoes, slightly burned, perhaps. The woman rose from the sofa, pouting sulkily. She brushed against Ben as she walked past him, kissing his ear, whispering something, her hand lingering on his thigh.

"Bratkartoffeln und Wurst," she said very loudly, as if instead of announcing the meal she was trying to peddle it from a streetcorner cart.

"Auf den Tisch, dann fahrt auf," Ben said sharply.

She smiled, and Colter couldn't tell if it was Ben's accent that amused her—it didn't sound that good to Colter—his own obvious discomfort, or if it was a feline, nearly subliminal sexual expression. But she smiled and then slithered from the room, the slip playing across her low, full buttocks.

"We'll eat now. Greta will take off," Ben said.

"Pull up a chair."

Colter did so. From where he sat he could see the woman, humming, swaying as she worked, preparing their meal. They were served great platters of fried potatoes and sausage and bottled beer. Greta had slipped into a cloth coat, and now she wrapped her arms around Ben's neck, kissing him goodbye. It seemed to annoy the agent. She fished into his trouser pocket teasingly, dug out the key to the Volkswagen bus, and left, smiling across her shoulder at Colter.

"Bitch," Ben muttered. Then he grinned and shook his head. "Eat up, Dubček."

Colter ate up. The food was substantial, but greasy and nearly tasteless. The beer helped. Finishing his meal, Ben belched, leaned back, and pulled a pipe from his coat pocket, filling it from a pouch. He lit it and puffed thoughtfully at the stem, filling the room with vaguely cherry-scented tobacco smoke.

"What the hell happened, Anton?" he asked. "Alvin was supposed to phone me. I waited four hours. Nothing."

"Alvin won't be phoning anyone again," Colter told him. "He got mugged in an alley. Fatally."

"Was it him they were after or was it you?" Ben asked, concern narrowing his eyes.

Colter shrugged. "Alvin thought they wanted him. It was a man named Krylov who did it."

"Are you sure of that?"

"Reasonably sure. He left something behind. Alvin had pointed him out to me earlier in the evening. Yeah, it was Krylov."

132

"That son of a bitch. He'll be going for a long ride one of these nights."

"What did Alvin have on him?"

"Not that you need to know," Ben said, "but Alvin was the terminus for party finks. He had the tap on all the French Communist Party members who were disaffected, and apparently Krylov got onto him. His place was searched, was it?"

"Torn to pieces."

Ben nodded. "That's washed up, then, I suppose. Alvin was a good man, but he was careless."

"How about you, Ben?" Colter asked. "Are you careless too?"

"Never. Don't worry on that score, Dubček. Fifteen years of this crap and they haven't tumbled to me yet. I'm close, and I'm careful."

"What about the girl?" Colter asked, looking toward the outside door the blonde had gone out of.

Ben stiffened, but his voice was controlled. "She doesn't speak English. Truth is, she's just a bit dumb, is Greta—but she knows some tricks in bed. Christ, I can't live like a hermit, can I?"

"No, I suppose not."

"Besides, it's nothing to you," Ben said carelessly, "you're leaving tonight."

"Tonight?"

"That's right. Over the border north of Bratislava. I've got a Czech to take you in."

Ben rose and walked to the wall. He tapped on it and a compartment swung open behind the wooden paneling. "You'll wear these." He tossed

Colter a suit of clothes, apparently much worn, with a few stains thrown in for good measure. This was what he had been measured for in Paris, he figured.

"What happens after I get across the border?" Colter wanted to know.

"You're going to be a Czech tourist going over the line."

Into the Soviet Union, he meant, and Colter felt a chill creep up his spine.

"That gun you're carrying—get rid of it," Ben said. "You've got your passport and it's a good one. You'll be traveling with a tour of Warsaw Pact visitors, so you don't have to worry about any other papers. Bus to Uzhgorod and from there by train and bus to your destination."

"Which is?" Colter asked, trying to sound calm. It seemed forever before Ben answered while he fooled with that pipe and stared at Colter, thinking who knew what.

"Batumi," he said at last. "It's very nice this time of year, they tell me. The Sixteenth Party Congress of 1930 *ordered* that the area be made the equivalent of Florida or California, and they tried their damnedest. Nice beaches, miles of orange groves, fine climate. Ten miles from the Turkish border—which is the way you're going out."

"Do the Turks know that?"

"Some of them do," Ben said ambiguously.

"This won't work," Colter said after a minute's morose reflection. "I'm going across with this tourist group and I don't speak Czech."

"The Czechs will assume you're Polish, the Poles will assume you're Hungarian."

"That sounds fanciful enough," Colter said bitterly. "All right—I get to Batumi and stand looking at the orange groves, the beautiful Black Sea beaches with the rest of the tourists from Europe. Say, for the sake of argument, that I manage to remain alive that long. Who, when, how, where?"

Ben squinted through his wreaths of tobacco smoke and turned the beer bottle in his hands meditatively. Finally he told him.

"It's Stepan Vesely."

SIX

Stepan Vesely. The name meant something to Mike Colter. It meant something because he had practically been raised on Vesely's poetry. When Aunt Katrinka had made her way out of Russia, she had had little more than the clothes on her back, the baby in her arms, but she had carried a volume of poetry written by a dazzling young man named Stepan Vesely.

"He is a candle in this dark world of ours, Mikhail, a great man. One who knows evil and sings of peace. One who lifts up his head to chant his words and so lifts our heads as well."

The boy at her knee had asked, "Where is Stepan Vesely, Aunt Katrinka? Can we see him?"

"He is lost in his epics, Mikhail. Lost in halls of splendor."

"Is he dead?" Aunt Katrinka had spoken of

Michael's mother and father in much the same language.

"No, Mikhail. I do not think even the Bolsheviks would kill him. But he cannot come out of his world into the sunlight."

Until now? But why now, Colter wondered. The old man—and he must be nearly Uncle Isaak's age—had suffered under that regime all of his life. Why now try to escape? And why did the United States want him out? Want him enough to propose this mad venture to Mike Colter? Did they perhaps hope to stun the world with another literary defection? Repeat the propaganda coup of Solzhenitsyn's emigration?

"Vesely is in Batumi?" Colter asked. Ben nodded and tramped toward the kitchen, returning with two fresh bottles of dark beer.

"He's been there for six months now. Living with his daughter, Anna. Here's her picture—" Ben handed Colter a grainy, long-lens shot of a slim, dark-haired girl with Slavic cheekbones and a haughty mouth. "And here's the most recent we have of the old man."

Vesely looked old and weary. There were lines around his eyes, deep grooves flanking his nose. He wore a white beard clipped short, the upper lip shaved clean. So that was he: It was like meeting a legend to Colter. Aunt Katrinka had described the poet imaginatively many times. The photograph jarred with Colter's mental image.

"Where are they staying?"

"They have a cottage in the country. They live

alone but for a housekeeper, an old crone, possibly KGB. Alone but not unwatched."

"Why watch Vesely? They suspect he might defect?"

"No."

"If they've been tipped . . ."

"That is not possible," Ben assured him. "No. It's a mystery to me, Colter." He shrugged. "If anyone in the company knows the answer, they haven't told me. General principles, I guess. But he is being watched, you can bank on that. So don't just march up to the front door and try to get away with presenting yourself as a traveling *rasolnic* salesman."

Colter smiled. "I don't believe you've ever eaten it or know what it is." He was silent for a minute. "Any suggestions on how I might go about it, then? Making contact, that is?"

Ben just shrugged. "The company likes to leave leeway for individual initiative."

"Funny," Colter muttered.

"It's the only answer I've got. Sorry."

"All right. You've got me to Batumi," Colter went on. "As a Czech tourist. How do I break out of that identity? A tourist turns up missing and Intourist notifies the local police who notify the KGB within twenty-four hours, or am I wrong about that?"

"No. I wouldn't think you're wrong. Listen, Colter—you've got to go in as a tourist for obvious reasons. As a tourist you can find lodging, rent an automobile with an Intourist chauffeur, purchase fuel . . . as a local citizen you would have to have masses of paper to get away with that. A Czech tourist, okay."

"Yeah. I can do all of that—but not while I'm with the tour, Ben."

"Right. This I looked into personally—I just asked at the Soviet consulate. You can leave your tour. You will decide that Batumi overwhelms you with its charm. You will request permission to remain an extra week and then rejoin the tour in . . ." Ben looked at a scribbled note. "Dnepropetrovsk. There's no problem as long as you continue to stay at the Intourist hotel where they can watch you."

"I become a hell of a lot more visible once I've left the tour."

"You do," Ben agreed readily. "But you'll soon become invisible again."

"How?"

"You're going to kick off there, Mr. Dubček." Ben's hands folded themselves together around his beer bottler. "Anton Dubček is going to die in Batumi. Without returning the rented Intourist vehicle, however." The agent allowed himself a thin smile. "And that car, of course, is your way out. Down the coast highway to the Turkish border. I'll show you the exact spot in time."

"Get back to my demise," Colter said. "I can't possibly arrange that on my own."

"No. You won't have to."

"We have people in Batumi?" Colter shook his head. It seemed unlikely.

"We have people," Ben affirmed. "What do you know about Batumi, Mr. Dubček?"

"That it has orange groves and nice beaches."

"Well, there's more to it. (By the way, Dubček, for a Czech, you're a smart ass). I've got a little history of Batumi here," Ben said, producing a thick blue volume from the table.

"Batumi," he read, "is the capital of the Atchar Autonomous Republic. The Ajars are Muslim Georgians. Batumi . . . has a subtropical climate . . . first mentioned by Pliny the Elder . . . Here we are. Nearly half the population of Batumi is Georgian, one third is Russian or Ukrainian, the rest Armenians, Greeks and Turks. In eighteen-seventy-eight, following the Russo-Turkish War, Batumi, having been dominated by the Turks for three hundred years, was placed under Russian authority."

Ben slapped the book shut. "Understand?"

"Not really. I did catch that about there being a large Ukrainian population, however; that will make it easier for me to blend in."

"Yeah, but you missed the main point. The Turks owned that area for about three hundred years, and much of the population is Muslim. As late as nineteen-eighteen the Turks recaptured Batumi—that didn't last long; the Russkis drove them out in a matter of weeks. Then even the British had it for a year or two, but that's aside. The point is the Turks still feel that they've been screwed out of Batumi, and the Turks who are living there yet under Russian rule cling to the hope of returning to Turkish control. That's a pipe dream now, of course, but there's a bitterness there and a bit of small-scale guerrilla work from time to time."

"That's where my help is coming from?"

"That's right. They've been given a cover story about you. You're supposed to be surveying the area for the CIA, measuring their organization's potential to see if they ought to be given covert aid."

"That's thin," Colter said. "Suppose they read through that, which shouldn't be too difficult."

"If they do, they'll cut your throat, I suppose," Ben answered casually, relighting his pipe. "But that's what Up Above came up with." Ben jabbed a finger at the ceiling.

"I wish Up Above was going in," Mike Colter said. He rose and walked to the window, looking out at the dark and dreary warehouse district, at the slowly flowing Danube River beyond.

"My contact's name?" he asked, without turning back.

"Mustafa. One name, that's it. The Turks are playing it a little cagy too, maybe suspecting a KGB scam."

"And that's it?" Colter asked, turning to walk toward Ben who was leaning back in his chair, arms folded, puffing contentedly on his pipe.

He spread his hands. "I'm afraid so, Dubček. I've got a few maps to give you to look over and a tour guide book. Also a Russian phrase book. We thought maybe you could be one of those travelers who insists on using only the local language, one of those 'immersion' types. It might help cover your language deficiency."

"Sure," Colter said with a bitter shrug. "Ben,

this doesn't do anything to warm my heart. The plan is patched together, relying too damn much on the disposition of a few Turkish malcontents and on my own improvisation."

"That's about the way I see it," Ben said cheerfully.

"You don't want to trade places, do you?"

"What? And leave Greta? No thanks—besides, I've had my fling, Colter. I can't say I liked it much, either." Ben handed Colter his rough clothing. "You'd better get dressed. We're leaving in an hour."

Colter just stood staring at him for a moment, before, shaking his head heavily, he began stripping. An hour. In an hour he would be on his way to Czechoslovakia. From there it was into Mother Russia, where Colter was to find a dissatisfied, elderly poet, and with the help of some Turkish rebels escape across the most closely guarded border in the world.

"It won't be dull," Ben said, as if reading his thoughts. "Have another beer, Dubček. It might be a while before you set eyes on German beer again."

"Among other things."

Ben nodded, unexpectedly placed a hand on Colter's shoulder, and shambled off to the kitchen, belching twice on the way. Colter finished dressing and then sat to the table scanning the maps of Batumi and environs. Ben placed a beer in front of him and then went to the window himself to sit in a wooden chair, watching for Greta's return.

"It won't wash," Colter said, but Ben was out of sympathy and conversation both. He sat staring out the window, lost in his own thoughts.

"Here she is," Ben said some time later. "Leave all those maps, right? Don't forget the phrase book."

They went downstairs and out into the cold dark night. Greta had left the Volkswagen bus running and Colter slipped into the warm cab while Ben paused to say goodbye to his woman. That involved a lot of neck tasting and haunch gripping, and Colter had nearly dozed off before the door opened and Ben, glowing, stepped in.

The Volkswagen bellowed to life and Ben took off toward the east. It had been a whirlwind tour of Vienna, Colter reflected, but it hadn't cost him much.

The little rat's name was Josef. They found him in the rolling hills south of the Bratislava crossing. Ben had taken a farm lane, rutted and winding between irregular patches of planted barley and oats. The night was dark as sin, with thin clouds covering the stars.

Ben parked the bus under a pair of ancient, wide-spreading oaks, turned off the lights and stoked up his pipe. After half an hour, the little rat came.

There was a low whistle from the shadows and after a minute he came forward, carrying a small bundle. He was short and ferret-faced, wearing a foppish little mustache. A heavy tweed coat dropped nearly to his ankles. He had muddy brogans on, but he managed to swagger in them.

"Josef," Ben said in a low voice. "Watch him, he's in it for the money."

"So am I," Colter said, and Ben shot him a hard glance. Josef stepped in through the sliding door of the bus and Ben and Colter stepped into the back, Ben switching on a faint light.

"Hello, I greet you," Josef said, smiling to reveal crooked yellow teeth.

"Have you got everything?" Ben demanded.

"Suitcase, newspapers, five thousand Czech korunas, photograph of family at home. Ticket for your bus, yes—all here that you asked for. All Dubček's name on everything, you see?" Josef smiled again. His eyes, Colter noticed, glittered and shied away from a direct look. When he held up the Czech currency they glittered even more.

"Did you remember change? I asked you for change. He can't try to change money."

"Yes." Josef lifted a little bag with a drawstring and handed it to Colter, who opened it up, briefly inspected the Czech coins, and tucked them away.

"Wallet," Josef said, handing a black billfold to Colter. He opened it, examining the papers. "A member of the Czech Communist Party, Anton Dubček. Works as a quality inspector in the Bratislava glass works. Married, two children."

Ben was examining the papers more closely, tilting them this way and that, holding them up to the light. "Not very good quality, Josef."

"The best," the little rat said. "The very best, Mr. Finn."

"Finn, huh?" Colter said. "What's the first name, then—Huckleberry?"

"Precisely," Ben said with a grin. Josef looked from one man to the other, trying to understand the humor of it. All he knew of Huckleberry Finn was that he was a tall foreigner—probably American—who paid well for Eastern Bloc papers and occasional smuggling assistance.

"One thousand Austrian schillings," Josef said almost pleadingly. Ben handed the money over. "And, Mr. Finn—for the Czech korunas?" Ben handed over more Austrian schilling notes. Josef rifled through them before stuffing them away in the pocket of his long coat.

"When do we go?" Colter asked.

"Now."

Colter looked at Ben, took in a slow breath, and nodded, looking through briefly the suitcase he had been given. Clothing purchased in Czechoslovakia, most of it properly used, neatly folded. He latched the suitcase and said, "I'm ready."

"Sure?" Ben asked.

"Yes," Colter, slightly puzzled, replied.

"I think you've forgotten something," Ben said, his eyes going to the bulging pocket of Colter's coat.

Colter looked at Josef and then back to Ben. He shook his head. "No, I haven't forgotten anything, Mr. Finn."

"All right," Ben said. He stuck out his hand. "Good luck then, Dubček."

"And luck to you, Mr. Finn."

Then Colter stepped out into the chilly night,

the scent of mown alfalfa rich in his nostrils, a northerly wind tugging at his clothes, chilling his flesh.

"Now? We go." Josef was beside him, his head coming to Colter's shoulder.

Colter nodded, putting on the cloth cap he had been given, hoisting his suitcase with his left hand. "Now we go."

He followed Josef off up a farm lane toward the low, darkened hills beyond. There were no visible towers, lights, or fences, yet Colter knew he was within a few hundred yards of the Czech border. Behind them the Volkswagen started up and drove away, carrying Ben back to his woman, and Colter was left alone in the night with the little rat.

"This way," Josef said, and Colter followed him, suitcase in hand.

They worked their way up a narrow gulley and now, on the hill above, stark against the sky, Colter saw the barbed wire in tangled profusion.

"Down," Josef hissed and threw himself to one side, clutching at Colter, who followed him reflexively. Josef lay still, his ferret eyes gleaming. Colter then saw him—a soldier in a great-coat and helmet walking a police dog, an Alsatian, over the hill, rifle slung over his shoulder, flashlight in hand.

They watched fifteen minutes after they could no longer see the Czech border guard, then Josef got to his feet, whispering, "Come."

They went on. The grass was to midcalf, heavy with dew now. A silver moon was rising, small and dim behind the clouds. They were traveling up a gulley still, skirting an outcropping of gray rocks. The barbed wire, hung in coils on X-shaped frames, was only fifty feet above them.

Josef halted and touched Colter's arm. It was a minute before Colter figured out what he wanted.

Before them was a tunnel mouth, black against the blackness. Colter looked at Josef, who was grinning hugely. He had never been caught coming over because he did not cut wire, try to go over it and past the eyes of the border guards. The tunnel, apparently watercut with later help from man, ran upslope, angling northward.

Josef held a finger to his own lips, ducked low and started into the tunnel, Colter following him cautiously. The earth was muddy underfoot, strewn with odd-sized rocks. It was also pitch black inside, and Colter had to hold onto Josef's coattail to keep from getting lost. Twice he tripped over stones and went down, once painfully banging a knee. A little way forward he rapped his forehead solidly on a low knob of stone and his growled curses echoed through the tunnel.

Finally Colter saw the light ahead. Pale blue, dimming as they neared it, it was the moon-illuminated sky, appearing brilliant from the blackness of the tunnel.

Josef touched Colter's shoulder and beckoned.

"I see," he whispered, and Colter was happy to let him see. They were now in Czechoslovakia—or under it. Josef scooted forward like some simian troglodyte, hesitated, and pulled himself up and out of the tunnel mouth, momentarily blocking out the sky. Colter waited, breathing raggedly, his nerves drawn taut.

In minutes Josef was back, his head hanging down into the tunnel from above. "Come," he hissed, waving a hand anxiously.

Colter went, but not with all that much confidence. He was on his own now, and it was a combat situation. Night infiltration, militarized zone. There was no amnesty for spies. The old feelings came back from somewhere, the warrior's intense alertness, the odd tightening of intestines, the dryness in the mouth, the clenched teeth. Signs of nervousness, of an organism recoiling at the mind's insistence on thrusting it into a position where it might be extinguished. Signs of an organism alert and prepared; atavistic heightening of senses, a rush of adrenaline.

Colter took a deep breath and tossed his suitcase up and out of the tunnel and crawled out himself. The organism had known. Josef was not alone.

Colter was jerked to his feet by two men. Josef stood before him, smirking. The smirk didn't last long. Colter kicked out savagely, lifting himself in the grip of his captors to do so. His boot drove into Josef's face and the little rat fell back screaming. Colter wrenched an elbow free and swung it back into the face of the man on his right, hearing the snap of bone as his nose went.

The other Czech kicked out at the back of Colter's leg, catching him behind the knee with stunning force. Colter went down, writhing in pain. The Czech with the broken nose was moving in silently, blood dripping from his nostrils. In his hand was a length of wood, in his mind the thought that it would be highly pleasurable to crush Colter's skull for him.

The little rat was still moaning with pain. The other Czech hovered over him. They were so near to the border that Colter could see the wire from the corner of his eye. They weren't twenty feet from the path patrolled by the border guards and their dogs. There was more danger of being shot by the border guards than of being battered to death by the little rat and his cronies. But their threat was more immediate. Colter didn't worry about the noise. As the wooden club was raised, he thrust his hand into his pocket and triggered off the Smith & Wesson, driving three nine-millimeter slugs into the body of his assailant. The second Czech took off at a run and Colter let him go.

The footsteps behind him brought the muzzle of the automatic around quickly. It was the little rat, and in his hand was a knife. Colter fired again, the Smith & Wesson spitting flame. The little rat was flung backwards. he landed in a sitting position and remained there, holding his gut.

From far away Colter heard the sound of an engine being started. It was a truck, and in a moment it was obvious that it was being driven toward them.

"My tour bus!" Colter gripped Josef by the shoulders and shook him violently. "Where does it leave from? When?"

"Go to hell, American," Josef said, and then the

little rat did a dirty thing. He died.

Colter was still holding him by the shoulders, and that was all that was keeping him upright. Josef was dead, as was the second Czech. And Mike Colter was left alone in a foreign land.

He stood and looked southward. It was there that the roaring of motors had sounded. Now he could see the headlights as the heavy truck rolled toward him. It was time to get the hell out of there. And time to get rid of the gun. Anton Dubček, CP member, quality control inspector at the Bratislava glass works, didn't carry American-made automatic pistols with him. Colter reared back and winged the Smith & Wesson up and over the barricades. Then, snatching up his suitcase, he took to his heels, running through the dark night toward Bratislava. The border guards, finding two dead Czechs, one of them with a pocketful of Austrian money, would likely think that a smuggling deal had gone wrong. Well, it had in a way—the little rat had gotten too greedy. Five thousand Czech korunas had caused his eyes to glitter just a little too much.

Colter halted, out of breath, on the rim of a hill above Bratislava. Below the farms and woodland gave way to concrete and brick as the city took form and pushed up out of the green earth. Bratislava was dark and somber and still at this hour— amazingly so for a Western city. But then, Colter was not in the West anymore.

He was in the East. In the East, headed for Russia, for Batumi, to find a poet. It had an air of unreality. None of it seemed possible or substantial. He was merely being swept along by chance and the will of the company. He no longer had any control over his existence, and it left him with an awesomely empty feeling.

Colter shook off the reflective mood, looked behind him again to see if there was anyone coming, and, seeing no lights, no armed dark shadows, hearing no shouts or whispers or on-rushing feet, he started off down the grassy knoll toward Bratislava, wondering if it wouldn't be proper for him to at least walk past the glass-works.

Sunrise found Colter exhausted, chilled, resigned, walking the streets of Bratislava, Czech-oslovakia. No one was abroad in the early morning. Colter hadn't seen more than three people since he had entered the city five hours earlier—and all three had been policemen.

He walked toward the center of the city, keeping a brisk pace, wanting to look not like a hooligan wanderer, but a respectable quality control inspector off for the bus depot. It would have helped considerably to know where the depot was.

The sun had grown warm on his back and shoulders. People had begun to emerge from the featureless red brick apartment buildings and collect at trolley stops, lunch buckets in their hands. Traffic on the streets increased and Colter began to feel real anxiety. He didn't like this situation a bit.

If he were stopped and questioned the game was up. If he couldn't somehow locate the damned bus terminal and find his tour, everything up to now was in vain, and there would be nothing left to do but to try slinking back across the border—another option he was less than crazy about.

He was aware suddenly of someone or something following him, and he halted dead in his tracks, turning to find a kid of seven or eight years old in a tan Youth Corps uniform, red scarf wrapped around his neck, military style cap tugged low, watching him seriously.

The kid wore a chrome whistle around his neck on a braided hawser. When Colter stopped and confronted him, he put the whistle between his lips, his face paling. Colter's must have paled a little as well. He didn't need that kid blowing his police whistle, attracting attention.

Colter, trying to appear stern and yet kindly, opened his wallet and flashed the Czech CP card he carried. The kid instantly relaxed, stammering something.

Colter shrugged and handed the boy his suitcase. The kid said something else unintelligible. Colter lifted an eyebrow and wagged a finger at the Youth Corps boy. Flagging a thumb back across his shoulder, he displayed the bus ticket to the boy, who sighed mightily, nodded, picked up the suitcase, and led the way down the street. Colter fell in behind him, fighting back a grin of relief.

His small guide took him down three blocks and over one to a gray, squat building where the international symbol for a bus had been painted above the Czech lettering. There the kid handed Colter his suitcase, accepted a three-koruna note, and took off, casting one last dubious glance at his silent comrade.

Once inside the terminal, Colter had no trouble at all finding his way. Behind the three long desks against the wall before him were boards with the times of departure and arrival for various cities. His bus, Number 43 for Uzghorod, had a white card tacked up beside it: "Sovyet Inturist." The time of departure was ten a.m., half an hour on.

Colter walked to the counter on his right, where two older, chunky women, scarves on their heads, paper sacks filled with possessions in their arms, stood. He slapped his ticket down on the counter and placed his suitcase up beside it. A young, heavy-featured girl looked at him worriedly, stamped his ticket, and took his suitcase.

She said something in a dull tone of voice and Colter nodded, smiling faintly. Then he moved about the terminal, looking at the newspaper racks, the snack machines, eyeing the Czechs, the occasional blue-uniformed policeman, the buses beyond the glass doors. At a quarter to ten people started queuing up before Gate Three. Colter worked his way over through the milling crowd and glanced at the tickets the people in line held. Uzhgorod.

He joined the shuffling line and filed through the doorway where the uniformed station attendant glanced perfunctorily at their pale green tickets. In another ten minutes Colter was on a bus riding eastward through the Czech countryside, bound for Uzhgorod in the Ukraine.

He sat beside a large woman in a red coat wearing a flowered red scarf. Colter's hands were slick with perspiration, his mouth cottony, and he thought he would have preferred parachuting into Batumi one dark night, taking his chances on being shot out of the sky.

The woman beside Colter said something to him in a pleasant, husky voice and he nodded. Then, yawning ostentatiously, he closed his eyes and pretended to sleep—people tend not to talk to a sleeping man.

The countryside rushed past, the bus growling up a long grade, smelling of diesel fuel. The woman beside him settled into her seat as Colter continued to feign sleep, a thousand violent scenarios running through his mind.

It was a mad mission, and being a few miles nearer to his objective didn't compel him to believe that he was any nearer to success, only closer to cataclysm. He yawned again, and somehow as the bus climbed higher into the foothills beyond the sun-bright, wandering Nitra River, he did fall to sleep. And the bus rushed on toward the Soviet Ukraine.

SEVEN

Hacha stopped to light his pipe, then he strolled on again, his eyes combing the ground. They had already found the tunnel and near it the bodies of two men. They lay there still, covered with tarpaulins. Inspector Hacha cleared his throat as if he would speak, but he said nothing.

"The trucks will be up later to fill the tunnel with earth," the uniformed policeman said. Hacha didn't reply and the guard fell silent.

"How many of them were there?" Hacha asked at last.

"Four, inspector."

"Four of them. And the two ran away."

"Yes, that's correct."

"And we haven't yet located either man?"

"No, of course these things take time."

"Yes." Hacha stopped at the high point of the border path to look down into Austria, the pipe clenched in his teeth, the wind lifting his sparse dark hair. "What did they smuggle?" Hacha asked.

"There is no telling."

"Something small, light obviously—or they could not have taken it with them. Something they could run with. Drugs? Currency. That's another point. Why didn't they take the money in the little one's pockets? Can these smugglers afford to sneer at a thousand Austrian schillings? Wait . . . what's that?"

"Where, sir?"

"Right there. Give me your binoculars, please, lieutenant."

Hacha was trying to find the small dark object in the field glasses, and, as he finally did, a smile spread across his face. "Here." Hacha gave the glasses to the uniformed policeman. "Have a look—just beyond that white rock." The policeman focused the glasses where Hacha had instructed him to.

"Yes, I see it now. Yes, inspector."

"Contact the Austrians. I am sure they will be happy to cooperate in a criminal investigation. Meanwhile, post a man here. I will not lose that gun, lieutenant, for unless I am mistaken that is the weapon used to dispatch our two friends there."

Hacha thought that everything was well in hand then. All he needed to do was trace the two other men involved, the two who had fled. The local smuggling community was very small, and some of those involved functioned only because

156

the secret police allowed it. Hacha had ways of discovering who was behind this. Once the dead men were fingerprinted and identified, the gun recovered, there was no real problem with closing this out. Why then, he wondered, did he feel uneasy about this?

"Something," he thought, relighting his pipe again, "stinks here, Hacha." But he couldn't put a name to what was bothering him, and so as soon as the guard who was to watch the pistol arrived, Hacha walked away toward the waiting car, his coat flaps waving in the wind.

"Something stinks here."

The Russian lifted his one good eye to meet Fetyukov's glazed stare. They had been up most of the night sifting through the facts in the Krylov case. Krylov himself had been interrogated again and then sent home to the USSR.

"I never did like it," Fetyukov said. "What am I, though, a policeman?" He lifted a helpless shoulder. "Only a diplomat, and so I asked for help."

"I can't find a line of coherent action here," Remizov said, pushing away the stacks of photographs Krylov's burglary team had taken.

"Pardon me?"

"My superior uses that term," Remizov said, standing. "What he means is that all events are elements in a continuum, or should be in an investigation. Riddles are what we deal with. The correct solution orders the parts of the riddle. I can't seem to do that here. I don't know what we're looking for."

The door opened and Tyurin came in, balancing three cups of coffee. He looked hopefully at Remizov, but saw immediately that there had been no progress.

"No milk," Tyurin said. "All those fat receptionists of yours drank it up," the lieutenant said with a grin. Then, "No luck?"

"No. Ideas?" Remizov asked, sipping at the coffee.

"Too many possibilities for me," Tyurin said, perching on the desk, his legs dangling like a schoolboy's. "Is there a security problem?" Tyurin asked, touching his index finger. "Did Alvin not have a roster of reactionary French CP elements? Did he pass it on to the man Colter? Who was the man Colter?" Tyurin was on his last finger, ready to drop the coffee cup in that hand, but he went on gamely. "Where is Colter? Why was the murder of 'Alvin' not reported to the police?"

"Colter was not CIA, and not diplomatic?" Fetyukov asked.

"No."

"Could it be that Colter had nothing to do with our problem? Could it be that Colter is not an American agent but something else? A private sideline of 'Alvin's'—dope-dealing, maybe, murder for hire, smuggling . . . ?"

"Unlikely to me," the one-eyed man said. "Tyurin?"

"All I have is more questions."

"We do know certain things. Shall we start over?" No one was eager to but no one objected. "Alvin met Colter, who had just arrived from America—New York. Certain articles 'Alvin' had in his possession were taken by Colter. The pistol," Remizov said, snapping a finger at the eight-by-ten photograph of the pistol that had been in 'Alvin's' room before Colter fled. "The money. French and Swiss francs."

"Colter could be in Switzerland," Fetyukov suggested.

Remizov shrugged. It was an obvious possibility.

"What if Alvin and Colter had the list of CP reactionaries and wanted to sell it to us? Alvin needed money, but he couldn't approach us directly. He wanted to use Colter," Tyurin said.

Remizov shrugged again. Anything was possible; but they hadn't been approached. But then if Colter thought the Russians might kill him, he wouldn't be eager to deal.

"We'll never solve this," Fetyukov said, lowering his vast bulk into a leather chair. "Colter has nothing to do with our problem. He was a friend of 'Alvin's.' He was up to something illegal too, and he fled rather than present himself to the police."

"The most likely hypothesis," Tyurin agreed, tossing his paper cup into the trash can where it rang, to Fetyukov's annoyance. Remizov was silent.

"You are probably right," Remizov said finally. "But what then? What is Colter up to? Who is he?"

159

"No one, a smuggler, a safecracker, a mercenary the CIA had on a leash." Fetyukov shrugged. "The possibilities are endless."

"They are. Why do you continue to say he might be a smuggler?"

"Is there a more profitable profession in Europe?"

"I was thinking of the Bratislava incident."

"I didn't hear."

"It was on the wire. Smugglers killed crossing at Bratislava. Killed with a nine-millimeter weapon." Again Remizov flicked the photograph on the desk. "Isn't this a nine-millimeter, Tyurin?"

The young lieutenant hopped down from his perch and came around the desk. "Smith & Wesson Model fifty-nine. Yes, nine-millimeter— the only caliber it comes in that I know of."

"Surely you can't . . ."

"I am only curious," Remizov said. "I admit the coincidence is difficult to accept. However, it costs us nothing to query Bratislava and discover what sort of weapon they have recovered. We can't overlook the coincidence just because we do not see the relationship."

"We can do better than find out what sort of gun it is," Tyurin said. He had a magnifying glass and was hunched low over the photograph.

"Yes?"

"I can make out the serial numbers, all but the last."

"Excellent. Fetyukov?"

"I'll send the wire." The big man rose from his chair, thinking very little of the course of the investigation. If a man named Colter had shot a smuggler in Bratislava, what did it matter? It happened every day. It had nothing to do with Krylov's indiscretion or the missing roster of disloyal French CP members.

Still he did what he was asked. There was something about this tall, one-eyed man, this Remizov, that made the alternative unthinkable. And then, he was Fyodor's man—and Fetyukov had once known Fyodor, known him very well. He had supposed him dead. He had that rare cancer of the retinas and was already nearly blind when Fetyukov had last seen him, and that must have been three years ago . . . he closed the door and went out. The two secret policemen were still excitedly hunched over the photograph of 'Alvin's' missing gun.

The return wire was very slow in coming. Fetyukov waddled back with it and Tyurin practically yanked it out of his hand. Triumphantly the lieutenant placed the message down on the desk, folded so that the numbers transmitted by Bratislava were beneath the serial numbers of the photographed gun.

They matched perfectly.

"Colter or his gun killed two smugglers last night in Bratislava."

"I don't see what this has to do with anything," Fetyukov said with some annoyance. He was tired after two consecutive sleepless nights. The secret policemen seemed more interested in this Colter than in solving the 'Alvin' problem.

"I don't know what it has to do with anything,"

Remizov said quietly, leaning back in the desk chair. "But there is something funny here. I am looking for it," he said almost to himself, "I am looking for the line of coherent action."

It was at three o'clock in the afternoon as Fetyukov sat dozing in his chair, Tyurin stuffing himself with sweet rolls, that the message from the KGB in Vienna finally arrived.

"They found the car," Remizov said.

"Where?"

"Vienna."

"Then it can't have been Colter in Bratislava," Fetyukov said, shaking his head. The two policemen ignored him.

"Where?" Tyurin asked around a mouthful of food.

"In front of the Hotel Regina. Abandoned."

"He wouldn't have checked into that hotel then."

"You're too much the professional," Remizov said. "I don't think Colter is."

Fetyukov, who had no interest in Colter, turned away muttering. Tyurin was excited. Fetyukov's entire conception of top-flight intelligence officers was being shattered by the brash young red-headed man.

"Okay, did Vienna check the hotel ledger?"

"They're working on it. One man, a Rudolf Keller, has been indicated as a possibility. The desk clerk recalls a drunken man, six feet tall, dark hair, large mustache. He checked in Thursday night and has never been seen since. There was no luggage in his room."

"Prints?" Tyurin asked excitedly.

"They'll have to have thought of that," Remizov answered. Then, "Better nudge them in case. I want fingerprints of Rudolf Keller."

Fetyukov was fed up with all of this. He went to his corner cupboard and took out a bottle of cognac. He took three glasses and placed them on the sideboard, but Remizov shook his head.

"No, thank you, Comrade Fetyukov." He was buttoning his coat already.

"But what is this? Where are you going?"

Remizov was on his way out the door; it was Tyurin, reaching back to grab a last sweet roll, who answered the diplomat.

"Bratislava—by the way of Vienna."

The land rushed past the train window. Vast velvet fields of oats and immense stretches of sunflowers growing head-high beside the tracks. The soil where it was turned over ready for planting was black, black and rich, seemingly capable of nourishing not only the crops of grain to be planted there, but the men and women who lived upon the land, toiling beneath the cold sun.

It was the Ukraine—vast, rich, war-torn, savage, gentle, musical and secretive, childlike and raw, pious and godless. From here Colter himself had sprung, he who had all of those qualities in his own soul. He who was a peasant and a haughty Cossack hetman at once, who was apt to cry at the sad songs, to break glasses on the hearth and march into war with his heart rising grandly to the roll of drums.

There had been no trouble at the border crossing. The bus had halted and Soviet border guards had mounted the steps, walking down the aisle, glancing at each face and proferred passport. They were young, amazingly young, Colter thought. Young, stiff, pink-cheeked, their necks shaved, eyes clear, complexions unmarked. They carried AK-47s and holstered pistols, yet they looked too young, too polite to ever use one on a human being.

All illusion. There is no estimate on the numbers of human beings killed by Soviet border guards each year, but it can be confidently assumed to be in the thousands. A border means different things to different peoples. To the Soviets it is an inflexible, strictly delineated reality. Those on this side must remain on this side—those on the other must not enter unless properly admitted, all legal conditions strictly met. And if those terms are violated, then it is perfectly proper to retaliate with weapons.

Colter's passport was taken, his face scrutinized by a pair of ice-blue eyes, his passport handed back. The bus then drove on into Uzhgorod, where they had a layover for a day in a fleabag hotel, then boarded the Uzhgorod-Rostov Railroad, where they slept four to a berth, the train stopping for each meal at a station, only pale dry biscuits and tea being served on board.

At Kryvoy Rog they laid over again and took a

tour of the steel mill, the old Polish castle at nearby Roslav, had lunch at a cafeteria with workers from the local commune, and traveled on.

Roslav hadn't been much of an attraction, but Colter was mesmerized. He had been born ten miles from the village. Birthed there, taken away before he could walk. He seemed somehow to know the country they had passed through, the narrow fields and small cottages, the honest, sun-darkened faces creased and folded by weather. He had been taken away and only now had he returned, an alien visitor. He stood in the sunlight at the old castle with its crumbling stone battlements where Polish barons had fought against the Cossacks and Tartars long, long before there had been a Soviet Union, when the Ukrainians had been a proud, independent people.

Maybe it was the barely remembered tales Aunt Katrinka had told him at bedtime that recalled the place so vividly, the patches of birch and pine forest, the wandering river, the dark, dark soil that still fed a large portion of the world.

Thinking of Katrinka blackened his thoughts. "I should have been there, Aunt Katrinka," Colter breathed, and his tour guide, a strapping, buxom blonde asked:

"What?"

"I wish that Czechoslovakia were so grand," Colter said, deliberately mangling his accent and syntax. He had already discovered, by listening, that his ear and his accent were excellent. It could be both useful and detrimental. The guide, a woman of twenty or so, smiled and nodded her head, obviously in complete agreement.

Her name was Tatyana, and she was a regular Intourist guide, traveling all the way to Batumi and beyond with the group. She spoke Polish and French, Russian, of course, and some English. Fortunately, she did not speak Czech.

From time to time Colter caught her looking at him, almost appraisingly. "Maybe," he thought, "she thinks I'm a hell of a fine-looking fellow."

Maybe she did, but Colter didn't like it, and he stayed away from Tatyana as much as possible. In the Union of Paranoid Socialist Republics, all foreigners were suspected of one thing or another— some smuggled in bibles, others cigarettes. Some prompted the local youths to hooligan antics by humming Rock and Roll songs. Colter didn't want to have Tatyana's vague suspicions, her watchfulness focus on him—still he couldn't completely avoid the busty blonde; that in itself was suspicious. He contented himself with staying on the edge of her group, from time to time making some trivial comment in his mangled "immersion" Russian, with falling in with the other tour guide, a young, narrow man, as much as possible.

Still something was happening. Tatyana's eyes were on him far more than seemed necessary or equitable. He couldn't help wondering what was going on behind those sky-blue eyes, that apple-and-cream-complexioned mask she wore.

They took the train to Kiev, a sprawling, bustling city of over a million and a half people, and the tour was put up in a decadently luxurious hotel on Kirov Street, which runs through the Staro-Kiev section of the city between the main avenue of Kreschatik and the many riverside parks where the spring grass was growing, where old men hawked balloons and children played.

Kiev. The Ukrainian capital. Where Prince Vladimir, after exploring all of the religions on earth, had settled on Greek Orthodoxy, married Princess Anna, the sister of the Greek emperor, and decreed that all Ukrainians from henceforth should be Greek Orthodox. Kiev, where contact with the Byzantine Empire through Christianity had brought the architecture of Constantinople to the Ukraine. A city devastated by fire and wild, vandalous Tartars, overrun by Lithuanian and Polish armies, ceded to Russia, occupied by the Germans in 1918; Colter knew all of this before Tatyana had begun lecturing them, taking them on her tour of the great city. Kiev had been home for those of his blood for centuries, and there was a blood memory, a memory fed by Aunt Katrinka, who knew much history that could not be found in books, much that the Russians did not allow to have happened, which they had expurgated, altered, ordered to be forgotten.

Kiev was a dreamlike place to Colter, yet it was gray and stony, and gray and stony people walked its streets. Their guided tour was made up of similar people. There was the head of a chemical plant in Warsaw, the chairman of the Gratislaw CP, the worker from Szeged in Hungary who had been given this tour of Russia in recognition of his production records.

And the man from the Bratislava glass works.

Colter begged off the tour of Kiev's Lenin Monument, the Schors Monument, the Arsenal Workers' Monument by pretending to be ill. He was ill in a way. Sick and tired of the politics that designated monuments, named streets, infected celebrations, transformed people into gray, stony things. If he heard the phrase "glorious revolution" once more, Colter thought, he would vomit. He was sick of chauvinism, of ancestor-worship, of everything.

He wanted to be in Batumi, to have done with this mad pursuit, or, alternately, in the Lake-watch, getting roaring drunk. Perhaps most of all he wanted to be where the small, lithe, warm-eyed woman was. Where the jungle steamed after the morning mists and birds screeched from the depths of the woodlands.

He had purchased a bottle of vodka of the sort they call *zveroboy*, or "animal killer," and he proceeded to kill the animal, lying alone in his hotel room, the window curtains drifting in the breeze, the subdued street sounds rising like foreign battle cries heard distantly to jar against his ears.

"So here is where you lie."

He had not heard the door open, but now he looked up to find her there, big, husky, her face aglow with good health and energetic scrubbing, her great breasts straining at the blue uniform she wore.

"Hello, Tatyana."

"Is not drink the curse of the working class?"

she asked lightly, sitting on his bed so that Colter rolled slightly toward her.

"If it is, then we are among the world's most accursed." Nowhere in the world did people seek to color their gray lives with the numbing hues of alcohol more than in Eastern countries, where there is no other color, no other hope at all. Colter realized after he had spoken that he might not have been expected to say such a thing, to phrase it so facilely. He didn't care. The animal killer was at work.

"They told me you were ill," she said, putting her cool hand on his forehead.

"I was ill. I am becoming more ill," Colter answered.

"Yes? That is not good. I found out you were missing and I became concerned about you, Comrade Dubček," Tatyana said.

She was so concerned that she was unbuttoning her uniform jacket as Colter lay, hand behind his head, bottle propped up on his chest, watching.

Tatyana threw her jacket aside and as Colter watched with rising interest and comradely feelings, she began taking off the white blouse that was all that restrained her great, jutting breasts.

"How is the tour getting on?" Colter asked.

"Ivan does this part," she said. Ivan was the other tour guide, a runt of a boy with moles all over his face and pink, watery eyes. Colter barely heard the answer. Tatyana shrugged out of her blouse and Colter stared almost with disbelief at the hearty, healthy breasts, smooth and so firm as to be almost muscular, at the taut, rose-pink nipples.

"So. Am I pleasing?" she asked. She tugged Colter's hand from behind his head and placed it on her right breast, warm, engaging, demanding. Her own hand helped Colter to knead it, to toy with the erect nipple. She smiled, unpinned her hair in one deft motion, and leaned forward, kissing him once.

Then Tatyana stood, her smile still warm, and she unbuttoned her blue skirt, which fell to the floor softly, leaving her in slip and pale blue panties. She slithered from these and sat on the bed again, resting her head on Colter's chest, her hand gripping his shoulder.

Colter looked down at the mass of cornsilk yellow hair, at the rise and tilt of her competent hips, the amazing, nearly pneumatic breasts, and he swung his arm out, placing the *zveroboy* on the rickety bedside table.

"And so," Tatyana whispered. "It is all right? I think I can make you well."

Colter rolled her mouth to his and kissed her deeply.

The woman was lusty, agile despite her heft. A hungry thing reaching out for colors from her own drab grayness, devouring them. And Colter was the foreign object, an entity guided along the tourist paths, shown secret, musty recesses where ancient rituals were performed, bright avenues of activity, the worker at play, at work, head thrown back exultantly, body arched and trembling, eyes shut, hands clawing at the deeper, swollen meaning of socialist accomplishment.

She lay against him slick with effort, her breathing deep yet unlabored, like that of a champion gymnast having finished her obligatory turns, her elective contortions, her leaps and splits, who now stood waiting for the judges' cards, her body exhausted yet fulfilled.

Colter stared blankly at the ceiling, thinking that she smelled like *bliny* and herring. Which made Colter realize that he was hungry and wished she would go so that he could eat. But she lay there, sweet and heavy, sated, murmuring sweet words to him as her finger toyed with the whorl of his ear, his hair, his small dark nipples.

At exactly four o'clock, however, Tatyana got up like a worker finished with her shift.

"I have the cathedral tour," she apologized, dressing quickly, buttoning up her astonishing body in a matter-of-fact way before bending to kiss him once on the forehead, handing him his bottle, and leaving.

Colter lay there in the descending darkness, sipping at the harsh liquor, wishing he was somewhere else, until shortly before six when his roommates came in and he rose, dressing to walk out onto the empty streets, the silent avenues of poor, dead Kiev.

EIGHT

When Tyurin got the folder from the embassy
in Vienna Remizov had already nearly put the
entire package together. He was content now, still
puzzled, but content. He was finding his "line of
coherent action."

"About time," Colonel Remizov said as Tyurin
entered the Bratislava police outpost, which was a
quarter of a mile away from the shooting site.

"These couriers—I think he stopped to see a
girl on the way."

"Is there anything in there?"

"I didn't look yet. Do you want me to?"

"We'll divide it up." Remizov took half of the
mimeographed papers. Their request had been
for anything the embassy and intelligence staff in
Vienna had that could be considered unusual for
the period just preceding, just following the
mysterious Colter's disappearance. Remizov didn't

know yet who Colter was, if that was his real name, but he was intrigued by what he had found out.

Fingerprints taken from Keller's Vienna hotel room matched those on the Smith & Wesson automatic. The bullets in the dead bodies matched those fired from the test gun at the police criminology laboratory.

"They sure think a lot of things are 'unusual,' don't they?" Tyurin grumbled. Remizov smiled. Crankiness in his lieutenant meant hunger. Nothing else was capable of disturbing his equilibrium.

Remizov himself had temporarily quit looking at the reports from Vienna. He was reviewing in his own mind the sequence of events, those movements of Colter that were verifiable.

Flown in from New York. He makes contact with Alvin in Paris. They conclude their unknown business and go out for a night on the town. The idiot Krylov kills Alvin. Colter flees to Vienna in Alvin's car, taking the pistol with him.

The telephone on the desk rang and Tyurin answered it. He nodded his head a few times, said, "I'll see," and covered the mouthpiece with his hand. "They've found a tailor in Paris who made a suit of clothes for Colter. Old clothes. Do you want to talk to Fetyukov?"

Remizov shook his head negatively. Tyurin said goodbye and hung up. "Well, that fits, doesn't it?"

"Yes. Did the tailor give them a description?"

"Six feet, dark, mustache. They're looking for

his associate, the man who makes the passports."

"They'll find out that he took Colter's picture, that he used the name Rudolf Keller."

"Well, they'll call back anyway. There may be something." Tyurin shrugged and rubbed his belly. "Did you see this one, sir?"

"What?"

"From Vienna—travel information. A man named Finn wanted to know if it is possible to leave an Intourist group."

"Check to see if a Finn has taken an Intourist ticket to anywhere."

"This is the first time we've given that consideration, isn't it?" Tyurin asked, rubbing his belly.

"What—that we are looking for a trail into the Soviet Union? Yes. But there may be no connection whatsoever. I want to know if this Finn ever took a tour, if he purchased a ticket, if so where to. What happened to him. Right?" Tyurin, who was scribbling a note in his book, nodded. "What's the full name, anyway?"

"Finn . . . Huckleberry." Tyurin looked up. "Isn't that . . . ?"

"Yes, it is. A fictional name. Better have them look into Finn right away."

"They'll never find him."

"Check the known-agent file and take any photos around to the embassy staff. Can someone do that?"

"The courier's still here. He can take instructions to—who is that in Vienna, Klevshin? I can never remember the man's name. Some sort of mental block."

"You're hungry, that's all. Yes, it's Klevshin."

"Unless you want me to do it myself, Colonel Remizov?"

"No, of course not. If they can't even handle that, they ought to get out of the business . . . Huckleberry Finn," he mused.

"Some American's idea of a joke, perhaps."

"Exactly. But which American's? Have the photo file scanned."

The door opened and Inspector Hacha wandered in, the pipe firmly between his teeth. It seemed sometimes to be rooted there. "Anything?" he asked.

Remizov briefly told the Czech policeman, who absorbed it all silently.

When he was finished, Remizov asked: "Anything from your side?"

"Something perhaps of interest. We've identified the dead men. I'm on my way out to their digs, want to come along?"

Remizov was on his feet, reaching for his hat before Hacha had finished the invitation. Tyurin silently cursed. Lunch was going to be delayed still longer.

Hacha's driver drove them along the long, straight concrete highway that divided the bright green fields. Remizov sat with his arms folded, his leather coat belted tightly, his good eye surveying the Czech countryside. He was fascinated by the Colter business, troubled and challenged. They had absolutely no idea of where the man had gone, of what his plans were. Probably he was simply a smuggler. The dead men had been known smugglers, petty thieves. But there was the tie-in with American intelligence. That bothered Remizov and made it their business. Colter had known 'Alvin,' and that made his movements of concern.

Fyodor had expressed it more bluntly when the colonel had advised him of the sketchy findings they had stumbled upon while looking into Fetyukov's little problem.

"Find the man," Fyodor had said in that tight, emotionless voice.

Whoever, whatever Colter was, he should not have run. "He is hiding," Fyodor had said. "If he is hiding he is doing something criminal. It may not concern us at all. He may be harming the Americans, he may be a lone wolf. But we must know. Look into this, colonel, please."

And then, as was his way, Fyodor had simply hung up.

"Here it is," Hacha said, and the driver took the dirt road to the left, bouncing over the ruts, rattling over an ancient, narrow bridge before swinging into the yard of a thatched farm cottage back among the huge plane trees.

"Who is that?" Remizov asked. Tyurin had come around to open his door.

"The woman? The wife of this Josef Stefanik—says she's his wife, at least, nothing shows in the recorder's office records. Common-law wife."

She was small, blond, her nose large and bulbous. She was extremely anxious to please and looked nervously at Tyurin and Remizov whenever they broke into Russian.

176

Inside the dilapidated farmhouse was a partial wall that swung open to reveal a workshop complete with engraving tools, printing press, cameras, stolen official seals. Colonel Remizov poked around, opening drawers while Hacha again questioned the wife of Josef Stefanik.

"She doesn't know anything," Hacha said finally. "I think the woman's not half smart. Either that or she's scared of prosecution—find anything?"

"No. Just the equipment, a few ruined papers. None for Colter."

"You think Stefanik provided papers for Colter? He already had the Rudolf Keller papers, didn't he?"

"He did. He switched. They're closing a lot of doors behind this man, inspector."

"Yes, that's true. He's changed papers again, if you're right. He came into Czechoslovakia, killed his forger for whatever reason and . . . ?" Hacha shrugged.

"Continued on to an unknown destination traveling under a new alias."

"How did he travel?" Tyurin asked, speaking up for the first time. "Car, train, bus, bicycle?"

None of the men was worried just now about *what* Colter was doing. There was no way of establishing that at this time. He was a killer, however, wanted for crimes against the state. And he was up to something else. Their primary concern was to find him.

"There's something he wants desperately," Remizov said. "A smuggler, a thief, would have turned and escaped into Austria, figuring the risk was no longer worth it. Unless we're dealing with a psychopath."

"Why not?" the Czech policeman said. "There's a world full of them."

"The explanation's too easy for an investigator," Tyurin chipped in. He looked at Remizov, who nodded.

"Yes, far too easy. No, Colter wants something. What, I don't know. Let's compile what we have and start again, gentlemen. Take the woman in. Maybe she will seem more intelligent in the police station. Take the papers here, go over the Vienna reports again, sift Fetyukov's account. Start again—we're missing something or we haven't come across it yet, but we will. We will succeed. Fyodor wants this man Colter. I want him."

Tatyana stayed away from Colter for the next few days as the tour traveled southward and eastward along the Black Sea coast, toward Batumi; but her eyes occasionally met his and he saw that hungry look she had fixed on him that night in Kiev.

Stupid. He told himself again and again that he had been stupid to allow things to develop in that way. He was no longer an anonymous Czech to the tour guide. Nor was it completely unnoticed by the others in the tour—this solicitude, this new interest Tatyana manifested toward the Czech, Dubček.

178

Ivan, for one, noticed it. The mole-infested Russian sullenly glowered at Colter, fastidiously ignoring any questions the "Czech" asked, going out of his way to assign Colter the worst seats in restaurants and theaters.

Colter had little time to worry about the Russian's piqued feelings. They had passed through Krasnodar the previous day and were now making toward Tuapse, a scenic coastal town of ancient Byzantine ruins where the people wore Eastern garments—robes and here and there a turban. Their faces were long and dark, their eyes deliberately blank. They were a day's travel from Batumi.

The Black Sea was a constant now on their right. Deep azure, with gently cresting surf that shot narrow bands of foam northward and southward as it broke on the rocky reefs. To their left were the Caucasus Mountains, with caps of snow still on the higher peaks, although it was well into April.

The villages and towns they passed through were no longer Russian. One saw Russian soldiers, Russian signs, the stern visage of Lenin, but the people were not Russian—they were Georgian or Turkish, descendants of Tartars and Armenians. Donkeys were led through the stone-paved streets, heavy loads of grain in their panniers. Here and there Colter saw mosques, apparently still attended.

The bus stopped at Tuapse, the last stop before Batumi, and Colter, feeling restless and irritable, found himself in a small room overlooking the sea

179

with the Pole, Gumolka, a man who resembled nothing so much as a prize pink hog preened for a livestock festival.

He had a porcine nose, protuberant belly and short legs. He had no liking for Colter, but Colter could not recall a single incident where he had run afoul of the Pole.

In silence they unpacked, Colter spending a long time at the window, which was tall, narrow, arched, located in a turretlike alcove.

From there there was a magnificent view of the sea, which at this hour was copper and red-gold, the sailing boats with sun-crimsoned sails gliding homeward. Distantly a mullah sang from a minaret as deep shadows fell across Tuapse.

Colter stood at the window until full dark, listening to Gumolka mutter in Polish, throw his articles into the shabby bureau, and mutter again.

Gumolka didn't seem to be having much of a trip. Colter had the idea it had been an honor that the Pole couldn't have graciously refused, and that he would rather be home with his stockinged feet propped up watching a potatolike wife make dinner for him.

"Good evening," Colter said in Russian as he walked abruptly toward the door. Gumolka muttered something else in Polish and threw his suitcase into the corner, watching the tall, dark-haired Czech go out.

Colter walked out of the hotel and across the street toward the wharves. The sky was nearly dark; the sea glowed with pale phosphoresence.

He walked down a long stone quay, and dark

eyes turned up to him from nets and holds filled with silver fish, from lines and patched sails. These people too were Russian if you believed your world atlas, but inside they were Turks, Muslims, followers of Allah, and it would take a hundred more years before the Soviets had processed the brains of all the young and produced a generation of true godless socialists loyal only to the Marxist-Leninist state.

Colter stood on the end of the quay, listening to the murmuring of the sea against the stone breakwater. He looked out across the harbor where Greeks and Swedes, Latvians and Turks, Thessalonians and Persians had anchored their fleets. Where nameless sailors from forgotten times, forgotten lands had waited upon the tide or a storm, looking across the deep, dark Black Sea to the Dardanelles and the Bosporus, beyond to where their families, their women, waited for the adventurers' return.

Colter stood there until the sea went flat and black and merged with the close draperies of the evening sky, and the wind went cold, the sea-scented breezes flitting across the harbor to tug at the flapping unsecured sails of the fishers.

Far to the south he could see a pale light gleaming, like a distant red star, and he wondered if that was Batumi. Batumi, where poets slept in their chains—or if that was too dramatic, where they withered away, seeing songs of blood, of earth and fire turn to dust.

At least, Colter thought, they *allow* poets in Russia. If they are censored, chained, outlawed if their dogma is erroneous, at least there is honor. Were there any American poets anymore? He knew he couldn't imagine anyone making a living at it, gaining honor or respect. The poetry he had heard lately was childish, unmetered, unrhyming, empty—and better left unwritten.

Why did they want Vesely? Colter still hadn't been able to conjur up an answer to that question. Why did Up Above feel it was important enough to risk an international incident, which it certainly would become if Colter were caught—he had a fleeting, vivid image of himself on some docket, with somber, fat, beribboned men beside him, of admitting to imperialist plots—and he realized that it could very easily be his fate to play out such a travesty. Assuming they didn't simply shoot him out of hand. He thought about success, hoped for it, but he realized he had never really expected it, not in this perverse game he had allowed himself to be pushed into. Maybe that was the appeal it had had for him; maybe Mike Colter was, after all, no more than a man pursuing his own end.

He turned then, poet-chaser, pseudo-Czech, tour guide seducer, Russian without a land, American without a home, and walked back toward the hotel where, with a little luck, he would be able to bribe the Intourist manager to bring him a bottle of animal killer. Not that the animal was ever truly killed. It only lay stunned at Colter's feet, flat on its side, slavering as it twitched in its sleep, waiting to leap and go for the jugular.

182

The bus for Batumi left at dawn, and Colter, with a massive headache, sat in the rear, his head pressed to the fogged window that glowed with orange sunrise light, hearing the jabber of different languages, the complaints of Gumolka, the roar of the diesel engine, the hiss of tires against the broken pavement, the rapid pumping of his heart.

He had spent the night with Tatyana again. There had been no reason for it and none not to. He had simply supported her hungry athletic body as it performed its heated contortions, leaping, panting against him.

Ivan had been near the door when Colter left her room in the early hours, and there had been pure torment and hatred in the little Russian's eyes. Colter managed to ignore the man completely, not feeling in the least responsible for Ivan's maligned libido. Yet he had made an enemy, that was clear, and that was something Colter didn't like. He had done a damn poor job of remaining inconspicuous on this journey.

Now the beaches flashed past, white and dull lemon in the morning sun. The Black Sea was a deep cobalt blue, glittering dully like undulating silk. From time to time Tatyana turned to look at him from her seat near the driver, and he could recall most vividly her soft, *bliny* breath near his nostrils, her kittenishly clenching hands, her seaching eyes.

"We must not imagine that we are doing wrong, Dubček."

"No," Colter answered muzzily.

"It is not sport for me," she went on. "You are a man who has sunk a hook into my heart, brought a primitive woman to the surface of the deep gray lake of my life."

"Sure." Colter yawned and closed his eyes. It was a good line, but Colter wondered if there wasn't a new angler each tour. He put it down to post-passion prose and stroked her back, keeping his own eyes closed to try shutting out attempts at conversation.

Once he had awakened in the night, chilled and confused. He thought he had heard a knock at the door, thought it was John Wayne and a squad of Green Berets. It was the night wind at Tuapse, slapping a shutter against the stone wall of an ancient hotel. There was a warm weight pressed against him, smothering him, and it offered no comfort at all against the chill of that bitter wind.

Batumi appeared as if emerging slowly from the dark sea as the tour bus rumbled down the well-maintained coastal highway. It sprouted slowly, taking on form and substance, becoming a conglomeration of the ancient and the modern, mosques and crumbling clay-brick houses side by side with modern, featureless factories glittering with glass. Colter saw a huge, silvery collection of man-sized pipes, long, inextricably wound together, and he remembered that there was an oil refinery in Batumi, a very large one, very modern.

The orange groves had begun to appear, lining the road, deep green trees with small bright orange fruit like ornaments hung carelessly. And beyond, the sea. He could see the coast as it

184

curved around toward the west, and he recognized that he was looking at Turkey across Batumi Bay.

The bus slowed, falling in with a column of army vehicles including a troop carrier and a dozen motorcycles with sidecars. Colter sat at the window, seeing the helmeted heads glance at him, feeling transparent and criminal. After a while the convoy turned off and the road became cobblestone, the buildings crowded together, and Colter's pulse began to race. Batumi—the place Anton Dubček had come to die.

He began to study Batumi, the lay of the land, with a more critical eye, mapping it in his head, seeing strategic points, the way the traffic flowed in the constricted heart of the town. And where, he wondered, did Stepan Vesely live with his dark-eyed daughter?

Colter closed his eyes, trying to recall the image of Vesely he had been shown. Oddly, the man insistently became his daughter, Anna, she with the haughty lips and intent eyes. Finally he even became Tatyana, and Colter gave up in disgust, opening his eyes as the bus swung around the corner and entered the rear courtyard of an off-pink, architecturally surprising Moorish hotel.

The bus halted with the hiss of air brakes, and the doors swung open. The tourists rose, stretched, bent over to peer out the windows, reached for luggage, and started shuffling forward. Dubček followed them out of the door and onto the paved courtyard, looking around at the faces of the gardeners, the handymen, who were all Turks, wondering if one of them was Mustafa. Mustafa—

who was to be responsible for killing Anton Dubček and keeping Mike Colter alive.

His room was plastered in pale blue, a single window, meshed over with copper wire, looked out upon a deep blue bay. There were bathers on the beach. The air was warm and balmy, the sky bright, the Black Sea placid and rich in texture, deep blue, silver, and gold. Gumolka, the Pole, cursed and laid out his clothes for a bath, casting a glance at Colter that seemed to blame him for all of his unspoken troubles.

Colter sat on the swaybacked bed and let a thousand hurried thoughts rush through his mind. Mustafa, Vesely, Dubček. Turkey, Aunt Katrinka, Tatyana, Ivan, Kiev, Cassidy. A procession of faces, a string of unrelated thoughts, an impossible mission, a wasted life.

He wasn't cut out for this at all. Not anymore. Maybe once, long ago, before he knew that life could crush you, that there were things worse than dying. Why not, he thought with a thin smile, just bail out? Sure—just continue the tour, return to Czechoslovakia, go to work at the Bratislava glass works, become a good party member, live with Tatyana, cut his own throat . . . he sat there gloomily while Gumolka, wearing only a towel around his hairless pink body, padded to the bathroom and began cursing the rusty, tepid water that issued from the pipes.

Colter rose, picked up his jacket, and went out into the Batumi afternoon.

He strolled along the sidewalk above the beach, pausing now and then to lean against the low concrete wall and look out at the bathers, all healthy, happy socialists in surprisingly skimpy bathing suits, the sun glittering on the sea beyond them, a light wind kicking up sand.

A dull-looking Turk sold *kvass*, fermented bread water, at a pushcart stand with a tattered, striped awning, and Colter gave him a two-kopek piece for a paper cup full of the stuff. Then he hoisted himself onto the wall, and, with his feet dangling over the beach, he watched the socialist maidens, their broad-shouldered, heavy breasted, scantily clad bodies bouncing and jiggling as they played on the sand.

Later he found a group of men standing beneath a cluster of cypress trees drinking vodka and arguing furiously about factory quotas. Colter stood nearby, listening. They were Ukrainians and he understood them perfectly, no matter how quickly they spoke. He had expected a certain amount of slang, but he heard nothing he did not comprehend, except for a few terms a gentle old woman like Aunt Katrinka would never have used—but these were graphically defined by the accompanying hand gestures the workers used. They were dark, strong-looking men with thick shoulders, fiery tempers, and quick laughter. Colter understood them, and he liked them.

"Are you with the Poltsava Oil Refinery?" someone asked him abruptly.

"No," Colter answered, "I'm just a tourist. I have an interest in meeting quotas—back home— and I heard you men talking. You don't mind if

I listen?"

"Not at all, comrade. Have some vodka."

And he did. It was *Ghorilka Spertsem*, a powerful Ukrainian vodka laced with pepper. Very harsh on the tongue, very comfortable in the stomach. Colter stood with the workers for an hour, drinking their vodka, which they pressed on him, and listening. The conversation veered away from quotas and factories and became pleasant. One man with a great booming voice, a florid face, and morose expression began telling of his extramarital adventures, another of catching the party vice chairman in the cloakroom with the secretary at the factory. The stories were warm, funny, and Colter found himself laughing with them. As the evening came on, the afternoon misting away, they drifted homeward in twos and threes and Colter was left alone on the beach.

Sighing, he started back up the beach, walking along the water's edge. There were but a handful of bathers left. They had taken weary limbs, sunburned bodies, red-rimmed eyes back to their hotels to shower and dress for the night. The sea hissed quietly against the pebbled beach.

"Dubček?"

Colter halted and turned. The young Turk was beside him, eyes sparkling expectantly in the near darkness. The thin mouth was compressed into a straight line. He came forward, studying Colter's face.

"Are you Anton Dubček?"

"That's right."

"Don't go back to your hotel."

"No?" Colter scrutinized the young Turk closely.

"No. Don't go there."

"Why not? Who says not to go there?"

"Mustafa. Mustafa says it."

"Are you Mustafa?"

"No. But Mustafa has sent me. He says you are not to go back to your hotel."

"All right." He nodded. "I don't go back to my hotel if Mustafa says not to. Where do I go then?" Colter felt a trembling in his legs and he tried to convince himself it was the wind off the sea that caused it.

"One hour," the Turk answered obliquely. "In one hour you will be on the corner of Oktybrya Street, near the Lenin Park. You can find it easily. Two men will come by in a truck that says 'Sea Catch' on the side of it. An old truck, you will know it when it comes. You will get into the back when the truck stops near the monument."

"All right," Colter said.

"You understand this?"

"I understand you. At Lenin Park, I wait for the truck."

"And you will do it?"

"Yes."

"You will not go back to the hotel?"

"No."

"One hour then. They will find you."

The Turk hesitated a minute and then walked swiftly away, a small, white-clad figure making his way along the beach in the gathering darkness.

Colter walked back to the sidewalk and asked the *kvass* man, who was just now closing up his stand, where Lenin Park was. The man lifted a hand and pointed to the south without looking at Colter. In an hour Colter was in the park, standing beneath the plane trees, watching the moon slowly rise. The monument itself had been defaced, Colter noticed. Someone had scratched the bronze bust of the revolutionary leader, crudely sketching a phallus, which disappeared into the Bolshevik's mouth.

The truck appeared punctually, slowly cruising the adjacent avenues until, caution satisfied, it rolled into the park precisely one hour after Colter had been contacted.

It was an ancient Ford panel truck, a '36 or '37 model with faded lettering on the side. "Sea Catch." Colter sauntered toward the truck, which had parked in the deep shadows of a monkey puzzle tree. The back door popped open and Colter was hurried inside by dark hands.

Three Turks squatted there in the smell of dead fish and damp wood, and on the floor was the dead man.

"Strip, strip," the Turk Colter had met on the beach said commandingly as the panel truck's engine started and it lurched forward, grinding a gear. Colter leaned against the wall and began taking off his clothes.

"All of it. Underwear too. Essential," he was urged.

They got the essentials. Colter was handed a robe like a monk's, and he slipped into it. The

Turks were hushed and still as the truck crept along side streets and back alleys. Through the small, clouded windows in the back doors Colter could see a street lamp, an illuminated storefront.

The Turks had gotten the body on the floor into Colter's clothes. He was a man in his mid-twenties, Colter's height and weight approximately, vaguely resembling him facially.

In another minute he resembled no one at all. The Turk nearest Colter produced a long knife and started to work on the face. One of his comrades grabbed his arm and held him back.

"This," he heard the other say, and a sledge hammer with a twenty-inch handle was passed between them. Colter saw the hammer raised, saw it fall. He closed his eyes but could not close out the sound like that of a melon bursting. He heard it again, mushier this time, and then again.

He glanced at the man—Dubček—lying there in his clothes, and he felt a pang of sympathetic remorse.

"Do not feel for the bastard. He was secret police," the Turk said. Then, merrily, he smashed the right hand to shreds of meat. "Fingerprints," he said. The left hand was done next, and then they decided more attention should be paid to the dental work. They used an iron bar.

The truck rolled on and Colter, trapped in a nightmare, sat on the floor, trying to avoid the eyes of the Turks, the sight of the mutilated body.

The truck stopped abruptly and the lights were turned off. Colter sat shivering in the robe, and this time he knew it was not from the chill of the night. Colter had seen death; he had initiated it, but he had never grown used to it. He despised gratuitous violence and the men who reveled in it. The Turks apparently had no such qualms. One man was the enemy—and so he was dead. The other was alive, since he was an ally who could help them. It was not ghoulish or bloodthirsty—it was necessary, no more, no less.

There was a distant rumbling sound now that Colter could not at first identify, until, with sudden animation, the Turks flung open the back doors and leaped from the truck excitedly, chattering to each other, waving their hands.

The body was dragged out, leaving a slimy purplish trail on the bed of the truck. One of the Turks sloshed a bucketful of water over the gore and scrubbed it down with a bundle of rags.

Colter, who had identified the distant rumbling sound by now, slid out of the truck to watch. There was a narrow concrete bridge over the railroad tracks, and steaming toward them was a forty-car freight headed for Kutaisi. The Turks were at the center of the bridge, crouched behind an iron railing. The revolving light in the nose of the locomotive lit the tracks below brilliantly, but did nothing to illuminate the bridge itself.

The train, clanking and rumbling, steam issuing from its iron nostrils, raced toward the bridge, and the Turks raised up, lifting their burden, rolling it from the bridge. Colter had a glimpse of Anton Dubček, arms and legs stretched out like a windmill, whirling through the air to land on the tracks before the locomotive, moments later to be ground to chunks of meat beneath the drive wheels of the Kutaisi Express.

No more Dubček.

In Colter's clothing, his wallet in the pocket of the coat, the anonymous man had become Dubček. Undoubtedly the body would be so identified. Dubček would be reported missing, and the dead man would subsequently be found. Suicide? Simply drunk. A tourist toppling from the unfamiliar bridge at night.

The Turks were grinning and chattering happily. A good night's work. One of them slapped Colter on the shoulder and said, "Now we see Mustafa."

The truck rolled on, out of Batumi proper and up into the darkened hills beyond. The road was dirt, the hillsides planted with grapes and olive trees. There wasn't a light anywhere for miles.

The headlights searched the dark, winding road as the truck rattled upland. Colter, peering forward, across the driver's shoulder, saw no habitations, no man-made structures at all, and soon the vineyards, the orange and lemon groves, the olives were gone. The country became rough and primitive.

Around another hairpin turn they went, Colter hanging on, and then the truck suddenly veered off the road. For a moment Colter thought the crazy Turk driver had finally lost control of the vehicle, but he discovered that there was a secondary road—hardly that even—a half-over-grown trail suitable for donkeys and little else that dipped down into a hollow and lost itself among

193

the tangle of dark trees.

They sputtered up a gulley where there was no visible trail at all and emerged onto a nearly level plateau where scattered cedar trees grew. The lights of the panel truck were extinguished as they achieved the flats.

They jolted along in silence for a long while— how the driver knew where he was going was beyond Colter, who could see nothing out the windshield. Finally they parked. The driver honked the horn twice and somewhere in the far distance Colter saw a light go on and then quickly off. The truck was started again, and within ten minutes they were parked inside of an ancient mudbrick barn, the motor off, the radiator burbling, the Turks clambering out, gesturing to Colter to follow.

Outside it was starbright, the moon only a haze on the distant horizon. The air still smelled of the sea, but more richly of pungent brush. There was also the smell of something cooking. Lamb, Colter thought, herbal and sweet.

The small colorless house with the thatched roof lay half hidden behind the shoulder of a high privet hedge, sheltered by tilting, gloomy cypress trees. A man standing so motionlessly that he might have been carved from stone was visible near the corner of the house. He held an automatic weapon in his hands, and it looked suspiciously like an Israeli-manufactured Uzi SMG, and Colter wondered how in hell Soviet Turk dissidents had come by them, but then weapons of all sorts, useful only in offensive action, are available on the world's market anywhere to anyone who has the cash to pay. Even the vast standing armies of this planet can't utilize the huge production of weapons cranked out by the world's competing arms manufacturers.

The Swedes the Czechs, the Americans, the Soviets keep factory after factory busy drilling and chambering, producing deadly new refined weapons, ammunitions, explosives for the use of terrorists or anyone else with a handful of cash and the will to kill.

The front door of the house opened and Colter was ushered in quickly. All was darkness until the door was closed again. Then someone hit the electric lights—powered by a faintly humming gasoline generator in the rear of the house—and Colter stood blinking in the comparative brightness of harsh neon.

There were blackout curtains on the windows, a braided rug on the earthen floor, a scarred, uncovered walnut table, and at its head a savagely scarred man with the hair shaved off one side of his head over his crooked ear. Or at first Colter had thought it to be shaven—now he saw the yellow scar tissue, and he knew that a wound had caused the baldness. Flame does that. Maybe the flash from explosives set with too short a fuse.

The man had gnarled hands though he was not much older than Colter. He wore a faded red cotton shirt and khaki trousers. Black expressionless eyes flanked a long, hooked nose beneath a narrow, protuberant brow.

"Mustafa?"

195

"Colter."

It was almost a shock to hear his own name again. He nodded. "Yes, I'm Colter."

"Sit down, my friend, we have much to talk about," Mustafa said in his strangely accented Russian. He gestured with a crippled hand and Colter sat, the others retiring to the corners of the room where they crouched, watching.

Raki was served, the harsh white Turkish spirit, and *kadin budu*, which means "the woman's thigh," and for some reason only known to Turks, the thighs are represented by meatballs and rice.

They ate slowly, each man watching the other, measuring without seeming to. Colter saw the strength of this one, the natural wariness. He had been a warrior, this Turk. He was a leader of men, a lover of his people. He had use for Colter only as long as Colter could serve him. And that meant living the lie that Colter was here for that purpose. It didn't do to think on how the Turks would react if they found out he wasn't there to help them against the Russians. Colter recalled far too vividly Anton Dubček and the hammer.

They had another course, lamb in an herb sauce, and followed it with three more small glasses of *raki*. The Turk was silent throughout the meal. Once a distant engine could be heard and two of the Turks slid out into the night to investigate, returning to whisper in Mustafa's ear.

"You are filled?" Mustafa asked finally.

"I am. Thank you."

"Good. A hungry man thinks of his stomach and not of the work at hand."

196

Mustafa gestured with a finger and one of his soldiers rose and walked to the small pantry off the dining room. Reaching inside a cannister containing flour, he returned with a pack of cigarettes, dusting them off on his shirt. It was a funny place to keep cigarettes, and since Mustafa had just lit an evil-smelling, dark cigar, Colter figured there was more to it than an after-dinner smoke.

There was more to it.

Mustafa took the cigarette pack, cutting cellophane and paper with an ivory-handled pen knife. He slipped the cigarettes out on the table and searched around for a moment before finding the one he wanted.

Glancing at Colter, smiling thinly, Mustafa slit the cigarette paper lengthwise and unrolled it. Inside was a tightly rolled piece of yellow paper, very thin, printed on both sides. Mustafa handed it to Colter and beckoned to his lieutenants to clean up the cigarettes and loose tobacco.

Colter smoothed the paper on the table's edge while Mustafa's eyes clung to him.

"Where'd this come from?" Colter asked.

"From Trabzon—the American Air Force base."

"How'd you smuggle it in?"

"All of my people are fishermen. It is no problem with a boat to get things into this country."

Colter scanned the first few lines of the message and then glanced up at Mustafa. He had the idea the Turk read English well and had already seen the message. They would expect him to read it.

That accounted for the camouflage that made up the first two-thirds of the dispatch.

AMX DC COMCON DECODE EIGHT
TRAB COMCON NO EYES SEVEN
FM EXCALIBER TWO TEN
TO SPECIAL THREE EIGHT

To field forces—
Attend evaluation Inside Force per weapon/cost/value. All assistance via yr recommendation. Countercause vital yr area. Commander most anxious cement alliance.

So much for the camouflage. Mustafa, his eyes somber with thoughts of Holy War, watched as Colter read the remainder of the message.

Second issue. Poet not needed. Only information fm Bulgakov. Rpt Bulgakov. Imperative. Destroy message. Out. Cassidy.

Colter sat staring at the message without seeing the words. He glanced at Mustafa and felt empathy toward the man. Both of us screwed, Colter thought. Both of us on impossible missions. Keeping blind faith.

Mustafa believed that Colter would study his group in action and report to the CIA on whether or not the Turkish subversive group should receive weaponry and money and other assistance. The Turk, like many others, had no idea of how the company operated. They sure as hell weren't going to give anything to people operating within the Soviet Union. But it was protection and guaranteed assistance for Colter if Mustafa thought they would.

Colter too had felt the shaft, although he had half-expected disaster, some sort of turnaround.

Poet not needed.

Meaning. We were simply shitting you, old man. We don't want Vesely out at all, nor does the poet want out of the Soviet Union. But he knows something, possesses something written by, spoken by, revealed by a man named Bulgakov. Pry it out of the poet, will you? A few yanked fingernails ought to do it.

Who Bulgakov was, Colter did not know. What the information might be was not important—oh, he knew vaguely what it would be. Atomic secrets, biological warfare data, miniaturization, code names, disposition of the Baltic Fleet. Military information. The company had felt they needed it and they had sent someone in. You couldn't blame them; that was the way they worked. They were saints compared to the KGB. Still—it had seemed to mean something, bringing the old man out. This meant nothing at all. Not to Colter personally. He was no crusader, only a hired man assigned to bring back information.

It was only a job, another dirty one, and Colter smiled at himself. They had gotten the right flunky, approached him in the right way. They had designed the mission to appeal to an idealist (an idealist who needed money, but an idealist nevertheless). He had been paid. It didn't matter, he supposed. But, damnit! They shouldn't have lied to him.

"There is something wrong, *effendim*?" Mustafa asked.

"No," Colter said hastily, "nothing at all." It was no time to be showing doubt, to drop his pose. Mustafa was friendly enough now, a gracious host—but Colter hadn't forgotten how their enemies could be dealt with.

"Good." Mustafa handed the message to a man at his shoulder. He walked to the fireplace and tossed it into the low, dully glowing golden flames where it curled and was consumed. Mustafa raised a glass of *raki* to eye level.

"To our success then, Colter."

"To our success."

NINE

"Do you want to look at it?" Doctor Yezhov asked. He seemed to be smiling behind his beard. His tiny green eyes twinkled as he rested a hand on the green body bag.

"No. Unnecessary," Vasili Blok responded quickly. Blok glanced at the bag, at the misshapen form of it, unlike anything human. He had spent fourteen years as the head of Batumi's police department without looking upon a corpse, and Captain Blok did not intend to test his sensitive stomach now—not on anything that looked as *that* must.

He turned instead to his assistant, Detective Orest Litinev, a serious-minded, mournful young man with a degree from Moscow University in criminology.

"What have we, Orest?" the captain asked, mopping his forehead. The morgue seemed incredibly hot. The scent of formaldehyde was oppressive. Blok turned and started out of the basement room, Orest Litinev at his shoulder, stooping slightly to speak into the captain's ear.

"Identification found on the body," Litinev said, "indicates that the deceased is one Anton Dubček, a Czechoslovakian citizen who was visiting Batumi with an Intourist group."

"Damn, a foreigner," Blok muttered. "There'll be trouble over this, wait and see." Litinev ignored the captain, who was congenitally pessimistic.

"For reasons unknown," the policeman went on as they went out and started climbing the stairs to Blok's second-floor office, "Dubček was pushed or fell from . . ."

"Or jumped from," Blok put in hopefully. That was by far his preferred solution. No one can be blamed for a suicide.

"Or jumped from the Chavchavadze Street bridge into the path of the Kutaisi Express. This occurred at nine thirty-five last evening. The engineer witnessed the fall and notified the police at the next station. Officer Klyuyev was dispatched from this station and he discovered the remains of Comrade Dubček in the brush alongside the tracks some fifty meters from the point of impact."

Blok nodded. They had reached his office and he swung the unpainted door open, leading the way into the cramped greenish room. His desk was littered with papers of one kind or another and the breeze off the sea through the partially opened window rustled through them.

Blok sagged behind his desk, his white shirt showing perspiration stains beneath his armpits. He wiped back his thinning gray hair and steepled his stubby fingers. He looked at the window for a long while, biting at the inside of his cheek.

"Have we contacted Intourist?" he asked at last.

"No, but we will."

"More problems," Blok said dismally. "Remember the purse snatcher last season? Or were you here?"

"I wasn't here yet," Litinev answered. He changed the subject quickly before Blok could start in on a lengthy story. Everything that had happened in the years before Litinev had arrived at Batumi was related by Blok if you allowed him an opening. And, he had an amazing mind for detail. "I'm trying to find someone to identify the body. Someone from the tourist group, I suppose."

"Poor bastard," Blok muttered sympathetically. He rubbed his stomach and leaned back in his swivel chair, lighting a cork-filtered Graznoy cigarette.

"Family?" Blok asked Litinev.

"We've held back on wiring Bratislava—that's Dubček's home—until the remains have been definitely identified. That," Litinev added to Blok's discomfort, "may take some time."

"Yes." Blok blew out a plume of cigarette smoke. "I really can't accept suicide, Orest. I'd wish it to be so, but—the railing is not that low on

203

the Chavchavadze bridge."

"Drunk, perhaps?"

"Was he drinking yesterday evening?"

"We're looking into his movements."

"Suicide isn't usually associated with a holiday, Orest."

"No, it isn't."

Blok leaned back farther yet in his creaking chair, puffing his cigarette, which he held between thumb and forefinger. "Well," he said, so low that Litinev barely heard him. "We can't go much farther until the doctor's through and the body's identified."

"No, sir."

"What else is up?"

"Smuggling, captain. The harbor patrol found ten kilos of hashish aboard a fisher."

"Turks, no doubt."

"Yes, sir. They were Turks. They've already seen the magistrate. Eight years labor."

"That ought to slow them down. Maybe it'll teach the other bastards a lesson. Still—let's lend the harbor police a dozen men, Orest. Let the smugglers see more uniforms. I'm tired of these Turks flaunting the law. Hashish—they always want that. What's their Koran say about that? How can they use drugs?"

"I don't know, sir." Litinev looked at his little notebook and continued with the briefing. "Comrade Speransky has reported his wife missing again. . . ."

"Ignore that! Haven't we enough troubles without Speransky constantly losing that bitch of

204

a wife he has?"

"I was going to send a detective out to their apartment . . ." Litinev said weakly.

"No. Forget that. Speransky knows where she is and who she's with. He just hasn't got the guts to go down and take her away from him. What else?"

"The KGB has lost a man."

"How's that?" Blok asked, cocking his head to one side curiously as he lit a cigarette from the butt of the old one. "How do you do that? Who was it? Kranz, I hope."

"Sergei Bakst, lieutenant, of the antiseparatist squad. He failed to report in last evening and failed subsequently to return home."

"Antiseparatist squad, huh? The Turks have got him, too. We'll find him with his throat cut. Why don't we round up all of those devils and put them in a work camp, I'd like to know."

"Probably," Litinev thought, "because the economy of Batumi would collapse without them." Aloud he went on. "Hooligans have defaced the Lenin monument again, Captain Blok. . . ."

Below was the empty sea, gray and rolling, and all around was the angry sky, a frothing, twisting sky with rain and sleet and spikes of lightning, and then you were dropping, dropping toward the tiny speck far below. The tiny speck, which became larger, in microseconds becoming vast and solid, a wall to hurl yourself against.

In the ears was the shrieking of mammoth

engines, the sounds of your own screams, the confused voices of people far away talking through the storm's crackling.

Then you hit the deck and the world was a ball of orange flame, terrible, jagged pain, the knowledge that you were dead. . . .

Colonel Remizov sat up panting. He looked around his Bratislava hotel room for a long minute, his heart thumping, the night empty and still, and then he knew finally where he was and that the botched landing lay far behind him.

The landing, but not the pain. Even now his leg throbbed, perhaps with recalled trauma. Even now his eyeless socket ached and he could remember the surgeon through an anesthetized haze telling the other doctor, "The eye must come out."

That was done, and the skull was patched back together, and then he had gone home to Moscow to work for Intelligence, to meet Fyodor, who had his own secrets, who was himself dying, dying slowly and horribly of cancer of the retina.

She hadn't wanted him then.

Not *her*. Or maybe she had already ceased to wait. Maybe it wasn't the eyepatch, the horribly twisted leg that had been set eight times, the scars across his chest, the scars on the abdomen where they had taken out the ribs. Maybe she had just ceased to wait . . . what did they want, these women?

"What is it, darling," the woman beside him murmured. "Come back to sleep."

But it was the wrong bed and the wrong woman

206

and outside dawn was arriving in a hazy, pearly mist. And there was a man somewhere who had to be found. Fyodor knew. He had hammered it into Remizov's head until Remizov knew what Fyodor had in mind—Remizov would replace Fyodor. He was the perfect replacement. Another cripple, another man who had nothing left to devote himself to but the hunt.

"I know," Remizov said to himself as he rose from the bed, and the woman there rolled over and snorted once before falling into a deeper sleep. "There cannot be any failure. Failure cannot exist.

"And so," Remizov said as he stood naked at the window, "I will find you, Colter. Whoever you are, whatever it is you are up to, I will find you. You threaten the state, you threaten me. And that cannot be tolerated."

Tyurin was already at Inspector Hacha's office when Remizov got there a little before six o'clock, but then Tyurin had the look of a man who has been up all night. Tyurin was still young—he could get away with that for a few more years. What, Remizov wondered, did Tyurin do on his nights out? Surely a man couldn't eat all day and all night too, but he had never heard Tyurin mention women, never seen his lieutenant take a drink. . . .

"The general bulletin paid off. Maybe." Tyurin said, making a hopeful gesture.

"Someone saw Colter?"

"It's not positive, colonel."

"Any coffee left in that pot? What is it then,

Tyurin—don't hold me in suspense."

"There's a possibility," Tyurin said, pouring Colonel Remizov a cup of dark coffee, "that a Youth Corps member, a boy of seven, saw Colter."

"A boy."

"He's very alert, colonel."

"You've spoken to him?"

"An hour ago."

"He's here?" Remizov sipped his coffee.

"In with Hacha now. Having breakfast." Tyurin glanced at his wristwatch. "They should be nearly through."

They were. When Tyurin and Remizov reached the police cafeteria they found Hacha sitting smoking while a young boy in a Youth Corps uniform finished mopping the egg from his plate with a piece of bread. The boy looked up at the approaching men and then to Hacha, who said something comforting, resting a hand briefly on the boy's shoulder.

"He's a little apprehensive," Hacha told them off to one side of the room.

"Why?"

"You know. Thinks he did wrong."

"Well, too bad. Let him know we don't think he did anything he shouldn't have. He full up yet?"

"Yes. He should be. That's his second plate," Hacha said with something like fatherly pride.

After the boy finished his milk they went to a small interrogation room on the second floor. Remizov opened the venetian blinds and swung the casement window open. Birds chirped along the window ledge. The investigator took a seat next to the boy on the leather bench. It seemed like a better idea than facing him across the desk. Someone had already gotten this kid pumped full of state fear.

"Did you have enough to eat?" Remizov asked.

"Yes." The kid sat, hands folded on his lap, bare legs dangling. His eyes were on the floor.

"Good. My name is Colonel Remizov."

"You are a Russian."

"That's right."

The boy started to say something else, but he didn't. The eyes that had flickered briefly up to Remizov's face now turned down again.

"You answered our general alert," Remizov began. "Let's see—you saw someone suspicious three days ago in the center of town." Remizov's eyes met Tyurin's. It had been three days since the murder of Josef Stefanik.

"Yes, colonel." The boy was trembling. Remizov looked away with frustration, disappointment, anger. When would they stop harassing these little minds? What did you end up with but neurotics?

"All right. Settle down now. Tell me what happened."

"I saw a man. He looked suspicious to me," the boy said. His voice was thin and high.

"Yes," Remizov encouraged.

"He was walking along the avenue. . . ."

Tyurin interrupted. "What made him suspicious?"

"It was very early. He was walking around with

209

a suitcase. I saw him go past my apartment three times. He was lost."

"All right. You went on down then to see who he was."

"I thought," the boy flushed, ". . . maybe he was an American spy."

"I see," Remizov responded with respectable gravity. "What happened?"

"When I got closer I saw that his coat and pants had mud on them. I thought he looked angry or . . . I don't know, lost maybe."

"What did you do?"

"I asked him who he was and he showed me his CP card."

"He had a party card?"

"Yes, colonel." The boy shrank away a little.

"And so you assumed he was not a spy. All right." The investigator smoothed back his blond hair, touching his eye patch, which seemed to fascinate the boy. "Please go on."

"Then I took him to the bus terminal."

"Wait. He asked you to take him?"

"Yes . . . no. He didn't really."

"What do you mean?"

"He couldn't speak. That is, he didn't speak, and so I thought he couldn't speak. Perhaps like old Mr. Tiso who had to have a hole cut in his throat when he couldn't talk. Maybe just a sore throat, I didn't know, but he said nothing to me. He just gave me his suitcase, you see, and we went along to the bus terminal."

"This was three days ago in the morning."

"Yes."

"Do you know which bus he took?"

"No."

"Did you see the name on the CP card?"

"No. I don't know . . . I can't think. Maybe Dolbek." The boy was growing frustrated and a little frightened again. Remizov let him go off with Hacha for a while to have an apple and use the bathroom.

"Well?" Tyurin said.

"It's him."

"You're sure?"

"I shouldn't be sure," Remizov said, going to the window of the police department office, "but I am sure, yes. He was forced to kill the forger. Then he proceeds to the bus station to make his escape."

"Or to continue on his mission," Tyurin pointed out.

"Would he?" Remizov frowned. He had been thinking along the lines of a brazen, clever escape. Going into Bratislava and not risking going back across the wire. What kind of man would continue on this mission? It was possible, of course . . . "Intourist," Remizov said suddenly, turning sharply.

"What's that?"

"Huckleberry Finn asked about Intourist travelers. We checked the Intourist rosters out of Vienna. What about those leaving Bratislava?"

"I'll see. The morning, three days ago?"

"Yes. Destinations, passenger lists."

"All right. What names? Colter, Finn, Rudolf Keller."

"And Dolbek."

"Dolbek?"

"The name the boy gave us."

"All right." He hadn't been very certain, but they would run that through as well. "I'll find the ticket clerk and baggage man who was on duty, check with the terminal police," Tyurin said unnecessarily. Remizov knew that Tyurin knew his trade.

"Now," Remizov said.

"Surely." Tyurin frowned slightly. Remizov's voice was sharp. He didn't like this one very much. He was enjoying the challenge all right, but something about it was bothering him.

"Tyurin?"

"Yes, colonel?" Tyurin had his hand on the doorknob, his hat in his hand.

"Sorry."

"Sure." Tyurin grinned and went out, closing the door heartily. Remizov went to the window again to stare out at the brick avenue. He was missing something somewhere, he felt, and he couldn't figure out what it was. Meanwhile Colter was . . . was doing what? *That* was what bothered Remizov. The United States just did not send single agents into the Soviet Union—with the exception of the diplomatic corps and various trade mission types, all of whom were well screened-out, anyway. This was wrong, totally wrong, and for the life of him Remizov couldn't figure it out.

"But I will, Colter," Remizov said quietly. "I promise you that I will find you." Hacha had returned with the boy and Remizov turned to question him again, to go over the ground twice and three times, to make sure nothing was missed, although he believed he already had the essentials. "Sit down," Remizov said, and then he settled down himself for another long session.

Colter stepped from the rusted Jeep. Mustafa, wearing green army fatigues, as they all were, lifted an arm, indicating the winding trail that led through the dry, dung-colored hills.

"That is the road. There is a checkpoint, but it is manned by men loyal to us."

Colter nodded. That was the road. It was ten miles down that road to freedom, to Turkey, to the West. Why not just have Mustafa drive him out of there? Or would he?

Colter didn't like the direction things were taking. Mustafa had taken command of events and preparations. Colter was completely at his mercy now, and probably that was the way the Turk wanted it.

"Is everything all right?" Mustafa asked with what might have been quiet irony.

"No, it's not. I wasn't ready to kill Dubček off yet. I had been told to rent an Intourist car before I disappeared."

"That was no good," Mustafa said disparagingly. "Where could you have concealed it until you were ready to drive across the border? The chauffeur would have had to be eliminated. No— we have transportation for you, Colter. Besides, when the opportunity presented itself we could not let it go by. This KGB lieutenant Bakst was too much interested in our group. He had to be killed. It was fortunate he could pass for you."

"Happy coincidence," Colter murmured. He didn't mind so much operating outside of the plan, which had seemed for the most part to be wishful thinking anyway. What he did mind was that he was now in a situation where he had to rely completely on Mustafa and his forces. They held the keys to escape, to success, and one slip-up with his cover and they would no longer be such warm allies.

The morning had been spent in the back country, prowling the hills in a jolting, creaking Jeep through clouds of dust, the hot sun blazing down. Colter had been shown arms caches, crates of explosives, printing presses, and leaflets urging the Turks to rise up against their Soviet masters. At each stop he had smiled and told Mustafa that all looked well, that the operation was certainly deserving of CIA aid. And all the while Colter knew he was looking at death.

There was not, in all the world's history, a single instance of any communist country's suffering a successful counterrevolution. Nor would it happen here. The shackles were real, enduring. Mustafa and his men were dreamers, and Colter had to encourage their hopeless dream.

They lunched at an isolated commune that was exclusively Turkish, and Colter was shown a secret machine shop, a cave where ancient vehicles were being readied for the war to come, the jihad, the Holy War.

Afterward Colter and Mustafa walked through the twilit olive groves of the commune, listening to the dogs barking, the children crying as the adults prayed to Allah and the sun was extinguished in the west.

"Tomorrow . . ." Mustafa began with a large gesture. Colter cut him off.

"I've seen enough."

"There is much more you have not seen."

"I know all I have to know about your operation," Colter said, grateful for the shadows the trees cast, shadows that might have hidden some of the deception on his face.

"May I ask then," Mustafa said, "what your recommendation will be?"

"My recommendation," Colter replied, nearly choking on the lie, "will favor your organization strongly. You don't have to worry. Aid will come. If there is anything at all we can do to help you . . ." But there was nothing. These people would go on being Russians. Their children would be Russians. Their grandchildren would despise their memory.

"What you can do you will do," Mustafa said with some relief in his voice. Colter had been so busy with his own thoughts that he hadn't realized the Turk must have been under some pressure. With aid, the dream could continue, without it, the war would rust away, a little here, a little there. "Now what may I do for you, Colter?"

"The other portion of my mission must be seen to," Colter told him.

215

"Ah, yes," Mustafa said, as if he had forgotten that which he damn well hadn't. The Turk forgot nothing, Colter would have bet. "The man Vesely."

"The man Vesely."

"All of that is arranged. In a few days . . ."

"Time is important, Mustafa."

"It is better if you stay out of sight for just a little while. My house is a poor one, but it is open to you."

"I thank you, but there is just no time to waste."

"Very well. It shall be done quickly."

"Thank you." Colter tried to read the Turk's expression in the darkness but failed. He heard a small, hissing sigh before Mustafa explained his plan.

"Tonight," the Turk said as they continued their walk, "we will take you to the Makhindzhauri commune. This is overseen by a comrade of ours. Most of the people on this commune are Turks or sympathetic Ukrainians. You will be given papers identifying you as a cousin of the overseer—he is Ukrainian. You will supposedly come from Tolpi. This is all quite in order, not unusual. During the harvest many more workers are needed. Do you know Makhindzhauri?" Mustafa asked, stroking his chin. His long face cut a striking silhouette against the dusk-purpled sky.

"No," Colter answered. "I've never heard of it."

"The name," Mustafa told him, "means 'the place of the maimed.' It was there many centuries ago that Georgian Christians were taken to be tortured until they vowed to accept the true faith, Islam. Those who did not convert to the faith were killed, of course. You see, Colter, this is something you must understand: Our war is a never-ending one. The Soviets do not understand this, because they do not understand our faith. They believe the war is over, but it cannot end, do you see that?"

"Yes, I think so."

"Yes. They do not understand the faith of the Poles, the Russian rulers. They do not understand the Afghanistanis, who will fight to the last man. They do not know us," Mustafa said. He turned his dark, brooding eyes on Colter. "It is a serious mistake to think that this is a game with Allah's people." Mustafa's voice was very low, the menace clear. "Do you understand what I have told you now, Colter?"

"Yes," he answered. "I understand it."

But Colter's understanding meant nothing. Nor did Mustafa's people's aspirations. Despite wishful, high-minded declarations, there is only one deciding factor in mankind's progress—the strength of those who rule or will take rule. The noble and the ignorant, the dedicated and the intellectual may wish to see this differently; but they have their eyes closed by a hope they hold out for mankind. They work from their ideal to reality, ignoring their own scientific doctrines. Empiricism, a short course in world history, reveals too starkly what we are and where we are going. And in the struggle of might against might, Mustafa's people even with the grace of Allah, had no chance at all.

After dark they came to the small room where Colter had been sleeping. He sat up, rubbing his head. Mustafa seemed dark and lean, hard-edged in the night. For a moment Colter thought something had gone wrong with his cover—that they were now going to take him out and shoot him— or worse. It was the night that brought such fears to life; this time it was nothing at all.

"You are ready to go to the commune?"

"Yes," Colter answered.

He got up and dressed. It was very cold outside, the stars high, blue, brittle. They climbed into the Jeep and it sputtered to life, rolling down out of the mountains by a series of goat trails.

They were silent. There was only the uneven rumbling of the Jeep. The land was empty, or seemed to be. And then suddenly, it wasn't.

"Get down," Mustafa said.

"What is it?"

"Down, damn you," the Turk repeated and Colter was shoved to the floor of the Jeep and hastily covered with blankets. "A patrol," Mustafa said beneath his breath. "Stay still. There may be shooting."

The army truck was grinding up the long grade, its headlights blinking as it ran across the deep ruts. Colter could hear Mustafa discussing it with his soldiers, but he couldn't understand what they were saying.

Their arms were shoved down on the floor as well, but they remained within easy reach. Mustafa said something and the driver of the Jeep

218

pulled to the side of the road and shut the engine off. Colter's head was throbbing with an erratic pulse. They knew! No, that was absurd—they couldn't know anything at all. He lifted the corner of the blanket and peered out with one eye. The truck rattled toward them still, and Mustafa and his men called out greetings in Russian, waving their hands.

The truck rolled on past, a few soldiers looking out of the back from behind canvas flaps. The Jeep was started again; slowly Colter let out his breath.

"All right." Mustafa patted him on the rump. "Get up. They're gone, pig infidels."

Colter sat up, and looking into Mustafa's eyes he saw a dark and horrible hatred as the Turk stared after the departing truck. "Go on," he said nudging the driver. Then Mustafa turned to Colter, his arm slung over the back of his seat. "You see, I hate."

"Yes."

"You see this?" He touched his face and head where the slick burn scar was. "They did it. With an incendiary grenade. That time two of my sons were also killed."

The Jeep roared off down the goat trail. Colter rode in silence. Two hours before dawn they reached the Makhindzhauri commune. Rows of small cottages, some with smoke rising from the chimneys as the workers rose for their daily duties, sat along a farm road. Two hundred acres of orange groves spread across the hills and deep valley beyond. A cock crowed somewhere in the distance and a dog began an insistent yapping.

The Jeep dropped down into the valley and made its way through the orange groves, coming up at the back of a white cottage with a thatched roof. They had been heard, apparently, for in the doorway stood a balding man in a nightshirt, his remaining sparse hair sticking up in tufts.

"Get out," Mustafa said sharply. "Trust this man, he is a friend."

"How will I get in touch?"

"Go on. Out!"

Colter stepped down and stood staring at Mustafa, whose hate for the infidels now seemed to have expanded to include Colter—or maybe the old memories had just come back too harshly. The Jeep lurched into motion again, and in a moment it was gone, disappearing through the trees. Colter turned and walked toward the house, toward the man he could "trust." He damn well hoped he could, because he was more alone now than ever, more cut off from any assistance.

"Come on," the man in the doorway said cheerfully. "There is tea and cake."

His name was Bulyev, a Ukrainian old enough to harbor dreams of a Ukraine nation. That was the old man's fixation. Colter didn't say anything, any more than he had said anything to Mustafa. It wasn't a part of his job to go around kicking dreams to ashes.

Bulyev's tea was hot and sweet. He had lived in Makhindzhauri for forty years, he said. Since the Russians had sent his mother and father to the work camps and his sister and himself to the south to plant orange groves. His sister was dead now; he was all there was of the family, of the nation he dreamed of, he and a few other old reactionaries.

"This is what I have planned," the old man said. "There is a flag with the emblem of the commune on it above the house on a flagpole. You will see it. I have also another flag with the Soviet emblem. You understand—the hammer and sickle."

"Yes, I understand."

"Good. We will have watchers. My people, those I trust most. If they see someone coming up the road you will hear the smith ring his hammer against the triangle three times. Then three times again. The Soviet flag will be run up the flagpole. If you see it, there is danger."

"I understand."

"Good, now I will tell you this. The Professor Vesely lives just across the road from us here. Yes, that is why this place was chosen, you see. If it were daylight I would take you out onto the porch and you could see the house. He lives there with only his daughter and a maid. The daughter does most of the shopping. Only about once a week does the maid go out. Into town to make her reports, I think. The KGB in Batumi. I don't know how you will do your part of the work. I think it will be quite difficult to see the Professor Vesely. But that is your part of the job. My part is to give you any assistance I can—if you need something, you must tell me."

"How can I get hold of Mustafa?"

"I will have to call for you. I have a telephone. I cannot give you his number, you see."

"You don't trust me?"

"Mustafa has said that this must be the way things are done, not I. I am sorry."

"You have no automobile? I might need one."

"We have only commune trucks. They are not very fast, I'm afraid," he said, with a wisp of a smile.

"Fine," Colter sighed. So everything still depended on Mustafa. He wasn't going to get out of Batumi without the Turk's help. "All right," he said, "where do I live?" He would just have to resign himself to these arrangements, Mustafa's arrangements. The Turk had Colter under complete control at the moment.

"We have a room for you here, in this house."

"Won't that look funny—the other workers are staying up the road, aren't they?"

"You are my cousin, are you not?" Bulyev said with a smile. "The other arrangement would never work out anyway. There are three families to each cottage. There would be many eyes and not so much secrecy. Here is only myself and the Little Old One."

"Little Old One?"

"My wife," Bulyev said. "Now she is cooking. She sees nothing, hears nothing. Do not worry yourself about her. I will show you your room now. Maybe you want to sleep for an hour."

Bulyev led Colter into a dark, musty cubbyhole where a cot had been freshly made up. Switching on the lights, he showed it to Colter.

"The window, you see," the old man said, "it looks out across the road. With these . . ." grinning, he produced a pair of binoculars, very old, army-style, but in excellent condition. "You can look practically in Vesely's window." He tapped Colter's shoulder for emphasis and grinned again. He was having a hell of a good time with the game.

Colter took the binoculars and frowned toward the window. He didn't run to it and peer out, which seemed to disappoint the old man. "Thanks. It's a good setup," Colter said out of politeness.

"You will see—it is all perfect. Simply bring the man Vesely here and I will call Mustafa."

Colter nodded. All so perfect, was it? Except that he did not now believe Vesely would come willingly. Nor did he see how Mustafa could respond quickly to calls for help. It stank, was what it did.

"What time do I go to work?" he asked Bulyev.

"All at six o'clock. There is time for you to have a little sleep." Bulyev leaned nearer, his breath stale. "Do not confide in anyone," he said. "Many of these people I have known for a long while, some not so long. There are some people here who have come just for the harvest."

"I won't talk to anyone," Colter answered. As far as he was concerned, far too many people knew what was going on anyway. The old man seemed satisfied. He tapped Colter's shoulder again and went on out, closing the narrow door behind him.

Colter sagged onto the bed, watching the darkened window, wondering what madness had prompted him to agree to this job in the first place. He lay back, watching the stars drift past the window. He had never felt so completely naked in his life. Never so drunk. He lay there, fully dressed, completely sober, watching with a gradually lifting pulse as the minutes passed and the skies began to gray.

A knock at the front door echoed through the house and brought Colter bolt upright, his heart hammering. Bulyev poked his head in the door.

"It is nothing, only the work foreman. You had better come out and meet him, though."

Colter went out to find a broad-shouldered Georgian with a heavy mustache glowering at him from across the room. He held a cloth cap in one hand, a clipboard in the other.

"This is my cousin," Bulyev said. You remember me telling you. The one that is from Tolpi."

"Yeah," the foreman said grudgingly.

"This is Comrade Repin," Bulyev said, and Colter nodded. Neither of them offered a hand-shake.

"I don't know what the hell to do with him."

"You can use him on the north quarter, surely," Bulyev said.

"We are shorthanded on the south plot."

"The north, I think," Bulyev said, without much subtlety. He was insisting, and Colter could see the wheels turning in Repin's square head. "So he can be nearer the house."

"I don't like to do things that way," Repin growled, "but you're the boss. Okay. North quarter."

"Fine." Bulyev smiled and rubbed his hands

together scratchily. "Now then, have you eaten?" At Repin's negative Bulyev called out loudly to the Little Old One and the three men sat down to the breakfast table.

Repin asked Colter a few questions, writing the answers down. Colter told him that he was Bulyev's cousin, from Tolpi, gave his name as Artem Novikov, which was the name used on the new set of papers he had been given. He was able to answer a few simple questions about Kiev, which was supposed to be his home town, Tolpi being only a temporary place of employment. After that Repin ate in silence, not even looking at Colter, which suited Mike Colter fine.

"He does not like you," Bulyev said after the foreman had gone.

"Maybe not," Colter shrugged. Repin didn't appear to like anyone. He was big and bluff, unhappy in his workers' paradise apparently. "Why did you insist on the north quarter anyway?"

"Ah—you will find out. From there you can see practically into Vesely's back yard. Besides, it's not good to let Repin have his way in everything. Go on now," he said, "it is getting light. The work will be starting."

Colter, wearing the clothing Bulyev had provided, was able to merge with the farm workers. The men wore twill trousers and cotton shirts without collars. The women, all above the age of forty, as fat as dumplings, wore shapeless dresses, scarves over their heads, once-white aprons and boots. Few of the workers knew one another.

Colter was only another strange face among many. The Turks among the workers carried prayer rugs, which the Russians glanced at scornfully.

Colter and a youth named Eino set off together in a truck filled with empty crates, burlap sacks, and two long wooden ladders. Eino was gregarious and eager. He was, he said, from Poltava, and was the secretary of his local Komsomol. Colter repeated his story of being an unemployed dockworker originally from Kiev now living in Tolpi. Again he was glad that he had recently visited Kiev. Eino had an uncle who was also a dockworker at that river port. He had freighted up and down the Dneiper himself. Perhaps Colter knew his uncle? Colter said he didn't and shifted the conversation to oranges. All Eino knew, he said, was that they picked those that were turning orange.

That was all Colter knew too, and so they got to it. They tied the burlap sacks to their belts and climbed the ladders, filling sacks. Then they climbed down again to empty the sacks into the crates in the truck bed.

From the ladder Colter could see the morning sun on the Black Sea, the smoke and shadows of Batumi as the town came to life. And he could see, as Bulyev had promised, directly into Stepan Vesely's yard.

She was there.

Young and slender, wearing a dark skirt and tan sweater. She couldn't have been thirty meters from where Colter worked. He knew Anna

Vesely immediately.

She was working in her vegetable garden, fussing with the eggplant, her lips pursed thoughtfully. She was the same girl as the one in the pictures, yet remarkably different out of the petrifying photographic image. The mouth that had appeared vaguely scornful now seemed merely full, intent. The broad, smooth brow was intelligent more than haughty, as he had first thought; her eyes were wide now that she was no longer squinting into a photographer's sun. She was supple and apparently energetic, applying herself with great intentness to each little function.

"Novikov! We must move on to the next tree now, if you do not mind!" Eino, hands on hips, was staring up at him, grinning toothily. He laughed out loud. "I know—I have spent time gazing at her myself. Lovely, is she not?"

"Lovely," Colter said. With a last glance at Anna Vesely he clambered down, helping Eino load the crates of picked fruit. He didn't see her the rest of the day, but neither did he forget her. That image, bright and alive, stayed imprinted on his mind, and he wasn't of much help to Eino.

"Come in, comrade," the policeman said.

Tatyana eased into the captain's office, holding her handkerchief to her nose. She had obviously been crying. Her eyes were red-rimmed, her little bit of makeup smeared, her nose pink at the tip. She had on her blue Intourist guide's uniform, over it a belted gray raincoat. Captain Blok looked her up and down and then asked politely:

"Would you like to sit down?"

"If you don't mind. For a minute."

"No, please do." Blok took her elbow and helped her to the corner chair. He was aware of the feminine strength of the woman, the trace of lilac scent about her.

"I'm sorry, I'm not myself," Tatyana sniffed."

"No. I understand. Would you like a small drink?"

"No, drinking is not good for me." She looked around, sighed with shoulder-settling heaviness, and said, "Well, there's no sense putting it off. Can we get to it?"

"He . . ." she looked at Orest Litinev, who was in the doorway watching, "told me that you had a man here. That the police think it may be a member of our tour."

"It may be, yes. That is what we want to know."

"And you want me to look at him."

"That is it exactly, yes."

"All right." She blew her nose and tucked her handkerchief away. "I can do that."

"Good." Blok smiled, glanced at Litinev, and helped the guide to her feet. He led her downstairs into the basement vaults. There Blok managed to excuse himself and leave Tatyana to Litinev.

Tatyana glanced uneasily at the tall, mournful-looking policeman. She was willing to help, told herself she was willing, but when Litinev pulled out the drawer she couldn't bring herself to look at the shapeless thing that lay, tarp-covered,

228

inside. She turned away deliberately and Litinev clicked his tongue.

"You must look now."

"I can't. I didn't know . . . he's torn to pieces, isn't he?"

"You must look now. Come." He took her arm and slowly turned her toward the tray. "I cannot show you the face, if that makes you feel any better."

"Then how am I supposed to identify him?" Tatyana asked sharply.

"You may be able to. We hope you can. We understand you knew this man very well."

"No, of course not. He was only a member of the tour. I knew him only superficially, I assure you."

"No. I don't think so. We have information that you were intimately acquainted with Anton Dubček, that you have slept with him, in fact."

Damn Ivan. "All right," Tatyana gave it up. "I knew him. I knew him well."

"And you have in fact seen him with his clothes off—you are . . . mm, familiar with his body."

"I don't know." This was turning into a nightmare, Tatyana thought. All they had said was that they needed someone to try to identify Dubček's body. Of course she had come. She had been worried about him since he had disappeared. No one said the police were going to bully her. No one said that he was—that he looked like that. "I don't know if I could identify him," she said hurriedly. "I don't see how."

"Shall we have a look?" Litinev reached out

and uncovered the body. It had been cleaned up and was not as bad as when they had received it; still, it was not pretty. Ghastly white with huge purple and red splotches, the hands badly crushed, the rib cage collapsed on the right side, innumerable small cuts and bruises. Tatyana swayed visibly.

"Well?"

"I don't know," she said.

"You must look, comrade. How can you say anything if you haven't even looked."

She did, cautiously, her eyes wide, her mouth open as she breathed through it, trying to fight back the smells of disinfectant and formaldehyde. He lay there, or someone did—a man naked, dead, white, battered. Could that possibly be Dubček, her Dubček, the one that had thrilled her blood, lifted her to heights of pleasure as he lay beside her, pressing his body to hers. . . .

"I don't know," she said in exasperation.

"Please, comrade. You must be sure."

"It's not Dubček," Tatyana said.

"No?"

"No, I said it wasn't, didn't I?"

"Yes, you said that," Litinev answered, "but you can't be sure if you haven't looked."

"I have looked, damnit!"

"Then please look again," Litinev sighed. "Do not turn your head away."

"It is not him," Tatyana said deliberately, spacing her words out carefully.

"How do you know that? Does Dubček have a

mole? Some identifying mark on his body? A scar, perhaps? There is a scar you do not see?"

"I do not know."

"You must know, comrade! I must know. This is a police matter. We must identify this man, and it is your duty to help us in this inquiry!" Litinev's voice rose for the first time. "Is it his sex organs you recognize? Or fail to? A birthmark, perhaps. This identification must be positive, comrade. It is not enough to guess at who this might have been. The police can do the guessing for themselves. Tell me what you *know*."

"It is not Dubček." Tatyana said almost hysterically. Why was this man browbeating her?

"You are sure."

"I am positive."

"You are positive?" Litinev asked.

"Yes."

"You do not know this man."

"No! Can't you cover him up, please. I tell you I do not know him." Tatyana burst into tears.

"It is of no help to cry." Litinev casually covered the body again, but he did not close the drawer. "Is it that you do not know this to be Comrade Dubček, or that you simply do not *wish* it to be him?"

"I don't know," Tatyana shrugged. She blew her nose again and turned red eyes to the policeman. "Perhaps that is so. Perhaps I just do not wish it to be him."

Litinev hissed through his teeth. "You do not know with any certainty whether or not this is

Anton Dubček?"

"No," she said in a very small voice. "I don't know."

Blok looked up from his desk questioningly as Litinev entered his office. "Well?"

"She is hysterical. She thinks it is Dubček, thinks it is not Dubček. She doesn't know."

"You have kept in touch with the hotel."

"Yes. He hasn't returned." Litinev sank into a chair, crossing his long legs.

"You have been able to trace Dubček's movements yesterday?" Blok asked.

"Somewhat."

Litinev opened a leather-covered notebook and read from it. "A *kvass* peddler remembers selling him a drink. Him or someone who looked like him, that is to say. Dubček apparently engaged in conversation with a group of workers from the Poltsava refinery. They shared some vodka with him. How much I don't know. He may have been drunk, none of them knows. They do recall him well enough to identify him perfectly—they somehow had the idea that he was Ukrainian, however, not Czech."

"Did they now, why is that?"

"He spoke Russian very well, but with a Ukrainian accent."

"You are sure this is the same man? It doesn't seem likely, does it?"

"The clothing description matched." Litinev shrugged. "The lady tour guide says that Dubček

232

was very interested in learning the language, however, that he spoke nothing else."

"I'll bet she taught him a word or two," Blok said.

"Still, it's funny the boys from the refinery didn't know he was a foreigner."

"Those boys don't know their own names once they start drinking vodka."

"That's probably it." Litinev consulted his book again. "Dubček was next seen walking on the beach. Southward. There were very few people on the beach at all then, it was getting cool, and he was quite noticeable, being in street clothes. It's almost certain that he was there at sundown."

"Wait a minute. At sundown?"

"Yes."

"On the beach."

"Yes."

"And one hour later he's off the Chavchavadze Bridge?" Blok asked with surprise.

"That's it. That's the way it works out."

"I don't like that." Blok shook his head and lit a cigarette. "What was he doing there, anyway?" he asked, waving out the match. "What is there for a tourist to see down that way?"

"Our obscene Lenin monument?"

Blok didn't smile. He was tapping his forehead. "He was just wandering around? Funny route to take, wouldn't you think? I hope the bastard wasn't thrown off that bridge by a bunch of Turks."

"You think he was murdered?"

233

"Don't you? Did you see the autopsy report?" Blok picked up a yellow sheet of paper. "I had to have this put into decent Russian—I don't understand the medical profession, Orest. Everything has to be obscure. What Doctor Yezhov tells us here is that the damage to the hands and face is 'not necessarily consistent with the incident as reconstructed.' What the hell does that mean, anyway? This is the second time he's written this out for me and I still can't see what he means."

"He doesn't want to make a mistake," Litinev suggested.

"Neither do I." Blok tossed the paper down and stood. "Something is wrong here and I don't know what."

"Have you talked to the KGB?"

"What the hell do I want to talk to those strutting maniacs for?"

"Lieutenant Sergei Bakst," Litinev said.

"Who? Oh, their missing man." Blok slowly swiveled in his chair, his expression brightening as he stared at Litinev. "You don't think so. . . ."

"We'd better get a physical description of Bakst, I think, captain." Litinev replied.

"You know, it just could be. . . ." He picked up his phone and nearly shouted. "KGB headquarters," his eyes on Litinev's. "If it is Bakst down there in the cellar, where the hell is our Czech friend, Orest? Answer that for me."

By four o'clock Blok was certain something was wrong, but he still wasn't sure what. His phone call to the KGB had gotten Sergei Bakst's description. It was near enough. The man in the morgue might or might not be the KGB officer. It was likely they would never identify the body now. A call to Bratislava turned up one startling bit of news. No one called Dubček, Anton, worked at the Bratislava glass works, nor had anyone called Anton Dubček ever worked there. There was no Anton Dubček belonging to the Bratislava Communist Party cadre, despite the fact that even now Blok was holding a CP card in his hand made out to Anton Dubček.

Doctor Yezhov's third report had been more substantive. After reexamining the body in question he had deduced that "the severe cranial damage suffered was most likely due to the vigorous and malevolent use of a heavy iron object (probably a sledge hammer)."

"Vigorous and malevolent," Blok grumbled, grinding his teeth together. He wished Yezhov would return to his veterinary practice in Brest.

Blok had no answers, but he had too many questions to suit him. Again he telephoned the KGB, and this time he unburdened himself of the Anton Dubček case.

The KGB captain's name was Gopchik. He too had questions. As soon as Blok had hung up he had a car take him around to the Chavchavadze Bridge, where he stood meditatively studying the high railing, the railroad tracks below.

"Blood." The technician said.

"What?" Gopchik had a pinched face, a tight mouth, hollow cheeks. He always looked angry.

235

Just now he looked pale and furious. That meant he was mildly interested in what the technician had to say.

"Blood," the lab man repeated, scraping a little of the maroon substance into a plastic bag.

"Sure?"

"Quite."

"Type it right away," Gopchik said imperiously. The technician glanced at the KGB captain. What did he think he had planned to do with it?

"Yes, sir."

"What was Bakst?"

"A-positive, sir."

"And this Dubček?"

"Also A-positive."

"All right. Well, that shows us one thing, doesn't it? This man was injured before he went over the bridge."

"Injured or dead. There's a lot of blood. Wonder why Blok didn't catch that."

"Blok?" Gopchik made a disgusted sound. "He spends his time on his fat ass or raiding the prostitutes to see what he can get. No wonder he can't identify this Czech. Through?"

The technician said he was and they climbed back in the black sedan to be driven back through the park toward Batumi. Gopchik was still meditative. Something was bothering him. Something out there on the fringe of awareness. Then it hit him and he practically stood up in the car.

"Dolbek!"

"Sir?" The technician goggled at his boss.

"That all-station alert for a man traveling

Intourist to an unknown destination. The list of possible names included 'Dolbek.'"

"Yes, but . . ."

"Dolbek. Dubček. You see. Didn't the report from Batumi police say this Dubček was carrying a Czech CP card?"

"I don't know, sir."

"Driver—Batumi police station on the way. I want everything Blok has on this Dubček. Something smells. I tell you this—something smells."

Back in his office Gopchik poured over the reports Blok had surrendered. By the time he was through, he was certain of several things. First of all, although he couldn't prove it, Bakst was dead. Bakst had been killed and given Dubček's identity. The second item he was certain of now was that Dubček was the missing Dolbek from Bratislava. It all fit. It would have taken them three days to get here. The similarity of the names. The CP card. The fact that Dubček's history was totally fictitious.

Gopchik looked as if he were ready to tear someone apart with his bare hands. His breath was coming in tight little puffs. In fact, he was humming under his breath as he dialed for an outside line and asked for Bratislava and the special investigator.

TEN

It was not quite dark when Colter returned to the house. Bulyev was out somewhere and there was only a small, humped old crone puttering about in the kitchen. She smiled at Colter toothlessly and he smiled in return.

He went to his room and closed the door, putting a chair behind it as he got the binoculars out from the closet shelf and settled in at the window, resting his elbows on the sill.

Nothing was visible, nothing at all.

He swept the garden and the area beneath the spreading linden trees on the opposite side of Vesely's cottage with the field glasses, finding nothing, no one.

Smoke rose cheerlessly from the stone chimney. The first star was visible against the pale haze of orange sunset. The front door of the cottage suddenly opened as Colter's glasses scanned past it.

A woman emerged from the cottage. Tall, severe, very thin, her grayish hair pulled back tightly into a bun. She wore an apron that fell to the hem of her long gray skirt. She stepped out onto the porch, turning her tight face left and then right as if looking for something, then began furiously shaking the small rug she held in her hands. The popping it made was angry, clearly audible. Colter withdrew from the window. The line of sight was too good—he didn't need to have the woman noticing the glint of late sunlight on the lenses of his binoculars.

When he looked again she was gone, the door closed tightly, the lamps behind the blinds lighted. Colter frowned and put the glasses up. Looking at himself in the gray, murky mirror on the wall, he decided on shaving his mustache.

Dubček had had a mustache; Artem Novikov would not. It might become necessary to go into Batumi, and although the only people who might know him should now be on their way to the next tour stop, it seemed judicious.

He borrowed an ancient straight razor from the Little Old One who stropped it for him and gave him soap and a towel. Flinching only a little, Colter did the deed, wincing mentally as his last bit of identity was scraped away.

"Well?" Bulyev asked Colter after supper, which had been *schhi* a thin cabbage soup, and *pyelmeni*, spicy meat dumplings.

"Well what?"

"What are you going to do? How long will this

take us?"

The old woman was clearing away the dishes from the table and Colter let her go into the kitchen with them before he replied.

"I don't know. With that virago housemaid of his, I don't see how I'm even going to get into the damned house."

"Thursday is shopping day," said Bulyev with a smile and a wink.

"The maid does the shopping."

"Not usually, but on Thursday, yes. She takes the bus into Batumi at eight o'clock in the morning and does not return until noon. Sometimes she does not come back until later. Those are the days she makes her reports to the KGB director."

Thursday was the day after next. "What about the daughter?" Colter asked.

"What do you mean?"

"What would she do if I showed up? Call for help? Is there some emergency warning system? A wire to the police headquarters, maybe?"

"No, nothing like that." Bulyev smiled. "At least I think not. I don't see why you're worried about the girl, anyway. Why should she get nervous? You are just a visitor who wishes to see the great poet. After you're inside then you don't have to worry anyway. You can handle her, eh?"

"Perhaps. Does Vesely have visitors at all? If I ask to see him will it seem unusual?"

"He doesn't have visitors, no. Perhaps no one knows where he is. Perhaps he discourages visitors. Maybe people are scared since he's banned, I don't know." Bulyev smiled as the Little Old One returned with a bottle of *tsinandali* wine, a dry white wine, which Bulyev took with lemon. Colter followed his lead, sitting thoughtfully in the warm room as night fell outside. From the cottages of the workers they could hear music, a balalaika and voices singing an old song. A Cossack song.

"They don't forget," Colter said, listening, and Bulyev, smiling sadly, nodded his head.

The edginess Colter felt, the urgency, succumbed to the warm, soft glow of the wine, and he was able to relax, to sit listening to the distant bala- laika music, watching the twisting flames of the hearth fire. Yet later that evening, lying on his bed, his heart felt as if it would explode with excitement. He had to sit up, to stand, to walk to the window, wiping a shaky hand across his damp forehead.

"Fool."

Here he was somehow—just then it wasn't quite clear how. Yet here was Mike Colter in a house in Batumi, USSR, trying to outwit the KGB. Then he remembered what it was that had caused him to feel fear in the night. A twilight dream, while he neither woke nor slept. There had been a light shining in his eyes in the dream, a glint of steel teeth, the sledge hammer had risen and fallen. . . .

Colter stood for a long while at the window, watching the cottage across the road through the night-shrouded trees.

"Are you cool?" Anna asked. His head came

around and again she was painfully reminded of his age, his condition. His face was pallid, deeply grooved, his hair snow white. His hands were crablike, his legs painfully thin beneath the lap blanket. Yet the eyes were alive. Fire danced in them. Another Stepan Vesely lurked in their depths. Playful, young, virile, boisterous, shouting his poetry to the night skies, to the empty steppes, laughing, rejoicing in life, suffering love. His vigor was gone now, but vestiges of it lived in his eyes—poor eyes, the cataract operations had not been totally successful.

"I am fine, Anna, fine," Stepan Vesely said. His daughter knelt beside his chair, her head on his leg, her hands holding his.

"You are sure you are not just a little cold, Father?" she asked, smiling up at him.

"I am always a little cold, it is nothing. Something left from the work camps."

"You have been writing," she commented, noticing the pad on his lap. "May I hear it?"

"It is nothing I am afraid, my Anna. In my feeble dotage I cannot find the old power. There are no longer any images worth relating in this old skull, no songs for the heart worth the singing, only an old man's maunderings."

"Still, I should like to hear it."

"Very well." Vesely smiled, obviously pleased. He rested a hand briefly on his daughter's head and, picking up his notepad, he read:

A froth of clouds across a changeling sky;
A night of thunderous remembrances . . .

"Comrade Vesely!" The harsh voice knifed through the soft, warm atmosphere of the room, and Vesely's eyes closed tightly. Anna stood angrily.

"What is it now, Comrade Uglich?"

The maid came into the room, her mouth tight and bitter. At times the Veselys seemed to forget who she was; they treated her as if she were actually their housekeeper. She glared at Anna, her eyelids dropping to hood her flat gray eyes.

"I must go into Batumi. There is a special message for me."

"All right, all right, Comrade Uglich," Anna said. She would have said more, but she felt the pressure of her father's fingers on her arms and she bit her lip, turning away from the KGB woman.

Uglich stood a moment more staring at Anna Vesely, then she turned on her heel and clopped away. A minute later they heard the front door slam.

"She is only jealous, Anna," Stepan Vesely said. "She is a dry and withered thing, a sere achievement of nature that never quite developed into a woman. In you she sees youth and beauty; I am afraid she despises us slightly for having allowed such an occurrence."

"She hates because she knows nothing else," Anna said a little venomously.

"That is what I have said, Anna," her father replied gently. "She is only a prison warder, and as prison warders go—" he chuckled dryly, "she is far preferable to some I have known."

"Yes." Anna's response was quiet but passionate. "Read to me then, Father."

"No. My eyes are tired. My song is a poor one. I wished to make one more statement, my Anna. Now that I understand more than ever the need for humanity to lift its head above its own filth. But that filth is creeping over me. I want to cry out, yet my own need makes me weary—can you understand that?"

"I think so. You would have a part of each of us be spiritual—if such a term is even thinkable in a world where the body, the celebration of youth, the support of the state seem to be all."

"We are only what we can conceive, Anna," Vesely said. "If I conceive of body, state, and work as being all of me, then that is all I am. I will not allow that, however!" he continued, showing genuine anger. "We must be more. It is essential. We must be more or nature has made a vast error in producing us. If we are not angels, then we are merely a superbeast rampaging across this magnificent world, preying on one another, destroying all that we have found pristine and beautiful. But . . ." his eyes glossed over, "I can no longer sing. My mind is no longer so virile as it once was, my words no longer so compelling as my dreams have been."

"You have already done so much. . . ."

"Not enough. It is never enough. The Englishman, Chaucer, wrote: 'No one can stop until there's nothing left.' Do you understand that, Anna?"

"Yes, Father," she said. "I understand," and

there were tears in her eyes. It was all too true that he no longer had his powers. More brutal and far more unnatural was the fact that his great works, those of his middle years, had been banned by Glavlit. Vesely himself had no copies of his great books. Books where Russia lived, where the crops were brought in, where the seasons turned from golden summer to blue-white, somber winter, where children and young lambs played and Cossacks rode across the vast steppes, where the River Volga sang its deep, constant song. . . .

He was asleep, and Anna rose, wiping back her hair. With a knuckle she swept away the tear in the corner of her eye. Her father's pad had fallen from his lap and she picked it up, placing it gently in his hands, seeing the words he had written there: "A night of thunderous remembrances."

Anna bent and kissed his white head. Then she walked through the house, wrapping a shawl around her shoulders. Stepping out into the night, she stood looking at the bushels of stars crowding the heavens, at the dark, burgeoning trees standing back against the velvet sky.

She walked through the trees, her head down, her legs swinging in a thoughtful cadence. She was attempting to not think of many things, of loveless life and long trials, disappointment and empty dreams. Anna paused, sitting on the circular bench girding a linden tree. She threw back her head and took a deep, slow breath, trying to still her rapidly beating heart.

"It is nothing," she thought. You look at the vastness of the universe, the depths of space, and you see the stars, suns that might even now be extinguished, dead, so long does it take light to reach us, so incomprehensibly large is it all. You see the band of stars—millions of them—the Milky Way, and that is only a small astral organism, only a splotch against the universe, another pinpoint of light. And none of it can matter very much.

Why would it?

A moment in eternity, the blink of a cosmic eye, the shifting of specks of dust, all so minute as to be imperceptible to infinity and eternity.

Why then did it matter—a moment, a dream, a whim, a wish? Perhaps precisely because they were so small. Anna leaned her head against the tree. She was, she supposed, her father's daughter to have such thoughts.

It was quiet in the garden. From the workers' cottages up the road came balalaika music. Starlight filtered through the dark leaves of the linden trees. Somewhere, it seemed, eyes watched her, approved, and they were not the eyes of the state at all, but were warm and—yes, loving—beyond all forms, political and social.

Anna Vesely sat there as the night went slowly cold, watching the white glitter of stars float past. Suddenly she sat upright, looking from shadow to shadow, an odd sensation, a knowledge, creeping through her.

Someone was watching her.

Someone, something. Inevitable eternity or one of Father's angels. Spook, spirit or sprite. The feeling was distinctly disconcerting, and she rose, drawing the shawl more tightly around her throat.

"It's nothing at all," she tried telling herself. "Probably just that skulk, Comrade Uglich." Needlepoints of irritation jabbed at her nervous system. She rose and started away, walking toward the house. Once, however, she paused and looked back, seeing nothing, hearing nothing, feeling—something quite indescribable and not very comfortable. The night had its eyes, it seemed.

Thursday dawned clear and bright. Birds sang in the groves, and Colter, yawning, came out of his room to sit across the breakfast table from Bulyev.

"Well? Today?" the old Ukrainian asked.

"Yes. It has to be. I can't let much more time go by."

"I thought so. Yes."

"What about Respin?" Colter wanted to know. "We'll have to tell him something if I don't show up for work."

"I've spoken to him already."

"Yes? What did you say?"

"I told him you were going into Batumi to get some medical supplies for us."

"How did he respond to that?" Colter asked, sipping at his sweet tea.

"He grumbled," Bulyev said with a shrug. "I asked him did he want me to send a Turk instead? Oh, no—that wouldn't do. He would deal with another Turk and we'd get bad medicine while our money went away to Trabzon. I told him, well, my cousin was in the house with me, I asked him to go." Again a shrug lifted Bulyev's shoulders.

"She hasn't left yet?" Colter asked, meaning the housemaid in the cottage across the road.

"It's too early for the bus. Not yet."

Colter ate a little of his *tost* and *maslo*, downing a second glass of scalding tea quickly. Then he returned to his tiny room, and, with the field glasses in hand, he settled down near the window to watch the cottage.

It was half an hour later that the door opened and the woman stepped out, shopping basket over her arm. Colter breathed a solemn curse. It was not the maid who was off to do the shopping—it was the daughter, Anna.

He saw her tie a yellow scarf over her dark hair and start walking down the road toward the main highway where the buses ran. Tossing his binoculars onto his bed, Colter snatched up his cloth cap and walked from the room.

"What's the matter?" Bulyev asked, reading Colter's expression correctly.

"The girl's going shopping."

"Not the KGB woman?"

"No."

"That is not usual," Bulyev said, stroking his chin. He was obviously worried. Anything out of the usual might mean trouble. "What will you do?"

"Write up a list of the medical supplies you need and tell me where to go."

"You mean to go into Batumi?"

"Why not?"

"I don't like it, Artem Novikov."

"Write the list."

Bulyev scribbled down anything that came into his mind, pressed the list and some money on Colter, and watched as he hurried out the door. Then he sagged into his chair and called for his wine. Tea was not going to get him through this morning.

Colter was running down the road before he caught himself and slowed to a trot. It didn't matter. He was already too late. The bus with the girl on it swung out onto the highway before he reached the bottom of the hill.

The next bus, he discovered by consulting the schedule on the post, wasn't due for an hour, and he waited impatiently beside the concrete road that wove its way down from the pine-clad highlands to the cliffs overlooking the beach.

To the north Colter saw the town of Tsikhis-Dziri standing on a cape that jutted above the Black Sea. Thirteen hundred years earlier the Byzantine Emperor Justinian had built a massive fortress there. Long destroyed, it had boasted hanging gardens, two underground redoubts and miles of below-ground passages that only recently had been unearthed.

The name Tsikhis-Dziri means "foundations of a fortress." It was that. Only the foundations remained, time had eroded all but the memory of the great castle. Orange and lemon trees now surrounded the fortress site, and a clean pebbled beach curved away to the south beneath the high-rising bluffs. The slopes of Tsikhis-Dziri Gorge, behind the city, are wooded with the remains of the ancient royal forest of Colchis. Pine, cedar, and oak in abundance. And farther up there is a splendid waterfall seventeen meters high with a walking path through the deep fern growing there. . . .

Courtesy of the Intourist guidebook to Batumi and vicinity, Colter thought with a ghost of a smile. An older woman standing with him at the bus stop moved away from him a little, imagining perhaps something sinister in his expression of amusement.

The bus rattled to the stop an hour and a half later. Colter stepped aboard and gave the driver a two-kopek piece for the privilege of riding with the chickens and hogs, the bundles of belongings the peasants carried.

Apparently Thursday was market day for everyone.

He sat there suffering in silence while the voices around him gabbled about the prices in the co-ops and the heavy taxes on the private sales they were now entitled to under heavily restricted circumstances. The bus rattled on, reaching Batumi an hour later.

It drove right through the heart of the market, which was away from town a little on the northern end, near the ocean. There booths and livestock pens had been set up. People hawked blankets and vegetables, mineral water, and wooden toys.

Colter stepped off the bus and stood looking around, moving with the crowd, neither slowly nor too quickly, toward the vegetable stands.

He spotted her quickly. Anna Vesely, laughing as she haggled with a crouching Turk over the price of his brown hens' eggs. She wore a yellow striped shawl over her white blouse. A knee-length green twill skirt and suede boots.

Colter moved nearer to her, listening to her voice, finding it pleasant. Anna glanced sideways at him and Colter grinned. She finished her business with the eggman and moved on past the brightly painted stalls heaped high with cabbages and carrots, beets and radishes.

Colter followed.

There was a tiny merry-go-round for the children to ride and it piped out tinny music from its bowels as Colter walked past. Red flags waved above the market. The sea air was brisk and balmy.

Colter stopped and bought half a dozen cabbages just to have something to carry. The Little Old One could use them anyway. Then he sauntered on, staying near to Anna Vesely.

Colter was passing a cart that advertised Narzan mineral water on its side when Anna Vesely stopped, whirled around, and, taking her lower lip between her teeth, stalked toward him. Her cheeks were touched with rose, her eyes sparked.

"What do you want? Why are you following me!" she demanded, halting directly in front of Mike Colter. She spoke so loudly that heads turned toward them. "You know I am not going to go anywhere with my father at home. What is the matter with you people!"

Colter looked down into her intent, flushed face, and he smiled softly. "I'm not a policeman."

"Then go away," she snapped.

"Don't men ever follow you?" Colter asked.

"Sometimes. Then I tell them to go away!"

"You are Anna Vesely?"

"Yes." She frowned slightly, looking into his eyes. Why did it seem she had seen this man before? "Good day," she said, turning to go. Colter caught her arm and she slapped his hand away.

"Please?"

"Go away."

"One minute. I really am quite harmless. I'm not going to attack you."

"What is it then?" she asked wearily.

"I asked you if you were Anna Vesely because I've wanted so much to meet your father. I've come a long way just on the chance that I might be able to do so."

"Where are you from?"

"From Kiev originally," Colter answered. The stiffness seemed to be falling away from her mouth. He found he liked it much better this way—soft, full, with a bare hint of some childlike quality.

"What is your name?"

"Artem Novikov."

"From Kiev."

"Yes."

"Walk along with me if you like," she invited, and Colter fell in happily beside her. "You know my father's work well, then?" she asked.

"Yes."

"His books have been banned for a long time. Not many people have read him."

"My great-aunt kept a collection of Stepan Vesely's poetry," Colter said. "I was practically raised on it."

"Why are you really here?" Anna asked suddenly, stopping Colter in his tracks. "You can't have come all the way to Batumi to find Stepan Vesely."

"Oh," Colter scratched behind his ear sheepishly, "I came down to work on the Makhindzhauri commune harvest."

"I see." Anna was looking at him oddly. Had he given something away?

Why are you really here?

He was damned if he knew, honestly. Because of the stroke, the two hundred thousand, the war in Cambodia. He was just here, that was all.

"Then you're one of our neighbors now," Anna said.

"Practically. Yes. I heard, you see, that Stepan Vesely was living across the road. It astonished me." Colter did his best to look astonished.

They had left the market and were now walking along the boardwalk above the beach. Anna was intent and silent, her groceries in her arms.

"Why aren't you in the army?" she asked suddenly.

She had halted and now she leaned back against the concrete railing. Beyond her the sea lapped at the quiet beach. A few languorous sun-

253

bathers formed spots of bright color against the sand.

"I was exempt from military service," Colter answered. "In Kiev I worked on the river docks. They called that a vital job."

"Did they?" Anna Vesely asked, lifting an eyebrow, and Colter was damned-near sure he had used the wrong term. "Vital job" hadn't sounded right when he said it, and now he thought even less of it. Whatever the term was he hadn't ever heard it. Anna had turned, faintly smiling, and she was looking out at the sea, which was calm, dark, dimensionless on this day.

It was warm, warm enough to prompt Colter to ask, "Do you swim?" He was leaning near to her as he spoke. He could scent the cinnamonlike fragrance of her. He liked the way a single strand of dark hair transected her pink, round ear.

"I swim. Why do you ask?"

"It's warm, a nice day for swimming. I merely wondered. I wouldn't mind it myself."

"Sometimes I come," Anna said. "Not very often, though. I hate to leave Father."

"That's a shame," Colter said, stepping even nearer. "Hasn't he someone else to look after him?"

"Oh, a housekeeper. But she's the sort . . . well, she's not very conscientious."

"One day we must have a bathe," Colter said.

Anna turned toward him, her lips pursed thoughtfully. "Yes," she replied, "we must."

"I would really like to see your father. I wouldn't disturb him," Colter said.

"I don't know. He doesn't usually see anyone."

"Why not?"

"There's no reason to," she shrugged. They had begun walking back toward the marketplace. The wind tugged at Anna's dark green skirt, drifting her hair across her face.

"Any time would be all right," Colter said.

Anna laughed, looking at the tall dark man, at those oddly cold blue eyes that gazed softly at her. "You are persistent, aren't you, Artem?"

"At times."

"Yes. I think so," she said with a quick little smile. She turned her eyes away.

"Well, then?" Colter persisted.

"I shall see. Perhaps. I do not know now."

"Are you going home now?" Mike Colter asked.

"Yes," she said. "On the next bus."

"Good," he replied with a grin. "So am I."

He hooked his arm around her waist and she did not object. It felt remarkably natural to walk that way with her, and Colter had to stop mentally and throw cold water on his thoughts. It was no time for games. No time for carelessness. He removed his arm, and again Anna looked at him, with amusement, it seemed, and then with puzzled contemplation.

They waited side by side, unspeaking, for the bus to Makhindzhauri.

The ride back was silent, although Colter was hardly ignoring Anna. He was near her, holding his bag of cabbages, just watching the girl, the quick alertness in her eyes, the extreme youth and yet age-old stoicism she possessed. Perhaps she had endured much; it was likely that she had. Or perhaps it was only the earmark of a Russian, this stoicism—that was their history: they endured. The bus rattled on and Colter sat there lost in a kind of waking dream, one he could not label, identify, categorize. He only knew that the dark-haired girl was a part of it and it was unsettling.

It wasn't until the bus let them off at the commune road and they began walking up through the trees that Colter spoke again.

"I'd like to see you again soon," he said.

"Yes? I thought it was my father you wished to see." Her words were slightly mocking, a little teasing.

"Yes. I want to see him, but I would want to see you again as well—very much."

"Why?"

"Do people need reasons for that sort of thing?" Colter asked.

"Yes." She was still smiling, and Colter wasn't sure if he was amusing her or if she found the world pleasant on this afternoon.

"I want to see you because I think we could become friends," he told her. "Is that enough reason?"

Anna shook her head slightly, shifting her burden. "Listen—the day after tomorrow I have to go to Zeloni Mys to finish a painting I'm working on. I don't know if you're interested in such things, but maybe you would like to come along? But you'll be working, won't you?"

"I can get off," Colter said quickly.

256

"Oh?"

"My cousin is the commune director."

"Well . . ." she seemed flustered, as if she hadn't expected him to be able to go along. There was also something about her, Colter thought, suggesting she was barely pleased. "Then we'll go together," she shrugged. "If you can make it."

"What time?"

"Seven o'clock. That's when the morning bus comes. I have to get there early while the light's good."

"All right," he said. "Seven o'clock."

Colter fell silent again, not speaking until they were within sight of the cottage. Then he said goodbye and veered off into the orange grove. The housemaid might have had an interest in a stranger's walking home with Anna Vesely. He didn't want to take a chance on being seen.

Anna watched him go, her dark eyes still amused, inquisitive, and, he thought, a little sad. It nagged at Colter that he was merely using her. She appealed to him a great deal, more than anyone in recent memory. Well, he told himself soberly, it won't last long after she discovers what you're up to.

He went into Bulyev's house, and, leaving the cabbages on the table for the Little Old One, he entered his tiny room to sit down with the binoculars next to the window, watching the Vesely cottage with decidedly mixed emotions.

"Anna?" The old man's head came around

from the desk as the girl entered his study. Sunlight bleeding through the linden trees patched the floor beside the french window. "Is it you?" Stepan Vesely asked. His eyes, he feared, were getting no better. She came, a dark, sinuous shadow through the spattering of sunlight, to rest a hand on his shoulder.

"It is me."

She bent to kiss his head, noticing that there were a dozen pages of yellow lined paper spread around the poet's desk, all of them covered with his slanting, shaky writing.

"The poem!" she said. "You've gotten a quiet morning for a change with me gone, and you've profited by it, Father."

"Profited? Perhaps, but I've missed you terribly, Anna. What an old fool I've become. Useless, really."

"But you have worked."

"Yes. I have worked. I don't know what miracle allowed it—it was just one of those mornings. A burst of energy, remarkable, really. A wave of creativity such as I haven't enjoyed for far too long came upon me. I worked, and I was young again. I worked and it flowed from me. It still flows, you see—that force that swirls around us—and it let me touch it once, as I used to . . . as it used to be. For a time, my Anna," he said with a weary smile, taking her hand. "Just for a little time. Perhaps it may even be allowed me to finish this last song."

"Is it . . . ?"

"It is good, child. Very good. I say that with

258

pride." Then his face darkened. "You will read it, Anna. It must be seen . . . by someone. It is necessary."

"The world will see it!" she said, bending down to look into Vesely's clouded eyes.

"No."

His voice was not bitter, but merely matter-of-fact. "The Empire," Stepan Vesely said, "has decreed otherwise. The Empire has said that no one shall read my poor songs. And the Empire, child, cannot rescind the decree. It would be an admission that there has been a mistake. The Empire does not make mistakes. The Empire is our God on earth, infallible, merciless."

Anna rose. She walked to the sideboard and opened it, taking down a decanter of claret. She poured herself a small glass of the wine and wiped away the tear at the corner of her eye. Vesely was behind her, staring at nothing, at the french window where the shadows of the linden trees danced, at eternity.

"Father," she asked after a minute, "have you ever heard anyone say: 'One day we must have a bathe.'?"

"Oh, yes." Vesely did not seem to find the question odd, although he wondered at the perplexed look on his daughter's face, and at the glass of wine, since she seldom drank, and only very rarely before nightfall. "I have not heard it for many years, though," the poet told her. "But when I was a very young man it was the proper expression for a swim in the ocean, the lake, or a public spa. Why do you ask?"

259

"I heard someone use that expression today," Anna said, drinking her wine distractedly.

"A very old person?"

"No. A young man. From Kiev."

"Oh?" Vesely's eyes brightened. "So you have been meeting a young man, Anna?" he joked.

"Yes," she said, much too seriously. "I have met a young man, but I don't know what to make of him, Father. I don't at all know what to make of Artem Novikov."

ELEVEN

From his perch atop the ladder Colter heard the blacksmith's triangle ringing and his heartbeat accelerated wildly. He glanced toward the house, half-expecting to see the signal flag, but the commune's banner was still up, twisting in the wind. The smith's triangle continued to ring, far more than the six times they had agreed upon for a warning.

Then what the hell was up? The workers were walking toward the barn where the crates of oranges were kept until delivery. Colter climbed down the ladder, stood frowning, hands on hips for a minute. Then he took off the burlap sack and heavy belt he wore. He walked toward the barn himself, not understanding this at all.

He caught sight of Eino, who was walking, hands thrust deep into his pockets, cap tilted back jauntily, toward the barn.

"What's going on?" Colter asked.

"Say, Novikov! How's everything? Seen that girl today yet?"

"Where's everyone going?"

"This—" Eino shrugged. "Just a production meeting." The young man laughed. "Isn't that something, Novikov? Everyone stops working so that we can go over and have a meeting to decide how to get more work done."

"Typical," Colter muttered with relief. He took a deep, slow breath, but his heart was still pounding as they reached the barn. The men inside stood around in groups or sat on empty crates. A group of women were perched on the tailgate of an empty wagon. The Turks, off to one side, stood silently, eyes dark and brooding. A portrait of Lenin had been hung on one wall of the barn. They all stood around talking, shifting from foot to foot for another ten minutes before the foreman, Repin, appeared.

The big Georgian went to the front of the barn and held up his hands for silence.

"Comrade workers! Comrade workers, please. Silence, if you will!" It took a while, but they gradually fell silent, moving forward a little to crowd around Repin. "I have been to speak to the agriculture commission in Batumi, and I'm sorry to report that we've fallen behind our quota."

There was an apathetic murmuring at this point. Colter stood, arms folded, watching the people around him stretch or yawn or whisper behind their hands. There wasn't a lot of production fervor showing. Repin was still talking.

"I know that most of you have been doing your jobs as well as possible, as carefully, as quickly. Unfortunately, there are several workers among us who show a tendency toward parasitism."

Colter glanced up to find Repin's eyes drilling into him. He muttered an oath—this was all he needed. A zealous foreman who took things seriously enough to go to Batumi and complain—that was implicit in his remarks.

"Some of us," Repin continued, almost mournfully, like a preacher seeing the sin written on his parishioners' faces, "have taken advantage of social connections to indulge ourselves, to foster antisocialist tendencies."

Repin continued to glower at Colter for a minute. Then he shifted gears rapidly and started berating certain unnamed female members of the commune who had been reportedly meeting certain male members back behind the sheds or in the truck garage when they should have been out boosting the harvest production. The workers started snickering and glancing around, trying to decide who was doing what and with whom.

After that they spent a good hour denouncing each other without naming names. Those who spoke up the loudest, railing against parasitism and antisocialist tendencies, were probably those who were the most guilty, Colter decided.

He didn't notice any increase in productivity that afternoon, but maybe Repin was happier.

Colter told Bulyev about it that evening.

"Yes, I know," the old man said across the supper table. He turned his tea glass thoughtfully between weathered hands as the Little Old One bustled about with a straw broom. "I was hoping Repin wouldn't be given the foreman's assignment this year, but they gave it to him because he manages to increase the output just a little bit each year. He's trying to insinuate himself into the good graces of the agriculture commission. He wants a seat on that board, and he'll undoubtedly make it one of these days. He's persistent enough."

"But has he been complaining to the people in Batumi about me, do you think?" Colter wanted to know. "Would he mention my name to the commission?"

Bulyev lifted a hand, lowered it, and sighed. "Probably. Knowing Repin, it is likely."

"If he has said something, what would the likely result of that be?"

"Nothing, probably." Bulyev didn't seem worried, but Colter didn't share his sense of ease. "Repin complains, and they probably fill out a card on you. Then," he shrugged, "the card is filed away like all such cards all around the world. Oh, you may get a letter informing you that you have been chosen for a reeducation seminar, but I doubt that. They wouldn't want to pull you off the harvest. Probably no one paid any attention to Repin."

"But he's got his eye on me, and I don't like it," Colter said, sipping his own tea. "It's dangerous. I have to take off again tomorrow. It's essential. I'm going to Zelyoni Mys with Vesely's daughter."

"I see." Bulyev rubbed his eyes. When his hand fell away he said, "You'll just have to break that date."

"Are you crazy? I can't break it, not when I've finally gotten a toe in the door."

"Repin . . ."

"Bulyev, I didn't come all this way to earn a reputation as a good socialist worker. I can't play Repin's game. I've got to get on with the job."

"He'll go back to the commission, Novikov." Bulyev shook his head in warning. "Don't you understand? One complaint is nothing, but you can't have him turn you in again. They may try to check back with your last employer in Tolpi—and you have none."

"It doesn't matter. Listen, I have to go ahead with this. Can't you come up with an excuse for Repin?"

"What can I tell him? What?" Bulyev raised his hands, palms upward, and sighed massively. "Look, Novikov, I'll try. I think you'll just have to be sick tomorrow. He might not like that, but what can he do if someone says he is sick? We'll close the door to your room, and I'll make sure he doesn't peep in."

"All right. We'll do it that way."

"But if he sees you . . ."

"If he sees me, that's that. Maybe we'll hand Repin over to Mustafa if that happens, huh?"

"No—it would look very bad if Repin turned up missing out here." Bulyev looked very worried.

"Well, he might have to turn up missing. You just keep him away from my room tomorrow, and everything will be all right," Colter told him.

"I will do my best," the old man answered heavily.

Colter hardly slept that night. He was plagued by odd dreams peopled by hammer-wielding Turks. He crawled out of bed and was dressed before dawn had touched the eastern sky with pearly gray, before Repin should be up. He slipped out through the window and crossed through the trees to the road. It was still dark, still very cool. He stood for a moment in the lane outside of Vesely's cottage, wondering if he should just steel himself and march on in.

Finally he turned and walked down the road toward the bus stop. He still had over an hour to wait for Anna when he reached the main road, but promptly at seven she came strolling down the hill, lithe and energetic, sleek, and far too appealing. She carried a collapsible easel and a large portmanteau. She wore a red sweater, a haversack, and a warm welcoming smile.

"I thought perhaps you would not come," she said.

"I wouldn't be anywhere else," he said lightly. He inclined his head. "Is that your canvas?"

"Yes." She glanced at the portmanteau. "I'll show it to you later. It's the sea from Zelyoni Mys." Anna smiled, and it was a delightful thing to see, both shy and confident, warm, and yet a trifle aggressive. What a place, Colter was thinking, to meet a woman like this.

"The bus," Colter said. It came rattling down the hill, billowing smoke. It was nearly empty when it reached their stop. Colter paid their fares while Anna wrestled her gear toward the back seat. The bus had started again before Colter, gripping the overhead rails, managed to join her.

"How long is the ride?"

"Not long. Fifteen minutes," she said, and then she fell silent, turning her eyes away from Colter's.

She sat, hands folded on her lap, gazing out at the tree-clad countryside. Colter sat watching her, liking the sleek neck, the long lashes, the handsome straight nose, feeling things he didn't understand and didn't like. It wasn't something simple like lust—that he could understand and deal with. Anna Vesely seemed to glow with life and feminine essence. Did she appear that way to everyone who saw her? Why wasn't such a rare creature spoken for? Then again, maybe she was—Colter realized he didn't know that much about her.

"Do you often let strange men go with you when you want to paint?" he asked.

"Never."

"Is there someone who would want to go?"

She turned her eyes to his, a faint smile drawing down the end of her nose, twitching the corners of her mouth, lighting her eyes.

"No one," she said. "No one for a long while." Since Moscow. She thought briefly of Boris. Boris and his artistic mannerisms, his youthful, open eyes and so tiresome unmassaged libido.

"He was more of a friend, actually."

"He doesn't live here?"

"Oh, no. In Moscow."

"So that's where you're from."

"Yes, Moscow. I was an art student there. My father needed to come south for his health, you see, and so naturally I came with him."

"I'm glad you did," Colter said.

"Thank you."

"I hope you'll allow me to meet your father soon. I do admire him," Colter said, feeling traitorous. He had a sudden mad impulse to break down and tell her everything.

"Oh, yes. Soon. One day when he's well."

"He is that sick?"

"Some days are not good," Anna said. They rounded a corner and her knee met his, her shoulder; the slight pressure was electric. She smiled brightly, "But there are good times. He is doing well now, or I wouldn't allow myself this day off."

"Then this is a good time to visit."

"Yes. Perhaps." She was studying his eyes, measuring. "You are sincere in this?"

"Yes," Colter said, choking on the word.

"Yes, I think you are. If you like, you may come to dinner this evening."

Colter's heart gave a little skip. "I'd love to. Thank you."

They rode in silence for a while after that. Colter stole a glance at Anna Vesely from time to time and was amazed to find her looking back at him.

Zelyoni Mys means "green cape." It is a seaport, and now a botanical research center. The hills around the town are clad with citrus trees. It was founded in 1912 by a visionary botanist, Professor Andrei Krasnov, who had decided Zelyoni Mys was the perfect site climatically for his venture—the world's largest and most comprehensive botanical garden. His dream was to turn the area into a garden exhibition, a microcosm of the botanical world complete with a Mexican boulevard and a Chilean town planted with date and coconut palms where Creole women in taverns would serve tourists liqueurs distilled from local fruit.

His imagination unbounded, Krasnov also wished to build a Chinese temple on top of the low, green promontory north of the town, and resettle pygmies from the mountains of New Guinea in a village of their own. Many of his plans went by the board, but a splendid Japanese courtyard was built, and the botanical gardens, with fifteen hundred varieties of trees now cover almost three hundred acres of land around Zelyoni Mys.

Anna had a sketchbook filled with charcoal renditions of fifty varieties, all done with amazing competence, all neatly labeled. "Blue gum," "Scots pine," "Spanish chestnut," and so on. Colter sat cross-legged on the grassy slope thumbing through the book as Anna painted the larger scene—the sweep of blue sea, the pale sandy spit below the bluffs, the orange groves, and the Japanese *torii*, which stood alone on the slope.

The sun dazed Colter. He sat there, warm and content, the ripe scent of grass filling his nostrils, the sea glittering beyond the green headland.

He sat and he watched the intent expression on Anna's face, the way she clamped her teeth on her brush and her eyes lit with small excitement as some stroke justified itself to her. He watched the line on her slender back beneath her white blouse, the concentration of her entire body as it focused on portraying the landscape before her.

"This must be boring for you," Anna said at length, and Colter, who thought he hadn't spent such an enjoyable morning in centuries, smiled and shook his head negatively.

"No."

"But there's nothing for you to do."

"And sometimes that is best," he replied. "Try it?"

She smiled and got back to her work. The brush poised and then was lowered. She turned to look at Colter, and he stretched out his hands to her. She put her palette down and took his hands. She settled beside him on the grass, smelling of paint and turps, her hair sun-scented, her faint cinnamon smell mingling with a more distant, earthy scent.

She lay back, holding his arms, and he sat looking down at her, gazing intently into those sparkling eyes, disbelief washing over him, joy, excitement, need. He bent and kissed her, and her lips parted to meet his.

"Lie beside me Artem," she said, and Colter lay back on the grass, her arm beneath his neck, her

270

fingers toying with his dark hair. He glanced sideways at her, seeing the flare of her nostrils, the rise and fall of her breasts, the distant proud look, which focused and sharpened and met his glance as she saw his eyes on her, felt the emotions behind the look.

"There is something here I do not understand," Anna said, and now she was looking past his face to the pale blue sky, her voice soft and muted. "This is like a passage from some prerevolutionary novel. A great, stark, rich romance. I cannot be coy—I feel an intense . . . love, desire? something I cannot quite define, for you, Artem. Yet I can feel beneath this unexpected happiness something else. I feel as if some deeper sense is trying to warn me of something—as if the earth is threatening upheaval. I feel menace, Artem Novikov. Can you understand that? It makes no sense, and what a time to talk of this. Can you explain it?"

He couldn't answer. She rolled toward him, her arm going across his chest, and Colter held her head, stroking that sleek dark hair, not understanding this himself. It was an obviously impossible situation, and the best thing to do was to shrug off the emotional side of it. Reduce it to something purely physical, purely temporary; make love to her, if she would let him, have a memory to add to his list of meaningless encounters, useful for reliving on cold Maine nights.

This would end, anyway. It would end in a very ugly way. There was menace, all right, and the menace she felt was Colter.

"I'm a spy," he should say. "I'm using you to get

271

to your father. That's what they pay me for."

He said nothing of the sort. He gathered Anna Vesely in his arms and lay beside her on the sun-warmed grass as the day drifted past.

After noon Anna packed her work up and they wandered through the Japanese Courtyard, where tourists snapped pictures of each other and spoke in loud, holiday voices. The two of them had sushi at a small restaurant, Colter fumbling with the chopsticks—it had been a while. They finished up with sake imported from Japan and tiny, wafer-like cookies with practically no taste. Later they bought a bottle of local *tsinandali* wine, which they drank in a quiet glade in the botanical gardens under a canopy of huge monkey puzzle trees.

The sun was warm, the shade cool, the fern, which grew everywhere, was sun-dappled, lush. Anna was close and beautiful and necessary.

"I love you so much," she said, her voice blurred with alcohol. "I love you already, Artem Novikov, but I do not know who you are."

And when she did know, there would be no more Artem Novikov and no more love possible. Colter held her tighter, his cheek against her breasts where he could hear the pulsing of her heart, the breath flowing in and out of her body. If he held her tightly enough then she could not leave him; if he did not think about time it would cease to exist, and they would lie forever in this dappled grove.

"Not allowed! *Nyet*, up you get."

Colter opened his eye and peered at the uni-

272

formed guard who was standing over them, waving his baton in a scooting gesture. "Not allowed here."

"All right." Colter rubbed his eyes and smiled at the guard, who was florid, past his prime, rheumy. "We're going."

"There are other places, comrade," the guard said.

Were there? Not for him, perhaps. Not again. Anna sat up, tucked her feet under her, and sat dazed for a moment, then she nodded and got up, wobbling a little so that Colter had to put his arm around her shoulders to steady her.

"Find another place," the guard said, and there was a touch of warmth behind his sternness.

They walked silently through the town, Colter carrying Anna's haversack. They stood side by side, arms around each other's waist, not speaking until the Batumi bus arrived.

"You are coming to dinner tonight?" Anna asked sleepily as they sat on the rumbling bus, her head on his shoulder as they were driven down the winding concrete road. The late sun was sinking toward the sea, gilding it brilliantly, scalloping it with dull crimson.

"Of course. That's if it's still all right."

She kissed him gently beneath the ear. "What do you think? That I don't want to see you? I want you to be by me as much as you can be. You won't get in trouble?"

"No, I don't think so."

"I shall have to cook," she said. "The maid is off tonight."

273

Colter's heart gave a little leap. Better and better. The KGB dog was off tonight. That meant that Colter had a chance of speaking to Vesely alone. And doing what? Bullying the old man, threatening? Colter clenched his jaw and took a deep, harsh breath. He had the chance to finish this up tonight. To finish it and . . . he looked at Anna and felt his stomach sink as if it were weighted down with stones.

"Damned fool," he thought savagely.

How could he finish this? It would be like slapping her in the face, crushing what she was offering to him. It was all happening too soon. He had just met her, and he wanted nothing more than to be Artem Novikov for a little while, to finish working on the harvest to . . . get himself shot, if he was stupid enough to delay and stay around here, waiting for any one of the hundred things that could go wrong to happen.

They walked silently up the hill after the bus had dropped them off, fingers intertwined, their shadows blending before the setting sun.

They parted with a brief kiss, and Colter stood watching her go, watching the quick sureness of her body, seeing her turn her head and cast one brief, meaningful smile across her shoulder. He swallowed a painful curse and turned toward the cottage. Cutting through the grove to avoid being seen by Repin, he came up on Bulyev's house from the back. His window was still open, and he crawled up over the sill. There was already a lamp on in the outer room. The light bled under the door. Colter went on in.

Bulyev was at the table with a bottle of wine. As Colter came in he took a huge swallow of the wine and rose, shaking his head bitterly, his mouth turned down. "The bastard found out you were gone," the Ukrainian said.

"Repin?"

"Who else."

"But how? I thought you were going to stand watch. How did he get into my room?"

"A truck broke down. I had to go out with another to tow it in. Repin came in while the Little Old One was alone here. She can't lie—it's beyond her. I found him waiting for me when I got back with the truck."

Colter blew out sharply and then shrugged, rubbing his head. "It probably doesn't matter. There's a chance I'll be gone by tomorrow."

"Do you think so?"

"I'm hoping so. There's a chance. Listen, Bulyev, you must call Mustafa. When you get through, tell him to wait in the trees behind the house until midnight. Tell him that tonight might be the night."

"I don't know if I can make contact with Mustafa tonight," Bulyev said unhappily.

"What do you mean? You have to get ahold of Mustafa. Christ, what kind of organization is this? I may have to make a run for the Turkish border tonight, can't you understand?"

"You do not understand. I am sorry—Mustafa was involved in some smuggling trouble. Not arrested, but they're looking for him. One of his people was caught with hashish on board his boat. The police know Mustafa is the leader."

"Jesus Christ." Colter just shook his head in disbelief. "This makes a lot of damned sense, doesn't it? What is the man doing trying to run a smuggling operation while he's playing revolutionary?"

"The smuggling is the source of their funds. Opium brought in from Turkey supports his operation."

"All right." Colter ran a hand through his hair. "There's nothing we can do, I guess, but try to get through to Mustafa or someone from his group. Phone him and keep phoning until someone answers. If you just can't get anyone, park a gassed-up truck in back of the house."

"A truck!"

"If I need transportation and you can't get ahold of Mustafa, I'm taking one of the trucks."

"All right . . . yes, if we have to. I'll try to get Mustafa." Bulyev ran a harried hand across his face.

"One other thing—I may need a gun."

Bulyev just nodded. He turned and walked to his pantry. From beneath a shelf he removed an oilskin-wrapped package that had been taped there. Inside was a Walther P-38K 9mm automatic.

"Here. I was told it is a good gun."

Colter took the weapon and checked the action. He pocketed it along with a box of cartridges Bulyev gave him.

"Tonight?" Bulyev asked almost mournfully. Maybe he regretted ever having gotten into this just now. It was too late for regrets. "You think tonight, Novikov?"

"Tonight." Tonight while there was still time. You had to take fantasy, wishful thinking, and balance them against reality, he told himself. Fantasy had no substance, it always lost. As Artem Novikov would lose. There was no Artem Novikov, there was no Anna Vesely, there couldn't be. There wasn't room in reality for her. Reality was the shaking down of an old and decent man, the bullying, the tears of Anna, the slow anger of the poet, the quick run toward the border, the weight of a Walther in your pocket. Reality was Mike Colter and survival.

TWELVE

The MIG-27 fighter aircraft touched down at Makhindzhauri Airfield at 5:12. The pilot coasted his shrilling jet to the military terminal and the cockpit lifted on hydraulic pistons. Before the whine of the jet engine had faded away a ground crew had attached an aluminum ladder to the fuselage and the two men inside began clambering out.

The pilot carried a small portfolio and had a brown raincoat over one arm as he reached the tarmac and began walking toward the low terminal building, unzipping the top of his flying suit as he went. He walked with a noticeable limp. He had left his flying helmet in the aircraft and his thinning blond hair was lifted from his scalp by the breeze that rose with sunset each afternoon at Makhindzhauri. He wore an eye patch.

Beside him and slightly behind was a younger

man in an orange flying suit, with a springy gait and reddish hair. Gopchik, in trench coat and a hat stood behind the iron railing watching their approach. When they looked his way he lifted a hand and the man with the eye patch nodded.

"What's his name?" Remizov asked Tyurin.

"Gopchik, captain."

"He is the one that sent the wire."

"Yes, colonel."

Fifteen minutes later when Remizov and Tyurin emerged from the flight room Gopchik was still in precisely the same spot. He stepped forward to shake hands.

"Gopchik. You have a car?"

"Yes, of course. Colonel Remizov, you would care to eat first?"

"No. Let's get on with work."

"Of course." Gopchik's pinched face looked furious. He was smiling again. Muraviev was in the car in front of the airport and the other KGB man got out to open the door for Remizov and Tyurin. "It is only six kilometers to Batumi," Gopchik said.

Remizov made no reply. He said nothing as the black Moskvitch automobile rolled down the coastal highway through the settling fog toward Batumi. He simply sat holding his portfolio, watching the orange groves flicker past shrouded in mist.

Tyurin sat listening to his own stomach rumble, glancing hopefully at Colonel Remizov. It did no good. Remizov was focused on his work, only his work. Then he was not aware of the need to sleep, the need to eat, but only to please Fyodor, to complete the given task.

The four men went into KGB headquarters together, up an unlighted concrete stairway at the back of the building. Inside everything was bright with neon. There were a few agents bustling around, perhaps trying to look their best for the man from Moscow.

"This way please," Gopchik said, and he led them to an inner office, which had a one-way mirror on one wall, a window on a second, a certificate from somewhere on the third, a portrait of Lenin on the fourth. All were precisely centered, and Tyurin thought he understood the Batumi man then. "Please sit down," Gopchik said. He himself took off his raincoat and sat rigidly behind his desk. "Coffee? Sandwiches?"

Remizov started automatically to refuse. He was already into his briefcase, withdrawing the papers on Dubček. The colonel glanced at Tyurin, who looked miserable and answered, "Please."

Then they got to work, as Muraviev slid out for snacks and coffee. Remizov had the chair across Gopchik's neat desk. Only the desk lamp and a single folder cluttered the polished surface. Remizov placed his own papers on the desk.

"Let us begin," he said.

"I wanted to . . ."

"Please," Remizov said. "Let me review this if I may. A KGB lieutenant named Bakst has been reported missing. Nearly simultaneous with this occurrence was the disappearance of a Czech tourist named Anton Dubček. A body has been found."

"Yes, Colonel Remizov. When I looked into the reports sent me by the local police . . ."

Remizov lifted his single eye to Gopchik. The man had been asked once not to interrupt. Remizov was in a brooding, hurried mood. He was trying to organize his own thoughts, his own chain of events, and Gopchik with his interruptions wasn't helping. Tyurin sat quietly to one side, his hands folded around one knee.

"We have then two men and one body," Remizov continued. This time Gopchik contented himself with a nod. "The medical reports indicate that it was certainly murder—the body was purposely battered. The medical officer, by the way, was very slow to notice this, or the local police very slow to pass the information on, yes?"

Since that seemed to call for a direct answer, Gopchik said, "Yes," rather dryly.

"Yes. It was certainly murder. The man's face had been clubbed with a hammer, eliminating the possibility of visual identification. Yes?"

"Yes, colonel."

"Dental work destroyed with an iron bar or some similar item. The fingertips smashed. This should have alerted someone to the possibility of deception."

"The body was very badly broken," Gopchik put in quietly. Remizov didn't respond.

"They did not wish the man identified, whoever the killers are. The next step in such a case is to find out why they did not want the body identified."

Tyurin inexplicably made a pleased sound and Remizov looked up to see the other Batumi officer with a tray of food and a pot of coffee. Remizov waited impatiently while Tyurin helped himself, grinning rather sheepishly at his superior.

"We might look where for the murderers of Bakst, Captain Gopchik?" Remizov asked.

"We think a gang of local Turks is responsible. Several are being held and questioned."

"With no result yet?"

"No, sir. Not yet."

"Very well. We have Bakst. Dead. Probably killed by persons known to you. For what reason?"

"He was a part of the antiseparatist squad, colonel. We have a small but persistent cadre of reactionary secessionists in Batumi."

"In this day and age?" Tyurin said with surprise. His diction was muddled by the half sandwich in his mouth.

"It's not that uncommon all along the southern border," Gopchik said a little defensively. "But seldom are these people as fervent as our locals."

"Anton Dubček," Remizov said, interrupting. He thumbed through the folder before him. "There is no Anton Dubček. His supposed place of employment in Bratislava has never heard of Anton Dubček. His party cell has never heard of Anton Dubček. You see then what we have," he turned to Gopchik, "if Dubček is missing, no one

282

is missing. Someone who was Dubček is now here under another name. Doing what?"

"We still haven't proven that Dolbek is Dubček," Tyurin pointed out, taking another sandwich.

"What is that?" Gopchik asked, frowning furiously.

"We have reason to believe that the man who was not Dubček is in fact a man named Colter, or Koltsov, as America now reports. Briefly, this is what we know," Remizov said, and he proceeded methodically, in a way nearly divorced from reality. Events and people were not real to Remizov, not truly existing or living. They were elements of a code, parts of a machine. It was this cosmology that made him what he now was, what Fyodor had intended. He was not deflected by human considerations. He understood human psychology, but only as a man understands the cogwheels of a watch. Intimately but without emotional involvement.

This was what Fyodor had constructed; this was what the man in Moscow, the dying man, had built from the crushed and useless naval flyer.

"On April eighteenth an embassy operative in Paris, a man named Krylov, was forced to eliminate an American agent named Howard French. Code name, Alvin. At this time Krylov reports 'Alvin' was guide-dogging another agent, or assumed agent, whom we believe to be named Colter. This agent subsequently disappeared, not even making a report of this incident to the local police—or the Parisian CIA."

How Remizov knew that was outside of Tyurin's ken, but he knew it. Remizov said nothing he was not sure of. Gopchik sipped at his coffee, very gently, as if afraid of disturbing the man's presentation. Remizov, thumbing through the pages of his compiled dossier, might have been unaware of the presence of the other men, so intent was his concentration.

"Bratislava," he said at length. "Two incidents in the time frame. One: a petty local hoodlum named Josef Stefanik, a Czech of Austrian descent then engaged in forgery and smuggling, was found dead within fifty meters of the Austrian border, his pockets bulging with Austrian currency. He had been shot to death with a nine-millimeter pistol, which was traced to Colter through fingerprints found in his hotel room.

"That same morning a Youth Corps member is struck by an odd occurrence, which he later reports in response to a special bulletin. A Czech CP member whom the youth thought was acting strangely enlisted the boy to take him to the Bratislava bus terminal. A check of the buses departing that morning reveals an Intourist-sponsored bus bound for Uzhgorod. A look at the passenger manifest produces the name—Anton Dubček!" Remizov glanced at Tyurin, who was still eating. "If we haven't proven that Colter was 'Dolbek' who became Dubček, we have at least reached the point of assumption. We have found a line of coherent action to follow," Remizov said, smiling ever so faintly as he used Fyodor's favorite expression.

"All of the descriptions tallied?" Gopchik asked. Remizov's answer was polite enough, but the look in the colonel's eye made Gopchik feel bad for having asked. The question was too obvious. What did Remizov think of him? There would be a report, no doubt. How would this look in Moscow? Not that anyone could attach any blame to him. That fool Blok had delayed things.

"The descriptions tallied," Remizov said. "The man seen with 'Alvin,' the CP member seen by the Youth Corps boy, Anton Dubček as seen by the Intourist people . . . all the same man. Here."

Remizov slid an artist's sketch of "Anton Dubček" across the polished desk to Gopchik. A dark-haired, high-cheekboned man in his early thirties. Blue eyes, heavy drooping mustache. It was characterless, as all composites were. The blank eyes of "Anton Dubček" stared out at the KGB officer.

"The resemblance is superficial, but . . . Muraviev? Please—a photograph of Bakst."

The photograph emerged from a filing cabinet and was placed beside that of "Dubček."

"Near enough," Tyurin said.

"The point of this is that the man I believe to be Mike Colter is now in Batumi—or has been here and gone—for what purpose? What is there to be learned here?" he asked rhetorically.

"May I say something?" Gopchik asked. At the colonel's nod Gopchik went on. "There is a Turk we have interviewed, a *kvass* peddler, who will swear that he was asked by the man we now assume to be Colter the way to Lenin Park. It was at dusk that this occurred. His tour was due to visit this park the next morning. Why did he go there at all?"

"He was instructed to go," Tyurin put in. "A meeting had been arranged."

"With whom?" Remizov asked, joining the game. The colonel stroked his chin, staring at Colter's picture, upside down before him, trying to see beyond the physical image.

"I don't know," Tyurin shrugged. "I can't guess."

"Gopchik?"

"No. But are we going at this the wrong way? Why is Colter here? I cannot understand why a man would come this far. What have we here? There is the refinery, of course."

"The Americans have nothing to learn from us concerning oil refineries," Remizov said unpatriotically. "I do not know what it is." He rose, spinning the photograph of Colter around. "I only know that he is here, or has been. That he has come halfway around the world for *something*. And there has been no trace of him whatsoever?"

"We are looking everywhere, colonel," Gopchik said, also rising, "but nothing has come in. I do not know where he could be hiding."

"It does not matter. I will find him," Remizov said with utter confidence. "We do not fail, isn't that so, Tyurin?" The colonel smiled faintly again. "Fyodor will not suffer failure in himself or in anyone else."

"We will not fail. We are practically in his shadow," Tyurin said.

"Yes. In his shadow." Remizov shrugged.

"There is nothing more to be done tonight. We must sleep. Double your searchers, Gopchik."

"But, comrade colonel!" Gopchik said with a dry laugh. "I already have *half* of my people looking for him."

The KGB captain was puffed up, waiting for the compliment that was sure to follow that revelation. Remizov walked to the desk, picked up his folder and said quietly, "Double your searchers."

Gopchik swallowed roughly. "Yes, colonel. Did you hear, Muraviev?"

The silent KGB man went out to implement the order. Remizov nodded curtly. "I will be taken to my hotel room now. Wake me if anything at all is accomplished. I want a summary of the case to date sent tonight to Fyodor. . . ."

"At this time of night, colonel . . ."

Remizov's eye flashed. He was not used to being interrupted like this, "I am awake. Fyodor, I assure you, is awake. Find a radio operator and send the summary. He must know what has been accomplished and what we have yet to accomplish. Above all you will find Colter. I will not tolerate the presence of an American agent here. Nor will Fyodor. Nor will *his* superiors!"

"Yes, colonel. He will be found."

Remizov turned and started toward the door, Tyurin at his heels. The colonel halted, his hand on the knob and said, "Also, I wish to have a woman in my hotel room. A blonde, not too young."

"Artem!"

She looked divine. She wore a simple black dress with long sleeves. The lamp inside the cottage backlighted Anna Vesely, casting a halo around her sleek head. "I thought you might not come," she said, leading him inside.

"You're always saying that," Colter answered. It was meant to be a light remark, but somehow his throat caught as he watched her face, remembered the afternoon and her touch. Anna glanced at him with concern.

"Something is wrong?"

"No, nothing really. Maybe a little too much sun and wine today."

"Yes." She smiled, went to tiptoes and kissed him lightly, quickly on the cheek. "Come in, please." She looked very lovely, too lovely for Colter's comfort, but there was also an air of preoccupation about her.

"There's something on your mind," he said. "I hope it's nothing I've done."

"No. Of course not." She took his hand and squeezed it. "Father is not well this evening, that's all. I worry when he seems weaker. Probably it is all my imagination," she added, in a manner that indicated it wasn't her imagination at all. The woman was very concerned.

"Maybe I shouldn't have come," Colter said, feeling smaller as this went on, *God, Anna, I'm sorry.*

"No, it is all right. Unfortunately, I don't think he will be able to see you, however."

"No, I understand. Of course not, under the circumstances," he said, glancing around the house. Which was the door to Vesely's bedroom? "Did you say the maid isn't here?" he asked as they went into the living room.

"I told you this was her night off," Anna said with a curious smile.

"Yes." Colter shrugged. "I'd forgotten, I guess."

"You have a particular interest in Comrade Uglich?" she teased.

"Who did you say?"

"The maid's name is Comrade Uglich. She is a KGB officer," Anna said outright.

"Is she?" Colter had decided that it must be the door to the left of the fireplace. Then the other would lead into the garden. His room was directly across from that.

"Are you listening to me, Artem?" Anna asked.

"Of course, Anna."

"I said the maid was a KGB officer, and you do not even blink. Doesn't that surprise you?"

"Not very much. No, it doesn't surprise me."

"I thought not," Anna said, and her voice had gone cooler, her mouth tightening a little. Colter didn't notice it. "Come, supper is warm. I hope you like *syomgas limonom*."

"Yes, wonderful. One of my favorites," Colter replied automatically. His thoughts weren't much on the salmon, nor were they even on Anna Vesely at that moment. It was best, he had decided, to shut her out. Don't think about her, what you're doing. *She has no reality.*

"Have you troubles, Artem Novikov?"

"Troubles? No, I haven't any troubles. Why?"

"Something is wrong. I thought perhaps you

had trouble on your job. You are absent from me. . . ." She hesitated, her eyes resting softly on his face, recalling that afternoon—this was not the same man. "Come." She led him to a small oval table that was set for two. Colter sat down and let Anna serve him vodka. Then, glancing across her shoulder at him, she went into the kitchen, tying on an apron as she went, feeling her heart shrink and grow cold.

Colter waited until she was out of sight. Then he slugged down the vodka, needing it badly. He rose and walked cautiously to the bedroom door. He opened it a crack, cursing silently as the hinges creaked. Looking in, he saw a deathly pale old man lying on a quilt-covered bed, his veined, gnarled hands folded together.

"Artem?"

Colter turned jerkily. Anna Vesely, a serving platter in her hands, was staring at him with narrowed, mystified eyes. "What are you doing?"

"I'm so sorry . . . I thought that door led out into the garden. I wanted some air," he lied unconvincingly. Anna simply nodded, turning her eyes away. She put the platter down on the table and began fussing with the silverware.

"She knows I'm lying," Colter thought, damning himself. "I must be lousy at it."

"Please, eat before it grows cold," Anna said, her smile only a shadow passing across her lips. She sat poking at her salmon with a fork, leaving the wedges of lemon untouched. Colter ate slowly. It was a delightful-looking meal. Smoked salmon, a little parsely fringing it, a watercress and kale salad. It tasted like wet cardboard to Colter. He had to force it down. There was no conversation.

When Colter had finished his meal, Anna served Turkish coffee. She sat across the table from him, stirring her cup, her eyes turned down. When they lifted to Colter they were moist and too direct.

"Who are you?"

"Artem Novikov."

"Yes. Artem Novikov, the fruit picker. From Kiev."

"That's right," Colter answered.

"Do you know how you sound when you speak to me? Do you know your language is filled with archaic phrases? Your speech is that of an eighty-year-old grammarian."

"In Kiev I suppose we speak . . ."

"Not in Kiev. Nowhere!" Anna's mouth drew into itself. She sighed and fingered her hair nervously. "You have a very unusual interest in Comrade Uglich, Artem, and yet you are not at all surprised to find out that she is KGB. Does that not strike you odd? It strikes me as very odd. Will you tell me—what is your name? Where do you come from? What do you want with us?"

"I just wanted to spend the evening with you," he said, reaching for her hand, which withdrew before his.

"It's my father. You want to speak to him. Enough to creep into his sickroom."

"You knew I wished to speak to him."

"About poetry?" Anna scoffed. "Only another

foolish woman . . ." she said, looking not at him, but at the table where her hands twisted her napkin. "I am not like this," she insisted, her voice breaking, "not Anna Vesely! I am not the sort of woman to be made a fool of. You must be very good at your trade, Artem Novikov. You have made me act so foolishly."

"Anna, it's not like that."

"How is it, then? You have told me the truth? You can't even answer me. You're not Ukrainian, I know this. Where are you from? Who sent you?" Colter still didn't answer. "Can't you and your kind ever leave him in peace? Just leave him in peace! He had a vision and he wrote it down for others to share. For that he has been locked away in prisons, for that he has been banished. For that he was made a non-person, for that he is tormented."

"I do not wish to torment him," Colter said, and his voice, gentle and sincere, brought Anna's head up again.

"Then what do you want?"

"He has information that is important."

"Important? Important to whom?"

"To . . . the people who sent me. That's all I can tell you. I must see him, Anna."

"He is ill, I told you."

"It wouldn't take long."

"And if I refuse you will force me with the gun you have in your pocket?" she sparked.

"I wouldn't force you to do anything, Anna."

"Then leave. I have made a fool out of myself. Leave me now. Leave my father alone; he has nothing for you. Go home—wherever that is."

"I can't."

"Just go. Go, go, go . . ." There were tears streaming down her cheeks now and she wiped them away angrily with her napkin. "To cry for you! I am ashamed. Go, Artem, go!"

She buried her face in her hands, and when she parted them to look up, she saw that Colter had risen and was crossing the room toward Vesely's bedroom door.

"Leave him alone! I told you to go away. My God, can't you leave him alone!"

"No."

She was across the room, knocking silver from the table, spilling her chair on its side in her haste, standing before him, blocking his way. Anna's cheeks were flushed crimson, and with a tiny yell of fury she lifted her fists and began pounding against Colter's chest until he gripped her wrists and held her, her face next to his, their eyes clashing.

"You are filth. A lying filthy beast." She tried to twist free and then gave it up. She hung limply in his arms.

"I love you," he said, and her head snapped up, her lips drawing back to reveal her fine white teeth. Her eyes were filled with angry tears.

"Love! Love? Are you mad! Where is the love in this?" she demanded hotly.

"Anna?" The voice from the bedroom was weak, and at first Colter did not realize that it was Stepan Vesely who had called out.

Anna realized it at once, however, and she tore

away from Colter and went into the darkened sickroom. Colter heard her voice, soft and caring.

"What is it, Father? Are you all right?"

"I am as well as a dying man can be," Stepan Vesely said with a small smile. His hands found Anna's and he looked lovingly into her eyes. Then his gaze shifted to Colter, who stood in the doorway watching. "Come in, young man," the poet said. "I heard you two talking just now. Perhaps love is something that should be shouted to the mountains, but I have never heard it done before tonight."

The old man's eyes were twinkling. Poor, clouded eyes. Anna knew he saw very little of her, or of Colter, now. They were only dark, moving shadows. Anna shifted the pillows that propped up Vesely's head, then she sat down on the bed beside him, her hand stroking his head.

"You are the foreigner that my Anna is in love with?" Stepan Vesely asked.

"I do not love him!" Anna objected violently.

"No?" Vesely smiled again. "Very well. You are a foreigner, however?"

"Yes, Mr. Vesely."

"Ah—you see, he calls me 'mister' and not 'comrade', Anna. What a delight that alone is. Mr. Vesely—yes. An old manner of address, however, young man. Your teacher was an older person."

"Yes. She was my great-aunt. She loved your work, Mr. Vesely. I had your poems read to me often as a child."

"In America?" Vesely asked.

"Yes."

Anna flinched and glanced fleetingly at Colter before returning her gaze to her father.

"I thought so. But what interest does America have in me, young man—excuse me, what is your name?"

"Mikhail Koltsov," Colter answered. "But it isn't you that my government wants, but something you may have belonging to another man."

"Who, please?"

"Bulgakov."

"Bulgakov." Vesely nodded his head and smiled sadly. "Yes, I might have known. Poor Bulgakov. He wasn't well. I am afraid he must be dead. He hated the very idea of destruction, the destruction of masses of people who are only trying to live out their time on this earth. Yes, and since he hated death and destruction, they must surely have taken him away to kill him. Is he dead?"

"I don't know. I thought so," Colter replied. "Who is he? *Was* he?"

Vesely looked at him with surprise. "You were not told this much? He was a scientist doing research in laser guidance systems. Or that was what they had made him become. Bulgakov was actually a mathematician—that and nothing more. If the world still has mathematicians in this computer age. He loved numbers, and he could have been happy with a slide rule and a limitless supply of paper and pencils. He was not a strong man, a very simple one in some ways. He thought his mind belonged to him; he believed he could withhold something from the Empire." Vesely had a faraway look, which dissipated as he sighed and waved a hand feebly. "Oh, well, that was Bulgakov. He was a friend of mine. We met in an ice pit called the Khabarovo Reeducation Camp, and there we shared our soup and there we endured together for a little while, Mikhail Koltsov."

"But he didn't die there?" Colter asked. Anna continued to regard him with disgust. He couldn't really blame her.

"No, not there. They came and took him away to Moscow. I suppose he died during interrogation. I don't know. I only know he never came back."

"But his notes?"

Vesely sat up a little straighter, although it cost him an immense effort to do so. He was watching Colter with an odd expression. "Please," Vesely said, "may I tell you something about Batumi. Something you may not know."

"Of course," Colter said, with a mental shrug. What kind of twist had the old man's mind taken? He wasn't here to listen to more travelogues about Batumi. His irritation must have shown, for Vesely smiled and said:

"I shall be brief."

"Father," Anna put in, "there is no need . . ."

"But there is a need. Please bear with me. You see, Mr. Koltsov, in ancient times this land around us was called Colchis, The Land of the Sun. It was to Batumi or near it that Jason and his Argonauts sailed to find the Golden Fleece, did you know that?"

"No, sir."

"No, but it is so. According to the myth. Can we believe in these myths, young Mikhail Koltsov? Should we repeat them? There is no task you can perform for me, Mikhail Koltsov, no way in which I as your King Aeëtes can reward you with golden fleece. There is none. I know nothing at all of Bulgakov's work, I am trying to say. If he had revealed all to me, I should not have understood it. I am no scientist, but only another pursuer of myths. I have nothing for you. Nothing exists."

"There must be something. . . ."

"No."

"Did he leave some notes?" Colter asked, almost frantically. He was ready to laugh, to scream. What the hell had they done to him? "Did he leave you some memento? Something that might not have seemed important at the time. A book, for example?"

"No, nothing like that. I have nothing of Bulgakov's, and even had I, I would be in a position similar to Bulgakov's, would I not? What a terrible choice I should have to make. Would I want the people in the Eastern hemisphere to have the information so that they might more effectively kill those in the West?" he asked, lifting his left hand. "Or," lifting his right, "would I wish the Western Hemisphere to obliterate the East— which, living here, would be quite uncomfortable for me. You see," he smiled, "I could not make such a horrible decision, any more than Bulgakov could. There will be wars, there will always be wars, and there will be new technologies surpassing Bulgakov's in efficient slaughter—but I, Mikhail Koltsov, intend to have no part in any such tragedy."

"There must have been something," Colter went on with a growing sense of hopelessness, of futility. "Otherwise none of this makes any sense."

"It makes no sense anyway," Vesely said kindly. "But I will tell you this—yes, there were certain notes Bulgakov had carried away with him from the research center and somehow hidden. I never actually saw the notes, you understand, but only the container he kept them in."

"The container?"

"Yes, only a small zinc-plated box half the size of a package of cigarettes. He showed it to me."

"And you know where that is?"

"Oh, yes," Vesely said. "I know where it is. Bulgakov showed it to me and then hid it in front of my eyes. He entrusted his secret to me. There was no one else at all, you see. I then assumed the responsibility for this information, for this war machinery."

"And?" Colter prompted.

"And it was my decision to leave it where it was hidden, to molder away beneath the snow. That was my decision; it is still my decision. It is in a place where no one will ever stumble across it, I assure you. You could not find it if I were to tell you exactly where it was, and if I were to point it out to you on a map, to precisely name the hiding place, you could not hope to reach it.

"In Khabarovo."

"Yes. In Khabarovo. Your quest is over, Mikhail Koltsov. There is no golden fleece to be found here. Please, make your escape while you can—go home to wherever it is that you live. While there is time, do this. It is a terrible thing for a man to die for a myth."

Then Vesely's eyes closed and Colter could only stand there watching him. "Did you hear him?" Anna Vesely said. "Go home! I tell you the same thing—go home, Mikhail Koltsov, we do not want you here. There is nothing for you in Batumi. Nothing in the house of my father."

Outside it was windy. Clouds drifted in from off of the Black Sea. The stars were milky and blurred in a pale sky. Mike Colter stood outside the cottage of Stepan Vesely, looking at the stars, the distances. Then he hunched his shoulders against the wind and started back toward Bulyev's house.

"Goodbye to all," he said bitterly. "It's been a lot of fun. Wonder what they're doing at the Lakewatch now. Maybe Consentino has stocked the lake. Goodbye . . . to all."

He was through with the spy business, and to hell with it all. He only wanted out of Batumi, the sooner the better.

He met Repin in front of Bulyev's house.

"Where have you been, comrade?" Repin asked, his voice rising with triumph. "I heard that you were ill, and I was so sorry! I came over to bring you a little something, but you were gone."

"Get out of my way, Repin," Colter said harshly.

"You talk this way to me?" the Georgian said. Colter held himself back with difficulty. He was in a foul mood and he felt like telling the comrade foreman where to get off. Or punching his ugly face in for him. Or both. That was no good and he knew it. Colter took a series of deep, slow breaths.

"Listen, Repin, I was feeling ill this morning," he said. "I was dizzy and had a fever. I thought it would do me good to get out and take some light exercise, to get a little fresh air, and so I went for a walk."

"You are a parasite, Novikov," Repin said, his confidence growing as Colter backed down. "I will tell you what happened. You were not ill at all. You were seen. You were out playing around with Vesely's daughter."

"Yes. I'm sorry," Colter said. "I couldn't help myself." He tried a man-to-man grin. "She was friendly and I had the chance to see her. You know how it is."

If Repin knew how it was, he wasn't going to admit it. "This is very serious, Novikov. Very serious indeed."

"It won't happen again. I'm sorry. Now please—I am feeling ill. I'd like to go to bed."

"You haven't heard the end of this, Novikov."

Colter had to fight back the temptation again, the temptation to slug the little Caesar. He grew contrite instead. "Look, Repin, I really am sorry. I'll not do it again. I promise you I'll be the best worker you've got from here on out if you'll only give me another chance."

"I don't believe you, Novikov. I don't believe you. I don't like you. You're not to be trusted, I think, and both you and your cousin, Bulyev, have not heard the end of this. I do have connections of some importance, you realize." Repin puffed up and Colter sighed. He only wanted to get past the foreman and into the house.

"I'm sorry. Look, Repin, I really am ill. Let me go in and lie down, will you."

"Yes, oh yes," Repin said mockingly. "I will let you go, Comrade Novikov. I will let you get your rest—though what you are resting from one can't even guess. But let me tell you this before you go: We will meet and speak again of this matter, and perhaps I will bring someone else to speak with you about it. You have had a soft job here. The climate is warm, the work not too hard. Perhaps you and Bulyev both will find new positions where conditions are not always so pleasant. This can happen, Comrade Novikov." He thumped Colter's chest with his index finger. "I advise you to sleep on *that* tonight."

Then, his face flushed with his small triumph, knowing he had done his best to increase productivity and intimidate the workers, Repin turned and swaggered off through the grove toward his cottage, no doubt planning on sitting up the rest of the night himself plotting glorious reprisals.

Colter walked through the trees to the house, pushed the door open, and went in to find Bulyev standing before the fire, his expression anticipatory, his eyes wide.

"Well?" he asked excitedly.

"I have to leave."

"But what happened?" Bulyev wanted to know. "Success or failure? Which?"

"I have to get out of here, Bulyev. Tonight. Did you contact Mustafa yet?"

"I haven't been able to reach him. This smuggling business. No one answers the phone."

"Look, have they arrested him?"

"No. It is someone else in his organization. Someone they cannot allow to talk."

"I want Mustafa up here!" Colter said angrily. "Him or someone else with a car. They agreed to do this, now damnit, they can't just drop me and go off on other business." Colter was wound up tight. His nerves jumped. The veins in his temples pulsed solidly.

"It does no good to shout at me," Bulyev said.

"No." Colter rubbed his face and shrugged apologetically. It didn't do any good to shout at Bulyev, none to shout at Repin. "You're right, keep trying, will you? I need to get out of Batumi tonight."

"I will continue to try." Bulyev shrugged as if he didn't expect much to come from his efforts. "These Turks . . ."

"Is the truck out back?"

"You don't think you will need that?" Bulyev paled.

"I hope not. But if you don't raise Mustafa pretty damn soon, yes, I'll need it. I'm not going to stay around here a minute longer than necessary.

Is the truck there?"

"Yes, it is there," Bulyev said, looking his age suddenly. "I will get back on the telephone."

Colter went to his room and sagged onto his bed. It was impossible to relax. He could hear Bulyev's voice in the other room. Colter rose and walked to the window, to stand looking out at the little cottage across the road.

THIRTEEN

The phone jangled in the night and Remizov groaned aloud. He sat up, pushing the warm, flaccid bulk of Eva to one side. He rested his head in his hands and sat naked on the edge of the bed. The fire had gone out and it was a chill night. He had to look around him to try to recall where he was. Batumi. Her name was Eva.

Who the hell was calling?

The phone rang again, and Remizov, reaching for his eye patch, rose to limp across the room to the alcove.

"If it's that fool Gopchik," Remizov muttered, but no, it couldn't be. He was too frightened to call in the middle of the night, too afraid of displeasing. There could only be one man calling at this hour, the colonel decided, and he mentally prepared himself, forcing his vodka-fogged mind to come alert. He turned on the dim electric light in the alcove and looked back fleetingly at Eva's sleeping, naked form. She hadn't been so bad, he thought.

"Colonel Remizov," he said into the telephone.

There was no apology for the time of the call and Remizov had expected none. The man himself worked all night frequently. He lived only for that work, and if Remizov was to take his place, as was expected, he would have to get used to that as well. Nothing else could be allowed to interfere.

"This is Fyodor," the flat, emotionless voice said. "Please listen to me."

"Of course," Remizov said, frowning. There was something in Fyodor's voice that set his nerves on edge. Something like censure. Had something gone wrong?

Remizov was standing looking into the mirror, seeing a spare, scarred torso, a patch-covered eye, thinning blond hair. *That is me*, he thought out of the depths of some night-inspired conundrum. That is the man the boy in me became.

He waited what seemed an interminable period of time, watching Eva, who seemed obscene in her sleep, one heavy breast uncovered. She whom he had ravaged, scored with his teeth, flung himself upon, torn at, buried himself in. A thing whose person was only a part of Remizov's mind.

Remizov heard the line click and come clear again. Fyodor had switched over to the scrambler link.

"I have the report, Remizov. The Colter report."

"Yes, Fyodor."

"Have you found him yet?"

"No, Fyodor." Remizov did not bother to make explanations.

"Your report, Remizov . . ." there was a long pause. That meant that Fyodor was having one of his attacks, one of those moments when the pain was like an iron spike driven through his skull. Remizov waited. He was used to pauses when talking to his superior. Now he would be fumbling in his desk for the metal box with the pain killer, now swallowing the yellow pills almost desperately. How long could he last?

"I am here now," Fyodor said, and his voice was dry. "I have the report. It is flawed, badly flawed."

"Fyodor, I assure you . . ."

"Flawed!" Fyodor said, and his voice shouted down the wires. Remizov was astonished. *What was wrong?*

"You are in Batumi and you do not have Colter. Have you removed his target?"

His target? What the hell was Colter's target? What was Fyodor going on about? Maybe the cancer had reached his mind. Fyodor never spoke like this, with anger in his voice. Never—except when there was a serious failure. Failure, which was not allowed.

"I have not removed his target, Fyodor. I was not able to determine what it is."

"An American agent."

"The oil refineries, of course. . . ."

"Shut up! Shut up, Remizov. I thought you

306

were the special one. All this time I have been grooming you. What in Batumi is worth this madness, this lone American agent? What? Answer me! Tell me!"

The words were like blows to the body as Fyodor, in a rage, spat them out. Demanding, taunting. Remizov closed his eye tightly, fighting off an attack of nausea. Too much vodka.

"Stepan Vesely. He is in Batumi!" Fyodor screamed.

The bells began to go off in the back of Remizov's skull. His blood began to race, his heart to thump too heavily. *Stepan Vesely.*

"Fyodor . . ."

"And through him . . . you do recall, colonel, that Stepan Vesely was confined at Khabarovo?"

"Yes, of course, I recall . . . *Bulgakov!*" Remizov banged his fist against the mirror. It shattered into a hundred pieces. His hand was bleeding. His stomach was knotted horribly. "Fyodor . . ."

"Do your work."

The line was disconnected. Fyodor did not want apologies. He wanted results. Remizov dialed Tyurin's room and barked out a few orders. Then he called Gopchik, telling him to get over to the hotel with transportation within fifteen minutes.

"You have the man?" Gopchik asked sleepily. Remizov just hung up. He dressed hurriedly, Eva watching him with a dull expression that made him want to club her.

He was out in front of the hotel in ten minutes, smoking a cigarette, pacing the sidewalk. Tyurin showed up with a donut in his hand.

"Evening, colonel. The good stuff?"

"I think so."

"Good. I want to meet this Colter."

"It's not so good even if we do catch him. It was Fyodor who found him—from a thousand miles away."

"Ouch. Not so good, colonel, sorry." Tyurin took another thoughtful bite. "But if we don't catch him—and he was here..." And then Tyurin did something Remizov had never seen him do. He shook his head and threw the half-eaten donut into the gutter.

"I know," Remizov thought. "I know."

Remizov's own nerve had come back by the time the car arrived. Gopchik was in it, and Muraviev, along with a driver.

"Find him?" Gopchik asked as the two men slid in.

"We hope so," Remizov answered. "Do you know where Stepan Vesely lives?"

"The poet, of course."

"That's where we're going, driver." And hope to God Colter hasn't already been and gone."

The driver had slowed and was peering out through the settling fog for the narrow road that led up through the orange groves. He spotted his landmark at last and swung left, dropping into low gear as the road turned sharply upward. Remizov noticed the hand-painted sign that read "Makhindzhauri Commune."

308

"What else is up here?"

"Only the orange groves, Colonel Remizov. A workers' commune and the Vesely house. Nothing else."

"Do you have any units you can call out?"

"Extra units, sir?"

"Yes. I want guards posted."

"Is that necessary, comrade colonel? We have an agent in place, as you know, this Comrade Uglich. . . ."

"Call on the radio," Remizov said, his voice cold, flat. "Get the house encircled, the road blocked. Use Batumi police if you have to."

"You think . . . ?" Muraviev's question faded away. He had the distinct impression that this Moscow bigwig wasn't going to tell him what he thought. Muraviev glanced sideways at Gopchik, seeing the tight-lipped consternation on his face as he reached for the car radio. Gopchik was used to running the whole show and he didn't like this a bit. Muraviev turned his face away, concealing his expression of satisfaction. Let Gopchik see how it felt to be bullied for a while.

"Is this it?" Remizov asked from the back seat.

The driver had already wheeled into the little drive before the cottage. There was a single light burning in the front of the house. Gopchik was speaking excitedly into the radio, receiving crackling, confused responses.

"The Vesely cottage," Muraviev confirmed. Remizov was already out of the car, leaving everyone but the equally quick Tyurin behind. He rapped on the door three times, very loudly, and waited a long time before the light, hurried footsteps approached.

When the door swung open he had a view of a beautiful young woman with dark hair and intelligent eyes. Anna Vesely. Remizov had seen her in photographs before. He remembered wondering what she was like. Remizov looked across her shoulder; everything seemed calm within.

"Comrade Vesely?"

"Yes," Anna answered.

"I am Colonel Remizov. I have come from Moscow to speak to your father."

"He cannot speak to anyone," Anna said wearily. "My father is very ill." She saw no hint of compassion in the one-eyed man's expression.

"Please," Remizov said, "let us in."

"He cannot speak to you. I've sent for the doctor. He is seriously ill, don't you understand?"

"It won't take long," Remizov said implacably. He pushed the door farther open and tramped into the house, the KGB men at his heels. He looked around carefully as he entered, noticing that the supper table had been set for two.

"Your father was not too ill to come to dinner?"

"A friend from the commune was over."

"Which is your father's room, please?"

"Won't you leave him alone? Please?" Anna said, looking at the tall blond man. "Haven't you people done enough to him?" She saw no sympathy in the single cold blue eye. Nor was there any malevolence. He was simply doing his job, which he probably did very efficiently.

People were factors in his equations, that was all.

Remizov had started toward the sickroom door and Anna could only tag along as the officer opened the door and entered. "We'll have a light on," Remizov said. Anna could hear someone else poking around out in the other rooms. Drawers were opened and shut. She had started toward the bedside lamp before it all came together in her mind.

Koltsov.

This man had come for the same thing Koltsov had wanted. That something that was hidden away in a northern labor camp. Did this one know about Koltsov? Could he? Or had she just told him? *A friend from the commune came over.*

Anna bit her lip and turned on the lamp. What happened to Koltsov was his own affair. Why should it concern her in the least? He was no better than this man with the eye patch. Predators, scavengers.

"Comrade Vesely? Can you hear me?" Remisov was bent over the sickbed, peering into the colorless, deeply lined face of Stepan Vesely. "Vesely, can you hear me? You must open your eyes. It is important that I talk to you."

Anna walked nearer, her hands clasped together. She saw her father's clouded eyes flicker open and stare without seeing at Remizov.

"Anna," Vesely managed to say, but his voice was weak and distant.

She sat beside him on the bed, touching his brow, which was very cool, very dry. The old man smiled.

311

"Tell him he must sit up and speak to me," Remizov said in a tone of command.

"I will not!" Anna flared. "He is very ill, as you can see—as anyone could see if he cared to. He can't sit up."

"He must answer my questions."

"He can't!" Anna shrieked, coming up from the bed, thrusting herself challengingly at Remizov. "Don't you see how he is? Who is that?" she asked, turning sharply toward the door. "I heard a car. Is that the doctor?"

"I think it is more of my men."

"Why don't you just go away?" she asked coldly.

"I'm afraid I can't," Remizov said with a sketchy smile. "My superiors would not like that."

Anna's answering expression was one of infinite contempt. She could see something in this officer's expression, something she at first could not comprehend. Now she did. It was fear! Fear. He was afraid of not performing his job adequately. If a dying man had to be hounded then he would be; because he was afraid! Footsteps padded toward them and Anna glanced at the doorway to see the doctor. Old, thin, black bag in hand.

"Finally," she cried out. "Please, doctor, come in."

He shuffled forward, glancing at Remizov once before he leaned forward and looked down at Stepan Vesely, nodding to himself, clicking his tongue.

"Doctor," Remizov said. "I must talk to this

man. It is urgent."

"No." The doctor turned his head toward Remizov. "That is not possible, sir, I am afraid."

"When will it be possible."

"I cannot say it will be possible," the doctor replied, glancing at Anna.

"What do you mean? What seems to be the matter with him?" Remizov persisted.

"The matter seems to be that he is a very old man who has suffered a hard life."

"He is dying?"

The doctor looked again at Anna and said softly, "Yes." Anna turned away. She had known this, expected it, and yet it struck at her heart to have it said aloud.

"I must speak to him," Remizov said again. "I cannot tell you how vital this is to our country. Do you have drugs that can temporarily restore him to alertness? Do you have something, doctor, that will stimulate him to allow us a few questions?"

"I do not use such drugs in my practice, sir," the doctor said icily.

"Ghoul," Anna whispered, but Remizov ignored her if he heard her.

"Do you think he will have periods of lucidity? Will there be remission?"

"I cannot predict such things," the doctor said. "It is vaguely possible."

"All right." Remizov now turned toward the door. A drab, bitter-eyed woman had appeared there. She wore a gray flannel coat and a man's cap.

"This is Uglich," Gopchik said.

"What is happening?" the woman asked. "I must know. . . ."

Remizov interrupted her. "Where have you been?" he demanded angrily.

"Who . . . ?" She grew briefly supercilious, and then she recognized the authority in Remizov, the way Gopchik had deferred to the man with the eye patch. "I was at my weekly briefing, comrade," Uglich replied.

"You are to go nowhere tonight. Nowhere at all. You are to stay with Vesely, and you are to telephone Captain Gopchik's office immediately if he regains coherent consciousness. Do you understand me, Uglich?"

"Yes, comrade," Uglich said, seeming to shrink before their eyes. "I will do as you say."

Remizov left the room without saying another word. He would have his own doctor here in the morning, one who did know how to use the sort of drug he had in mind. The old man would talk; as long as he could draw a breath, he could talk.

Anna trailed after the colonel and stood watching from the doorway as the doors to the Moskvitch slammed shut and the black car roared off down the foggy lane, its taillights winking as the car bounded down the rutted road.

"Well?" Gopchik asked above the roar of the car's engine.

"We need a doctor. Have you one?" Remizov asked. Gopchik nodded. "There isn't much time, captain. The old man is dying. He must not die until we have spoken to him. Find a doctor as soon as possible. Notify me then. I want to be with him when he comes. About the man Colter . . ."

"We have not yet found a trace of him, Colonel Remizov."

"He may have come, done his work, and gone," Remizov said sharply. "With that incompetent bitch up there anything is possible. She wouldn't have been any problem to get around. What is her name, Uglich?"

"Yes, Colonel Remizov."

"I thought so. All right. We can do nothing here for the moment. We must find Colter. It is imperative."

They had to slow the car as they approached the main road. A truck had arrived and was now pulled up to the side of the lane. Soldiers were clambering out and a handful of local police, setting up the roadblock. Gopchik looked expectantly at Remizov, perhaps waiting for a compliment on his efficiency. There was none.

"Where could an American hide?" Remizov asked himself again. If only he knew Batumi better. It was not a large city, but there were 125,000 citizens. Enough to make a house-to-house search impossible. Remizov rubbed his forehead unhappily. It was almost as if Fyodor was watching now, hanging over his shoulder. He had worked so hard, so long, to put himself into Fyodor's good graces. He was the logical successor to that throne, everyone knew that. Failure. One failure shouldn't weigh so heavily. But he *couldn't* fail.

"I want to see your file on Dubček again. And get that police captain—Blok?"

"Yes, colonel, Blok."

"Dubček has to have some contacts here. With the criminal element, perhaps. He had to have help in Batumi. Transportation, lodging, how could he do this all himself? How is he going to make his escape—if he hasn't already done that? He must realize that he can't use any public transportation. Without an Intourist authorization he'll never hire a private car."

"The forger, sir," Tyurin said. "Maybe he has an Intourist card."

"He'd still need a driver. Well . . . check on that, Gopchik. Tonight. Get someone down to the Intourist office. If he can't find a car, then what? We are on the sea. A boat?" Remizov quit thinking out loud and started brooding silently. The chance for success here seemed suddenly very slim.

There were two possibilities, he thought morosely. Either Colter had already spoken to Vesely and was now making his escape with the information or no one would ever again speak to Vesely, Colter included. Unless the doctor was very good. Remizov had seen unconscious men brought to acute alertness in moments under the skilled hands of his Moscow medical corps. It was ruinous to the health of the subject, but as an interrogation tool it was occasionally useful. Vesely was not in Moscow, however, nor would the poet survive transportation there.

"If you would like to eat, Colonel Remizov," Gopchik said, turning around, throwing his arm over the back of the seat to face Remizov, "we could . . ."

"I would like to see your file again and talk to Captain Blok. I would like to see a doctor dispatched to the Vesely house," Remizov said with irritation. "And please notify the border guards and shore patrol that it is necessary to increase their watchfulness."

"Very good," Gopchik said. He turned around very slowly, taking the radio microphone from its dashboard clip. He began calling his office and field units, biting off his commands. Muraviev bit his tongue to keep the smile from forming on his lips. Colonel Remizov and his aide sat silently in the back seat, gloomily watching the city lights of Batumi approach.

"Do you have to sit there with that pistol on your lap? This is really absurd. Absurd! What do you think is going to happen here? He is a sick old man, he is dying," Anna said, struggling to get the last word out. She felt the lump growing in her throat again.

"You heard my orders," Comrade Uglich said, smoothing her colorless skirt over her bony white knees.

"They gave my father no peace in life; they give him none in death."

Comrade Uglich, who had been prepared to leap into a denunciation of reactionary elements, changed her mind and leaned back in her chair, smiling thinly. Let her bury herself. She understood nothing, this child. She watched as Anna picked up her father's hand and kissed it, holding it next to her cheek.

Anna placed the hand down on the bed covers and rose with a shake of her head. Uglich dispassionately noted the tears in the girl's eyes.

"I'm going to clean up the dishes," Anna said. When Uglich did not answer, she turned and went out, knuckling away the tears that had gathered at the corners of her eyes. Sniffing, she began clearing the table, looking at Colter's plate, his napkin, before, angrily, with much clattering, she stacked the plates and took them into the kitchen where she dumped them noisily into the sink.

From the kitchen window she could see, through the orange trees, the small dark window that was Colter's. She looked at it in fascination for a long minute and then, angry with herself, she started the water running, the spigot sputtering as water burst forth in a savage fountain.

He was the same as Remizov, this colonel from Moscow. Just the same. There was no difference. Koltsov and this colonel. Two carrion birds. She picked up the dirty pans beside the sink and threw them down again. Anna sprinkled soap powder from a blue box over the dishes, spilling quite a bit of it. Then she stood, eyes closed, leaning against the sink.

When she went back to her father's room, Uglich was gone. There was a light under the bathroom door and the sound of running water.

318

Anna looked idly around, and, seeing the stack of yellow, lined paper on the bedside table, she picked up a sheet and began to read.

A froth of clouds across a changeling sky;
A night of thunderous remembrances . . .

Anna glanced toward the bathroom door and then picked up the stack of papers and went out into the living room. Looking around, she found the portmanteau she had dumped in the corner after returning from Zelyoni Mys. Recalling that afternoon brought a pang of inexplicable melancholy. She took out her cheesecloth-covered canvas and set it aside, placing the sheaf of poetry in the portmanteau.

They could not have that! They could not destroy that work. There he breathed, there his heart beat and his living, ageless blood coursed. If they could, they would take it away, examining it for codes, for military secrets, and, that done, they would file it away in some mausoleum beneath the streets of Moscow where the blood of Stepan Vesely, his soul, would become a state secret. And then, and only then, would Stepan Vesely be dead. She would not allow it—they would not kill him.

"What are you doing?" Uglich appeared in the doorway, her automatic pistol still in her hand.

"I wanted to take out my painting so it can dry," Anna said, keeping her face from Uglich. She set up her portable easel and placed the undraped canvas on it, stepping back to examine it as Uglich watched from the shadows of the doorway.

Finally the KGB officer shrugged and turned away. Anna looked with something like revulsion at the painting before her, the sea, the *torii* crimson and bright, the grassy knolls, thinking of the dark-haired, smiling man who lay out of frame, watching her as she painted, as the sun beamed down, as the sea breezes flowed in and carried the salt scent of the water, the sweet fragrance of the grass to her. . . .

She turned and walked rapidly to the door, taking a deep breath of fresh air. The fog was twisting its way up the slopes, creeping through the groves, long, milky tentacles lying against the dark earth.

"What are you doing now?"

"Getting some fresh air, Comrade Uglich."

"Don't go out of the house."

"No, Comrade Uglich."

The KGB officer didn't have to worry. She was going nowhere. Where was there, after all, to go? She just stood looking at the house across the road, at the darkened window and the slowly creeping fog.

"You'd better come in here," the KGB officer called from within, and Anna turned around, her heart pounding. She forced herself to walk and not run, crossing the room on swift, silent feet.

"What is it?"

"Nothing," Uglich said from the bedside. "I thought he was going to kick off there, but I guess he's still alive."

Anna sagged onto her bedside chair, watching her father. His eyelids fluttered slightly. She could clearly see the blue veins in them. His flesh was nearly transluscent now. Bloodless, lifeless. Such a shame, such a shame. A husk where a fine, strong thing had thrived. And the world would be peopled now by those who were somehow a little less fine, a little less strong.

His fingers twitched as if he were trying to reach for her, and she took his hand, squeezing it, feeling or imagining she felt a slight responsive pressure.

"He's breathing, isn't he?" Uglich asked.

She thrust her horse face next to Vesely's, listening, and Anna had an almost uncontrollable urge to leap up and shove her away.

"Yes, I guess he's breathing." With a bored sigh Uglich took her seat again. Anna lay her cheek on her father's chest, listening to the erratic beating of his great heart.

It was beating and then it was not. Anna didn't move. Her eyes opened wide, her own heart began hammering in her rib cage. She squeezed his hand so tightly she heard a knuckle crack. Uglich yawned in the corner chair. Still Anna did not move. She couldn't. It was impossible.

Something good and noble had risen up out of the steppes of Russia and they had crushed it, torn at it until it was broken and withered. Now he was dead; the night whispered a silent, agonized word. Uglich cleared her throat and Anna stared at her with dark anger.

She rose, looking down at her father, seeing the

peace on his weathered face.

"What's the matter?" Uglich demanded.

"Nothing."

Anna turned and walked out into the living room, her heart flooded with grief, her mind spinning crazily. Now what? Now what? Questions, interrogations, back to Moscow, more interrogations, and the pointless life at the university—if she were lucky.

And the book . . . her eyes shifted with something like panic to her portmanteau, where the manuscript of Vesely's last great poem was hidden.

"What are you up to?" the voice at Anna's shoulder said. Anna jumped at the words and spun to look at Uglich. "What are you looking at?"

"Nothing."

Uglich herself was now looking at the leather portmanteau. "What's in there? If you're holding something back, some information, you'll be sorry."

"There's nothing in there."

"You little liar," Uglich said harshly.

"I swear to you . . ."

"We'll just see." Uglich brushed past Anna and Anna grabbed at her arm.

"There's nothing, I tell you."

"Then get out of my way!" The KGB officer pushed Anna away, and Anna, reaching out for balance, grabbed the sleeve to Uglich's blouse.

Uglich swung around viciously, trying to club Anna with her pistol, and both women fell to the floor. Anna hit the ground hard, jarring the wind from her body, and she was slow getting up. Her hand was in something sticky as she braced herself to rise, and it wasn't until she was on her feet that she realized what it was.

"Blood." She stared at her hand with shocked awe. Slowly she lowered her hand, staring at Uglich.

The woman still lay sprawled on the floor, her mouth twisted into a toothy grimace. She had fallen so that her head had hit the sharp corner of the low table beside the easel, and she wasn't moving.

"Comrade Uglich?"

There was blood on Anna's hand and on her sweater. There was blood oozing from the wound on Uglich's scalp, staining the wooden floor. Anna stepped across the body and closed the open front door, leaning her back against it as she stared at the sprawled, motionless figure on the floor.

Was she dead? Anna couldn't bring herself to check. Dead or not it was trouble of the most serious kind. Anna stumbled forward and walked in a daze to the sickroom. There Stepan Vesely lay, still, unbreathing.

"What shall I do?" Anna murmured.

She got to her knees and placed her head on her father's hand. *Dead.* He was dead, Uglich was probably dead. The world was a vast dying place, an arena of death.

She lifted her head, wiping her eyes with both palms. Rising, she sniffed, stood staring at her father's peaceful face. She bent then and kissed his cool brow and went out of the room.

Uglich had not moved, and it didn't look as if she was going to move. Anna picked up her coat and then walked to the corner. She found her small leather satchel and unzipped it. From the portmanteau she took the yellow sheets of manuscript, stuffing them into the satchel.

She stood looking around the room then, satchel in hand, as if she had forgotten something, but there was nothing left to be forgotten. Nothing that mattered.

Anna went out into the cool night, glancing up and down the lane. Earlier she had heard the trucks at the bottom of the hill, seen a searchlight of some kind, but now there was no one around. She crossed the lane quickly and then she was into the orange grove, working her way through the heavy fog toward the house beyond.

Colter sat up out of a jungle nightmare to hear the pounding on his door. He slipped the Walther out from under his pillow and responded quietly.

"Come in," he said, and the pistol slowly came up as the door opened.

There was a light behind her silhouetting her—the faint glow of the fire, red embers and golden, dying ash. She stood there, sleek, dark, her eyes shining darkly, a small satchel in her hand. Colter lowered the gun, rose from the bed and walked to her, seeing Bulyev in his nightshirt a few steps behind the girl.

"Anna." He went to her, putting out his arms, but she stepped back.

"I didn't know where else to go," she said.

"I told her you were not here," Bulyev said, "but she insisted on coming in. What was I to do?"

"All right, Bulyev." Of Anna he asked, "What's happened?" He looked into her eyes, finding them bitter and empty at once. "It's your father."

She nodded silently. Her lip began to tremble and she clamped her mouth shut firmly to stop it from giving her away.

"There's something I must talk to you about." Anna looked across her shoulder at Bulyev.

"You can trust him."

"It's Uglich. The KGB officer." Haltingly Anna told Colter about it, about the visit of Colonel Remizov earlier in the evening. Colter felt his stomach turn over, his mouth go dry. "I didn't know where to go," she said, "who can I turn to? I have no one, and so I came here."

Time's up, Colter thought. The cards were on the table and the opposition had the better hand. "Call him again," Colter said to Bulyev. "Get through. We're all out of time!" The old man went away, shaking his head. "I've got someone who's supposed to take me to Turkey," he told Anna Vesely. "I want you to go with me."

"Yes," she said, in an unprotesting, small voice. "What does it matter? I'll go."

"You'll go if you want to stay out of prison." Colter took her arms and shook her slightly. The woman was in shock. He wanted her to understand the seriousness of things. "You'll be tried for killing Uglich."

"Yes, I know," Anna said wearily, pushing her hair out of her eyes.

"All right. What have you got there?" he asked, nodding at the satchel.

"It is my father's. His last poem. It must go to the West, somewhere where it can be published—you see, I must go with you."

"I can't get him on the telephone!" Bulyev called from the other room.

"I'm taking the truck then," Colter said, walking by Anna into the living room.

"You can't! That is madness. You can't make it to the border in that truck. And you'll never be able to cross without Mustafa. Those are his people at the checkpoint."

"I can't stay here, Bulyev. Where is Mustafa! We can't wait. You heard a part of what the girl said."

"All right." Bulyev looked from Colter to Anna and back again. "Take the truck. Leave it at the Zemloy Garage."

"Where's that?"

"I know where it is," Anna volunteered.

"Leave it there. You'll never make the border in a truck, but at least you'll be off the commune. I'll tell the authorities I had to have the truck repaired if anyone asks. The people at the Zemloy are all right. You just stay there. I'll be on the phone until I get Mustafa. He'll pick you up before morning and you'll be on your way home."

"If you ever get hold of him," Colter said angrily.

"I'll get him."

"There's no choice, I guess. You're right about the truck—it's no good for crossing the border."

"The roads all around here are blocked," Anna told him. "How can we go anywhere?"

"What about the back way?" Colter asked Bulyev. "The way Mustafa brought me in."

"You can't make it up that road without a Jeep."

"I can try."

"All right then!" Bulyev pulled at his own hair as if he would yank it out. "Try it. But get to the Zemloy Garage. It's safe there. I'll get Mustafa somehow."

"You'd damn well better," Colter said, and his voice was hard and slightly menacing.

"I will," Bulyev said. "You be careful."

"We will. Thank you, Bulyev."

"For nothing. Good journey," Bulyev smiled, thrusting out his hand. Colter took it in a brief, firm clasp, then he put his arm around Anna's wrist. She recoiled briefly but left it there temporarily.

The Little Old One watched them dazedly as they turned out the house lights and went out the back door, Bulyev peering out first.

"It's clear," he said. "Very foggy."

"Make sure you get Mustafa," Colter said. "Make sure he meets us there or we're dead, Bulyev."

Then Colter stepped out the door into the foggy yard, gripping Anna Vesely's wrist tightly. He wasn't going to lose her now.

The man beneath the trees had been waiting. Now he separated himself from the shadows and came forward confidently. Colter breathed a slow curse.

"And now what are you up to, Comrade Novikov?" Repin demanded. "You, with this woman? Where are you going?"

"Get out of the way, Repin."

"You tell me to get out of your way, comrade!" Repin laughed and stepped in, gripping Colter's arm below the elbow. Colter let him have it. His right hand bunched into a fist and came up hard in Repin's wind. The Georgian doubled up, grunting, and Colter lifted his knee into the foreman's face. Repin went down in a heap.

"Let's go," Colter hissed.

"What is it?" Bulyev called, rushing toward them. "What has happened? Oh, God! Who is it?"

"Repin. Tie him up and stow him somewhere."

"I can't!" Bulyev was aghast. "When he comes around . . . what will my explanation be?"

"Tie him up, or I'll have to kill him," Colter said. He was aware of Anna's sharp intake of breath. Probably she was having second thoughts about going off into the night with a hardened thug.

"I don't know what to do," Bulyev moaned.

"I can't have him talking to anyone tonight. You tie him up or he'll have to die."

"All right, all right!" Bulyev looked to the skies for help. "Go," he said miserably, "just go."

Bulyev, too, was having second thoughts about things, but it was far too late. If the Ukrainian had any sense he would see to it that Repin just disappeared on this night never to be seen again. Bulyev's face reflected the same sort of thought. Colter rested a hand briefly on Bulyev's shoulder and then turned away.

"Come on."

He half-dragged Anna after him. The dark bulk of the commune truck loomed out of the darkness. Colter helped Anna up the step and then climbed into the cab of the truck himself, sliding under the steering wheel. The truck started after a frantic minute's pumping of the throttle. It hadn't occurred to Bulyev to keep it warm. The diesel engine finally rattled to life and Colter jammed it into gear. The truck lurched forward into the foggy night. Anna sat beside him silently, staring at nothing through the misted windshield, the satchel on her lap.

Colter glanced at her, changing gears and stamping down again on the accelerator. He looked at her and he wanted to talk to her, wanted to kiss her, to tell her she was wrong about him. The truck jolted over a rut and Colter cursed softly, turning his attention to the dark and winding road.

FOURTEEN

The ancient truck groaned up the narrow road, the transmission and differential whining as Colter dropped back another gear and flattened the accelerator pedal against the floorboard. The fog was thick outside the cab of the truck; at times Colter had to lean out the door to make out the road. Anna hadn't said a word. She sat there numb and silent, her arms folded around the satchel.

"It'll be all right," he said tentatively. There was no reply. "If we can make this grade we can swing back toward the coast highway and come into Batumi from the south. If they're looking for us at all—and that seems likely by now—they'll be looking for us to come in from the north."

No answer.

Colter dropped still another gear and cursed slowly, fluently, in English, utilizing his full knowledge of his mother tongue to ornament and embellish his profanity. She wasn't disturbed by that. She said nothing. She never would speak again. Not to him. Colter slammed his hand against the steering wheel in frustration.

The truck was beginning to tilt now and in a moment it was at a perilous angle as it climbed up out of the canyon toward the hilltop, which showed as a dark island floating on a sea of milky fog.

There was just enough room for the truck now on the narrow road. The outside wheels were flirting with disaster as they ran along the edge of the soft shoulder. Below the drop-off was very steep, something like a hundred feet, if Colter remembered. Just now he couldn't see the bottom for the fog. Maybe that was for the best.

Twice Colter almost lost it as the truck refused to proceed up the incline and started rolling back. The second time the engine stalled and there was a frantic moment while he tried to brake, restart, and find a gear all at once. Through it all Anna sat passively, accepting whatever was to come.

Finally the truck crept up onto the flats and Colter stopped, looking right and then left through the fog bank. "Do you know the roads back here?" he asked. "Anna! Which way, do you know?"

"Half a kilometer on. The road drops down past the desalinization plant."

"Thanks," Colter said bitterly. He popped the clutch out and the truck jerked forward. The going was easy across the flats despite the fog, and he found the road he wanted without much trouble. There was a cluster of low, blue buildings to the left and the scent of chemicals. Straight ahead dull, vaguely orange lights marked the coast highway. The moon shone on the Black Sea, the hills were lost in fog as Colter rolled up onto a frontage road and then onto the two-lane concrete highway, turning north toward Batumi.

"Anna? I'm sorry about your father." There was still no answer. "I'm very sorry. It was the last thing I wanted. Damn it!" he spat out in English before calming down, "I do love you. I never meant to hurt you. I want to explain it all to you when there's time."

There was no response. Colter drove on. There was almost no one on the streets as Colter wheeled the truck into the city. The only traffic they saw was truck traffic, produce moving out of the city, and that was comforting. It was good cover.

"Which way?"

"Six blocks or so ahead, then left," Anna said. "The street is called Bilgya. It should be marked."

Colter glanced at Anna. She had tied a scarf over her head, but her position was no different than when they had left the commune. Her sharp, pretty profile was cut distinctly against the window. Like one of those carnival silhouettes clipped out of black paper. With about as much life.

He found Bilgya and crept up the street. "On the right," Anna said. "The next block, I think."

Zemloy Garage. A drab, brown brick building with four huge doors opening onto the street. The place was locked up, dark.

"I hope there's someone here," Colter said, expecting no answer, getting none.

He parked the truck at the curb and slipped out, looking up and down the foggy street, his hand not straying far from the pistol in his pocket. He walked swiftly down the narrow, stinking alley beside the garage and found the door that had "office" painted on it. He pounded on it three times and stepped back to wait.

It was a full five minutes before a light went on and the door opened a crack, a narrow, sleepy Turkish face peering out at Colter.

"What do you want?"

"There's a truck outside that needs some work. It belongs to Bulyev."

"Come back tomorrow. I don't know Bulyev."

"Do you know Mustafa? He wants that truck taken care of tonight."

"I will call and find out."

"Let us in first. There are other people who want that truck."

The Turk looked at Colter with open suspicion, then nodded his head. "All right," he said, "I'll open the front doors. Then I'll call."

Colter walked back through the fog to his truck, half expecting to find that Anna had gone. She hadn't. She sat there, immobile as a mummy still, not even bothering to glance in his direction

333

as he climbed back in.

"I found someone. He's going to open the door."

Colter sat tapping nervously on the steering wheel for another two minutes. The garage man must have called first anyway. Finally the corrugated door rolled up, the Turk pulling frantically on the chains that operated it, and Colter gunned the diesel to life, driving the truck forward into the dark, oily interior of the Zemloy Garage.

Colter turned the key off and the engine clattered to a stop. He could hear the door closing behind them. He sat in the dark silence for a minute, not moving. Then he touched Anna's arm.

"Let's get out. Maybe he's got some tea."

The Turk was standing there waiting, flashlight in hand. His expression altered briefly when he shined the light toward the truck and illuminated a well-shaped feminine calf as Anna climbed down.

"This way," the garage man said.

They followed him up a flight of iron-railed, concrete steps, through a steel door, and into a small, warm, tobacco-scented apartment. There were two rooms, one with a narrow, low bed, the other containing an uncovered round wooden table and three chairs.

"Make yourself food," the Turk said, gesturing. "Make yourself tea. I will go and watch."

He went out after turning on the light—a forty-watt bulb dangling from the stained ceiling, and Anna sagged into a kitchen chair. She looked very small just then, small and exhausted. Just now she was losing the battle with the world.

"Tea?" Colter asked, and she nodded. "There's some cheese here too, and some salt crackers."

"All right."

A few silent minutes later Colter served her and sat down himself to the steaming tea. "We'll make it," Colter said. She didn't find it all that reassuring. He reached across the table and covered her hand with his.

"Another successful mission," Anna said, looking up sharply into his eyes.

"Not *another*. My first. And last."

"Really?" Her eyebrows drew together.

"Yes."

"They made you come?" she asked hopefully.

"No. They wanted someone who could pass for a Russian. They asked me and I accepted." He shrugged.

"Was it for money."

"Yes. Partly for money." He explained about Aunt Katrinka and Uncle Isaak.

"That's terrible! Wouldn't the government take care of him? They had to force you into this job?"

"It wasn't that way," Colter said, knowing what she wanted to hear. She wanted to know he wasn't some hard-boiled operative, a cutthroat spy, but a dupe of his imperialist government. "There just wasn't anything I cared about anymore. They offered me money—and maybe a chance to kill myself without having to take the gun in my own hand and putting it to my temple. I found that somewhat appealing."

"You don't mean that!"

"Maybe not. It's just that I was dying anyway—it didn't matter much really."

"You were dying?" She shook her head. "I don't understand. You were ill?"

"Very ill. For a very long time," Colter told her.

"Why are you taking me with you, Koltsov?" Anna asked without looking at him.

"I love you."

"Don't talk foolishness!"

"I'm not. And when I get home you'll stay with me. I'll take you to the immigration people and get your papers all straightened out. There won't be any trouble. The government owes me one. We'll go up and see Uncle Isaak, and then we'll take a long vacation—honeymoon, I should say. Fishing. Do you like to fish?"

"Why are you doing this?"

"Doing what?"

"Telling me lies like this, Mikhail Koltsov."

"I'm not telling you lies, Anna. Why should I tell you lies now?"

"I don't know," she said hesitantly. "I know you don't love me. I can't discuss this anymore. I'm too upset."

"All right. We won't discuss it. I just wanted you to know what was going to happen." Colter sipped at his tea, watching the top of Anna's bowed head, studying the raven-black hair, the white part.

"*Do* you love me?" she asked. Her face lifted. There were tears in her eyes. Her mouth was slack and childlike.

"Yes."

She was around the table in a flash, knocking her chair over backward, spilling her tea. Then her arms were around Colter and her tears were mingled with her kisses. He tasted her mouth, her cheeks, her nose, her eyes, holding her to him so tightly that she gasped for breath.

Then they crossed the room and sat together on the Turk's bed, silent for the rest of the night. Colter sat there, her head against the hollow of his shoulder, her breathing soft and tranquil as she slept.

"I do love you, woman," he said very quietly. He kissed the top of her head. "I do. I only hope to God there's time for us." She had become reality. Everything else had faded to fantasy and myth. Stepan Vesely had been wrong. He had his treasure, his golden fleece, his woman and his life. "I do love you," he whispered again.

"Who was that on the telephone?" Remizov asked.

"The doctor, comrade colonel. He's on his way. He had to stop at a pharmacy."

Remizov glanced impatiently at his watch and then at the window of Gopchik's austere little office. Blok, the Batumi police captain, sat across the room smoking cigarette after cigarette. Remizov threw the file on Colter down on the desk.

"There must be more! Damnit, where is he? Where is the key to this man? He can't be working

337

alone. It's impossible for a foreigner."

Blok cleared his throat tentatively and Remizov glanced at the police captain, who hadn't spoken three words until now.

"Turks," Blok said.

"What?"

"The captain means," Gopchik said, "that we have a severe problem in Batumi with dissident Turks. I have, I think, already sketched this problem for the colonel. You see," Gopchik essayed something distantly like a chuckle, "at one time in centuries past Batumi belonged to the Ottoman Empire, and some of our locals are convinced that it still should, though I hardly see what these hooligans have to do with the Colter case."

Remizov let Gopchik have his say. Glancing at Blok, however, he saw that the policeman had meant something more.

"Captain Blok?"

"I mention Turks for several reasons." Blok stubbed out another cigarette, blowing smoke through his nose. "First of all, I can't conceive of any local people except the Turks helping a fugitive. More likely they would capture this Colter and bring him in here beaten silly. Then, too, when you think of escape routes—why it's got to be to the southern border, doesn't it? To Turkey. Possibly by sea. Two-thirds of our fishing fleet is Turkish owned. As Captain Gopchik points out, there are Turks with a grudge against the state. They would be willing to help a foreign agent, I think."

Remizov stared at the squat police captain, wondering why in the name of Stalin's ghost the KGB couldn't recruit men like that instead of the Gopchiks of the nation.

"That is all speculation, Blok," Gopchik said, waving a hand of dismissal.

"Of course," Blok agreed readily, "but it seems that speculation is what is needed at this point— some possible threads of investigation. I do not say it is a fact that Colter is being aided by local Turkish hooligans. I do say, however, that I would look into such a possibility if it were up to me."

"Which it isn't."

"No."

"You never said anything about these theories before," Gopchik said almost angrily. He knew that Remizov was more impressed with the idiot Blok's comment than he was with all of his own efficient efforts to root out Colter if he was still in Batumi. He had men working up and down every street, knocking at doors. Remizov appreciated none of that.

"I never said anything because I was not concerned with the case anymore after turning it over to you," Blok said calmly. "But I think I am right. I think it must be to Turkey that Colter escapes, or tries to. The border guards may even know our dissident friends. Yes. That will be the way. The Turkish border or the sea."

Remizov felt in his guts that Blok was right. There was proof of none of it, but his theory seemed sound. "You have a file on these dissidents. Gopchik?" the colonel asked.

"Thousands of files," Gopchik said lightly. The colonel did not smile in return.

"I suggest you go through them immediately. Immediately. Bring in every available man to help you." Remizov paused, tapping his finger on his knee. "Does anyone come to mind—a ringleader big enough to pull this off, fanatical enough?"

"Mustafa," Blok said. "But then no one ever seems to know where he is. If we knew we could lock him up for life."

"What's his game?"

"Everything there is. Arms, opium smuggling, black market . . ."

Gopchik emitted a gurgling sound, and when Remizov looked at him he thought the man was having apoplexy. Gopchik waved a hand wildly and nearly shouted: "I had one of Mustafa's people brought in tonight. A man named Hashim. He has been accused of smuggling and I wanted to hold him while we searched his boat."

"Well? Bring him up here."

"I signed his release fifteen minutes ago."

"You did not feel he was important?"

"I didn't. Now—God! Five years ago," Gopchik panted, "Hashim was implicated in the murder of another Turk. His friends all swore that he was with them praying at the time. We had to let him go."

"Yes, yes?" Remizov said impatiently.

"The man that was killed. He was murdered with a sledge hammer."

The three men started for the door in hurried

unison. Tyurin had been coming in, coffee in hand. Now he dropped the cup and rushed after them. Their shoes clattered down the deserted corridors as they raced toward the processing desk where prisoners were checked in and out, Remizov filling Tyurin in as they ran.

The officer behind the desk came to his feet as if he had been sitting on a spring, his eyes wide. "What is it, captain?"

"Hashim! Checked out?"

"He left just this minute, captain. He went out toward the back parking lot. That door. If you hurry . . ."

Gopchik was pulling his gun from his belt holster as they reached the back door. They burst through into the night to stand looking across the parking lot. It was a while before they saw the Jeep parked near the street, a tall man, his arms folded, leaning against it. And striding quickly toward the Jeep, Hashim.

Mustafa was leaning against the Jeep, waiting for Hashim, as he had been for four hours. Finally they had released the fisherman and he was making his way through the parked cars toward Mustafa, grinning.

Mustafa saw the door to the KGB headquarters burst open, saw the four men shoulder through.

"Hashim!" one of them shouted and Hashim began to run. A hail of bullets from the doorway cut Hashim's legs from under him and he began crawling toward Mustafa, his face contorted with pain.

Mustafa was already reacting. At the first sight of the KGB men, Mustafa had reached into the Jeep and pulled out his AK-47. Flipping it to full automatic, he leveled a storm of lead at the four policemen. He heard a cry of pain and saw one fall as the others quickly withdrew, dragging the injured man after them.

"Mustafa!" The man on the ground lifted a pleading hand, but Hashim wasn't going to make it. He had stopped crawling now and was lying on his belly in a pool of his own blood. Mustafa recognized the hopelessness of his situation and simultaneously saw the windows being broken out of the KGB headquarters, saw two men running in a crouch toward his position. Mustafa opened up again with the chattering AK-47, and leaped for his Jeep as the guns from the building opened up, spraying the parking lot with bullets.

Mustafa wrenched the Jeep into gear and jack-rabbited it forward. A man with a shotgun loomed up in front of him and Mustafa ducked, jamming his foot against the gas pedal. The windscreen was blown out of the Jeep as the KGB man's shotgun was fired, flame gouting from the muzzle, the lead pellets whining off the Jeep's metalwork. There was a solid thump as the vehicle impacted with a human body, and then there was no sound but the screaming of the Jeep's engine.

Mustafa sat in the shards of glass racing down the streets of Batumi, heading for the docks. He intended on driving the Jeep into the Black Sea, making toward one of his cousins' fishing vessels and getting out to sea before they had him positively identified.

He saw the flashing blue light in the center of the road dead ahead of him and he cranked the steering wheel around violently, the tires screaming. Bullets flew up the street, and Mustafa turned into a narrow alley, barreling through the trash there.

He turned again up Goveashvili Street, but that was blockaded too. Swearing savagely, he U-turned the Jeep again and headed back into town. He wasn't going to make it to the docks. Where then?

An idea occurred to him and he headed back through Batumi at flat-out speed, ignoring all traffic signs, swerving sharply to avoid a truck emerging from a cross street. There was blood on his head and it kept trickling into his eyes. Mustafa drove on, cursing all infidels, Russians, communists, and all of Allah's creatures indiscriminately.

All four wheels left the ground as Mustafa hit the concrete dip at the corner of Bilgya and Revolution. The Jeep landed with a kidney-jolting thud and Mustafa had to fight for control.

He could hear what sounded like dozens of sirens toward the docks, but Bilgya was deserted as he roared up to the Zemloy Garage, leaning on the horn.

The street door opened before Mustafa reached it, and he rolled the Jeep in to sit trembling behind the wheel, his blood still leaking into his eyes, the screech of the closing iron door behind him loud

343

and grating.

"Mustafa!" the garage man said in dismay and shock. "What happened?"

"I want the Land Rover. Take this Jeep out and get rid of it. Quickly."

"Where is Hashim?"

"Dead. Do what I told you. Make sure both gasoline tanks are filled on the Rover. I have to leave the city, and I have to leave now."

"There are people here."

"Get rid of them."

"From Bulyev."

"What! Tonight? What's happening, anyway? Where is he? Did you say there was more than one?" Mustafa asked, climbing from the Jeep.

"Yes. Two of them. The man and the girl."

"What girl!"

"I don't know, Mustafa."

"All right. Where are they, in your room? I'll talk to them. Now do what I told you. Then you'd better leave yourself. It's possible they know about this place."

"Yes, Mustafa."

Mustafa, his automatic weapon slung over his shoulder, was already running up the steps to the garage man's quarters. He burst through the door to come face to face with Colter, who was holding the 9mm Walther level with Mustafa's belly.

"It's you. Thank God," Colter said, lowering the weapon. He couldn't miss the blood smeared all over Mustafa's face, staining his shirt, nor the wild look in the Turk's eyes. "What's happened?"

"Never mind. I have to get the hell out of

Batumi. Now. You coming?"

"Yes."

"All right. Not the girl, though," Mustafa said.

Anna was sitting on the bed, her face puffed with sleep, her eyes dazed.

"She goes," Colter said.

"No. I can't take another."

"She goes, damnit. She's what I came here for. If you ever expect any CIA help, she goes with us."

The Turk was silent for a long moment, then he gave in. "All right," he grumbled. "Bring her and let's go. It's going to be a rough night, though."

"It already has been," Colter said under his breath. He took Anna's hand and they headed down the steps to the garage where Mustafa was already gunning the engine of a pale blue Land Rover. The mechanic was opening the outer door once more.

"Get in," Mustafa said sharply, and they crawled into the back seat. The car door hadn't closed behind Anna when Mustafa found a gear, and with the squeal of tires the vehicle jumped forward, wheeling into the alley beside the garage, speeding eastward toward the foothills beyond Batumi.

Blok's blood stained the wooden floor of the corridor. The doctor, luckily for Blok, had just arrived at headquarters as the shots were being fired. He now had Blok on the cafeteria table, trying to stanch the flow of blood from multiple gunshot wounds.

Remizov stood, hands behind his back, staring at the open door of the communications room. Gopchik's bleating voice went on endlessly, issuing commands that closed all major roads out of Batumi, authorized an immediate search of all fishing vessels in the harbor and the arrest of all known or suspected Turkish separatists.

When he emerged from the communications room, Gopchik's face was glistening with perspiration. There was blood on his white shirt collar, Blok's blood most likely.

"We'll get the bastard," Gopchik promised.

Remizov nodded noncommittally. If Gopchik hadn't started shooting when he had, they might very well have gotten the other one alive. They had turned and started walking toward Gopchik's office when a communications officer stuck his head out the door and called to the KGB captain.

"Comrade Gopchik—urgent communication."

"They've got him," Gopchik said with a wink. Leaving Remizov in the hall, he walked back into the communications room. In a minute he returned, his face pale.

"Well?"

"A call from the Vesely house, colonel. Stepan Vesely is dead, and so is Comrade Uglich."

Remizov cursed slowly, bitterly. "What happened?"

"It's not clear at this time. Vesely seems to have died naturally. Uglich may have been murdered."

"What does the girl say? Anna Vesely?"

"She . . . seems to be gone, Colonel Remizov."

346

Remizov shut his eye. He could smell the disinfectants the doctor had used on Blok, hear the clattering of teletype machines in the communications room. *We must not have a failure.*

"Vesely's dead. The girl—did she leave alone?"

"No one knows. There are no indications."

"Damnit, you had men posted around that house!"

"Someone was obviously negligent, Colonel Remizov," Gopchik said rather eagerly.

"Yes," Remizov was thinking, "and we both know who it was." Huge beads of perspiration stood out on Gopchik's forehead. A clock hanging on the wall overhead ratcheted once and the minute hand moved. Time was getting away from them. Remizov himself was stunned nearly to immobility. What was there to do? Where had they lost the game?

"Do you think the American has the Vesely girl with him?" Gopchik asked finally.

"I don't know. If he does, then we must assume he has Bulgakov's data. What other explanation is there? Colter eliminated Uglich and fled with the girl. Promising her rewards in America." Remizov rubbed his forehead. "I want to know where Colter is," he said very softly. "I want to know."

"The Turk . . ." Gopchik began.

"Forget the Turk. If your field forces can't find him, we can't do anything further. The incident may be totally unrelated. We have to concentrate on Colter. I am here to find Colter and recover certain information. It now appears that the only way I can stop that information from leaving the country and being delivered to a hostile power is to stop Colter. I want an army liaison officer brought down here immediately. I intend to seal the border. Meanwhile, let's get every available man on your dissident files. I want Colter!"

Three hours later they were no closer to finding Colter than before. The army liaison officer had come and gone. The Turkish border was sealed and the border force reenforced by regular army troops. Helicopters were up, although they were of little use until dawn.

"Sir?" A KGB man in a rumpled blue suit and crooked tie came into Gopchik's office, and Remizov looked up from his stack of folders.

"What is it?"

"We found the Jeep."

"You are sure?"

"Yes, sir. It had been sprayed with buckshot. Glass all over the place, traces of blood. A fingerprint check confirms that Mustafa was operating it, if not tonight, then recently. Another set of prints was also found. They belong to a man working for the Zemloy Garage on Bilgya. I've sent a team over there."

"Very good, thank you," Gopchik said.

Remizov listened and then got back to the files, still hoping to turn up something. Finding the Jeep had been decent police work, but it didn't bring them much closer to finding the Turk. Not unless he was hiding on the premises, and that seemed unlikely. Since they had located the abandoned Jeep, it was reasonable to assume Mustafa had another vehicle by now.

Was there a connection between Colter and the Turk? Remizov couldn't ignore the possibility, but neither did he want to waste his time on irrelevancies. He wanted Colter!

Remizov's hands and eyes worked independently of his mind as he sorted through the stacks of files. He was not interested in the bulk of them, since they concerned Turks and their various illegal or reactionary activities. Colter was no Turk. He had passed for a Czech.

The chance seemed to be a long one, but Remizov had hope. He knew exactly what he wanted. A transient, someone new to the area. But what trouble could Colter have gotten into? He would have been extremely cautious. Still, it didn't take much to find yourself on file, on one of the various lists. It was a way of stopping serious trouble before it began. Gopchik had thick files on traffic offenders. Good—that was a possibility, someone who didn't know the traffic laws, who had made a trivial mistake in the past week or so. A man who might have been a Ukrainian. Remizov was at the bottom of the stack. Nothing. Angrily he shoved the pile of reports aside.

"Are there any more?" he asked Gopchik.

The KGB captain looked up with blood-red eyes. "Interagency stuff. Noncriminal complaints."

"Political reports?" Remizov asked, wincing. Denunciations were habitual with many Soviet citizens, and he had waded through such reports before, by the tens of thousands. Ninety percent of them were motivated by jealousy, vindictiveness, or a perverted instinct toward self-preservation.

"Let's have them up," he said with a heavy sigh. There was no other course of action open. The streets were being searched. They could only look here, in the vast files of the State. Tyurin was still going through his stacks, looking pale and drawn. "He knows things are bad for us," Remizov thought.

"Do you want to take a break to eat?" the colonel asked.

"No."

Gopchik was back with a metal cart loaded down with files in paper boxes. "This is the last month's," he said. "There's nothing from the field forces."

Remizov hissed through his teeth and reached for the fresh files. *We cannot suffer failure.* Yet he was failing. Everything was going down in front of his eyes. His career, the respect of his superiors. With ferocity he attacked the political folders.

Nothing had been turned up two hours later although there were two faint possibilities. The first was a temporary laborer at the Makhindzhauri Commune who had been reported for parasitism. His description vaguely matched Colter's, and Remizov had two officers dispatched to the commune immediately, mainly on the weight of the commune's proximity to the Vesely house. The second possibility was a man born in Czechoslovakia whose legal name was Dubček. It was an hour before someone remembered that he was the local Party secretary.

"Sir?" The officer in the rumpled blue suit appeared again as Remizov was stretching his weary arms overhead.

"Yes?"

"They've been through the Zemloy Garage. Shards of glass, spots of blood on the floor. The owner has apparently fled. He's not at home."

"Anything else?"

"Nothing unusual. I made up a list of the vehicles parked in the garage. May be some connection." The KGB officer shrugged.

"May I see that?" Remizov took the list, checking the registered owners. The name leaped at him from the smudged notepad. "Here we go," he said with barely suppressed excitement. "Makhindzauri Commune. Damn!" He dug through his reports again, finding the report on the parasitic worker at Makhindzhauri. Artem Novikov, native of Kiev. Six feet tall, dark hair, blue eyes, thirty to thirty-five years of age.

"Radio those men we sent out there and have them approach with caution," Remizov said.

"Captain Gopchik!" It was the communications officer again. "A message from Makhindzhauri. They say it's urgent."

They were down the hall and into the communications room in seconds. Gopchik got on the radio and began talking to his field operatives.

". . . Hell of a mess," the radio crackled. "The

351

man who turned in the report, Repin, he's dead, shot through the head. The manager of the commune is also dead—appears to be self-inflicted gunshot wound. The only witness is a scatterbrained old crone who's dancing around here like a chicken, moaning and carrying on so that I don't know what she's saying, whether she saw anything or not."

"Demented?" Gopchik asked.

"Close to it. What do you want us to do?"

"Stand fast." Gopchik glanced at Remizov.

The colonel shrugged, "Bring the old woman in. Maybe the doctor can calm her down."

"Did you hear that, Zadkine? Bring the old woman in."

"Yes, captain." The radio crackled to silence.

"Colter," Gopchik said, handing the microphone back to the radio operator.

It was Colter all right, had to be. He had been at the commune, made contact with Vesely and his daughter. After getting the information he wanted, he had killed Uglich and fled in the commune truck. Repin and possibly the commune manager had been in his way. He had finished them. The truck was driven to the Zemloy Garage, and there they met Mustafa.

It was all very neat as a reconstruction, and absolutely useless as a lead to his present whereabouts. They were no closer to Colter than they had been eight hours earlier. Remizov stood glaring at the window where the first gray of morning lightened the skies over Batumi.

"The border must be impenetrable," he said

quietly. "Nothing, no one must be able to cross. That is where he is heading. I am certain of it. We cannot allow it, Gopchik. We are slowly sinking, you and I. The ground is shifting under our feet. And if Colter makes it into Turkey, it is the end for us. He must not be allowed to escape. He must not!"

FIFTEEN

The helicopter made another low pass, its rotors chattering, the sun glinting off the plexiglass of its windows. Colter pulled his head back, tortoiselike, and held Anna to the ground. It was the fourth chopper in half an hour—or the fourth pass by the same one. As it drifted away, olive drab against the clear blue sky, its staccato sound growing faint, Colter rose and looked back into the cave where Mustafa crouched miserably by the dust-filmed Land Rover.

They had spent the night bouncing up and down these dung-colored, dry hills, using goat tracks for roads, as Mustafa worked his way southward. At dawn they had taken shelter in the cave.

"He's gone," Colter said.

"He'll be back," the Turk answered.

Mustafa's enthusiasm was waning. By now, he

felt sure, they had implicated him in the assault on the KGB officers. His only chance was to escape into Turkey, and it looked like their chances were somewhere between slim and none.

Colter took the field glasses from the seat of the Rover and returned to the mouth of the cave. Anna sat cross-legged on the ground, looking up at him.

He scanned the dirt road that marked the border, seeing the picket line of men stretched out as far as the eye could see, seeing the Jeeps, trucks, tents. He followed the telegraph poles to the crossing road where he could just make out the red-and-white-striped kiosk that was the Turkish checkpoint.

Anna slipped her arm around his waist and Colter lowered the glasses, offering her a patently false smile of confidence. "After dark, I think we can make it," he said.

"You think so?" Mustafa's voice was challenging. He seemed to hold Colter responsible for all of his troubles. "Where is the CIA? Why don't they come? Why don't you call in a helicopter to get us out of here?"

"How would I do that, Mustafa? Look, getting us out was your part of the bargain," Colter reminded him. "You said it was simple."

"Yes. Maybe." Mustafa spread his hands. "Before the entire Soviet army was posted on the border! Look at them."

Another chopper was coming up the long, barren valley and Colter withdrew into the cave. Anna sat on the running board of the Rover and

Colter stood beside her, watching the low-flying, thundering helicopter buzz past the mouth of the cave.

"Why don't you tell her the truth—we'll never get across the border now."

"Because it's not the truth," Colter said angrily. "We will make it."

They had to. Life had only begun again three days ago, the day he had first seen Anna. He would not let it end here in some ancient nomads' cave in these empty hills south of Batumi.

"They'll hear the Rover if we try it," Mustafa grumbled.

"Yes. We can't use it."

"Afoot? The woman will never make it."

"Quit finding reasons why we can't make it," Colter said sharply. "You're in this as deeply as we are. You know what will happen if they capture us. What choice do we have except getting across? We'll make it!"

"Yes." Mustafa turned away, crouching against the earth to stare out at the sunny, dry hills.

There was nothing else to do but wait until dark. Colter sat next to Anna, holding her hand, knowing better than Mustafa did what sort of chance they had. He had done some night fighting once, a long while ago, in another life, and he knew too much about nightscopes, infrared scanners, and seismic radar to have any confidence in their ability to creep across the border undetected.

He turned, lifted the wing of Anna's dark hair, and kissed her smooth forehead. He wanted to protect her, to keep her away from any horrors. He knew he would always want that.

"Read to me," he said, nodding at the satchel. Mustafa shot him a disparaging glance.

"Are you sure?"

"Yes. I want to hear it." At least once. Anna removed the manuscript and began to read slowly, softly, the power of her father's words apparent behind her gentle tones, and Colter sat back, lost in the poem, in the woman's voice, waiting until dark.

At sunset Mustafa was like a caged animal stalking the cave, checking and rechecking his AK-47. Colter felt the edginess creeping up his spine. His head thrummed, his heart beat in erratic cadence. Anna sat passively, but her face was deathly pale.

"Well?" Mustafa demanded. There was only a single long filament of crimson coloring the western skies. The hills were deep in shadow.

"One hour," Colter said. The hour passed with merciless inexorableness, yet with aching, tedious slowness, the sweep hand of Colter's watch alternately creeping around the dial and seeming to spin crazily. He held Anna, seeing the tension on her face. Her mouth hung open as if she could not breathe. There were still ten minutes to go when Colter, unable to stand it any longer, rose.

"Come on," he said, and Mustafa hissed through his teeth with some savage emotion.

They walked together to the mouth of the cave and stood looking down the dark canyons, seeing the flicker of lights on the border road.

"Good luck," Mustafa said quietly.

"Luck," Colter answered.

Then they were off, half-walking, half-sliding down the long slope before them. It was cool on the valley floor below. Colter ran in a crouch, his Walther in his right hand, his left gripping Anna's wrist. He could hear her soft, ragged breathing. She had the satchel clutched tightly in her left hand. Mustafa was only a vague dark shadow ahead of them.

They were relatively safe as long as they kept to low ground. Scanning nightscopes could not find them. But to reach the border they would have to emerge from the canyon and cross a hundred yards of nearly flat ground. Anna stumbled and fell and Colter jerked her to her feet. Mustafa had continued on, and now he was out of sight. Colter only hoped the Turk didn't open up with his automatic weapon. He seemed ready to start shooting at the slightest provocation.

They rounded a tight bend in the narrowing canyon floor and came face to face with the lone Russian border guard. The man started to bring his weapon up, but Colter leaped at him, going for the throat. He got his forearm behind the guard's neck and jammed up hard beneath his chin, hearing the chilling snap of his spine.

The guard dropped silently to the ground and Colter stepped back, his facial muscles twitching. He couldn't see Anna's expression, did not want to. He took her wrist and led on.

Five minutes later they were within sight of the border road. They lay panting in a small depression, looking toward the Turkish kiosk. They had elected to cross at the checkpoint rather than at a remote location for two reasons. First, Colter hoped it would be unexpected. Secondly, he did not think the Soviets would have any compunctions about shooting or capturing them simply because they had legally crossed into Turkey. With Turkish border guards watching that was a lot less likely.

Colter still could not see Mustafa. He lay against the hard earth, hearing Anna's breathing. He could hear a voice from the kiosk, a hundred yards away, speaking in Turkish. Not much farther away a Soviet army truck was parked. It appeared to be empty. In the other direction Colter made out three Russian soldiers standing together, speaking in low voices.

It was then that he saw Mustafa. The Turk was pinned down within fifty feet of the Russins. He must have been trying to cross when the soldiers had approached and decided to stop for a cigarette and a talk. He was lying beside the road in the thin shadows of the low-growing brush. Colter could see light glinting on the blued barrel of his weapon. And if Colter could see him, the Russians would too.

Colter rolled toward Anna, putting his lips next to her ear. "At the first sign of trouble, run for the kiosk. Keep running no matter what."

Colter's hand, wrapped around the butt of the Walther automatic, was slick with perspiration. He dried it on his pants leg and shifted position slightly, moving carefully, his eyes alert, constantly searching.

The now-familiar chatter of helicopter blades brought Colter's head around. It was coming in low, following the border road, twin white searchlights turning night into day. The soldiers looked up at the chopper, one man waving.

It passed overhead not more than fifty feet from the ground and suddenly Mustafa was no longer lying in shadows. He was fully exposed, lying in a pool of white light. One of the soldiers gave a sharp exclamation, audible even above the roar of the rotors, and tried to unsling his rifle.

Mustafa came up from the ground, the blinding light washing out his features and coloration. He had his AK-47 at his waist, and, as Colter watched, he sprayed the soldiers with bullets, the muzzle flash of the automatic weapon flame-red.

"Now!" Colter said, and Anna scrambled to her feet. He pushed her forward and began running beside her. A machine gun had opened up from the chopper and Mustafa was riddled with bullets. He danced madly like a marionette as the slugs jerked at his body. Then he was down and motionless, along with the three soldiers he had killed. The chopper still hovered overhead, its rotor blast stirring up dust, its searchlights probing the darkness beside the road.

Anna tripped and went down, and simultaneously Colter saw a soldier leap from the truck parked to the north of the kiosk where the Turkish border guards stood watching it all impassively.

Colter flung himself to the ground as the

Russian soldier opened up with an automatic weapon. Colter returned the fire from the ground, missing badly twice. Then, lifting himself to one knee, steadying the Walther with both hands, he fired again and the soldier was flung back against the truck's radiator. Colter was to his feet again, running toward the kiosk, Anna clinging to his hand, stumbling, the helicopter turning to bring its machine guns to bear.

The kiosk, safety, seemed a thousand miles away. The white glare of searchlights followed them as they ran, their lungs aching, hearts swelling and throbbing in rib cages too small to contain them. There was something in Colter's way, something red and white across the road, and letting go of Anna's hand he leaped it, feeling her fall.

He hit the ground hard, scrambled back and dragged her to him as the angry searchlights, white-hot, seared eyes and flesh, as the guns fell silent.

Silent? Colter hugged Anna to him, shook his head and looked around. The chopper was withdrawing, and now Colter could see that the red and white obstacle was a long pole across the road. A wooden sign dangled from it. In English and Turkish it read: "Halt! You are now leaving Turkey."

The border guard hovered over them and Colter looked up, blinded by the sudden comparative darkness. His hand tightened around the butt of the Walther. The Turkish guard's voice was soft and pleasant.

"Your passports, please?"

"Yes. Yes, I see." Remizov hung up the phone and looked at Tyurin and Gopchik. "They got away. The Turk was killed crossing, but Colter and the woman are gone."

"What we must do then . . ." Gopchik began.

"There is nothing to be done," Remizov said quietly. "Nothing at all. We have failed, that is all."

He picked up the telephone again and asked for the Moscow number. It took a long while to make the connection, a very long time indeed for someone to answer. When Remizov did get through it wasn't the voice he had expected to hear.

"Yes," they heard him say. "I'm sorry. Of course."

He hung up the telephone and looked at the two men with him in the room. "Fyodor is dead. A few minutes ago."

SIXTEEN

Cassidy got out of the car, pushed his glasses up on his nose, and stood regarding the old house. It had a new coat of paint on it and new screening around the porch.

"Is this the place, Cassidy?"

"Yes, sir."

Cassidy's companion grunted. He would rather have been in Washington playing golf on this pleasant summer day than making this follow-up call.

It was all quite pointless. If the man had had anything to say, he would have said it during that three-day session held on his return.

"Mikhail?"

Cassidy looked around to find the old man wearing gardening gloves and an affable, slightly blank smile.

"Uncle Isaak. You remember me?"

"Yes. Mikhail? He is in the house. He is home, go on up."

"Thank you," Cassidy said.

He was indeed home. The door was open and Colter called out to them to come in. They found him tying flies at the kitchen table.

"Oh, no!" Colter laughed. "Cassidy! Get out of here," he said, but he was grinning as he said it. Cassidy's superior was introduced, and the three of them went out onto the screened porch to talk. From the back of the house the faint sound of someone typing was audible.

"A beer?" Colter asked, taking one himself from an ice chest. Both government men refused. Colter sat on the old-fashioned glider, looking expectantly at the two men.

"This is a follow-up debriefing," Cassidy's superior said. "On your unsuccessful journey east."

"Unsuccessful?" Colter repeated, his mouth lifting slightly. "Hardly that."

"Something has come to light?"

"No. There's nothing new."

"We had hoped that your wife had recalled something, discovered something we had missed going through her father's papers."

"Sorry, afraid not. Sure you don't want a beer, Cassidy?"

"Then there is nothing, just nothing you can tell us about the project that we don't already know?"

"No. I'm sorry."

Cassidy's superior shrugged. "That's all we expected, really. It's just that it's best to check."

"Sure."

Colter rose from the glider. The two government men were already moving toward the door. Uncle Isaak stood in the yard, a sack of tulip bulbs in his hand. Above the pines a flight of mallard ducks winged toward the silvery lake beyond the trees.

Colter stood watching as the two men climbed into their car slamming the doors. He was still there, on the screened porch, when Cassidy's superior said, "That was a waste of time."

"Yes, sir."

"Strange man. Did you get what he was talking about? Couldn't make heads or tails of it myself. A successful mission?" Cassidy's superior shook his head uncomprehendingly.

Cassidy started the motor and backed the car around. He glanced at the porch of the old house, seeing Colter standing there, and at his side a beautiful, dark-haired woman. "Yes, sir," Cassidy said quietly, "I think I do know what he meant."

Cassidy's superior glanced sharply at him, looked toward the house, seeing nothing but Colter and his Russian wife, the foolish old man waving goodbye to them, and shrugged again. Maybe it would still be possible to get in nine holes if the plane out of Lewiston was on schedule.

Cassidy pulled onto the highway and began

winding his way down out of the deep green Maine forest. When he glanced in his rearview mirror he could no longer see the old house. Cassidy began whistling a tuneless little song as he guided the car along the uncrowded highway. He whistled it all the way back to Lewiston.

NEW ADVENTURES FROM ZEBRA

DEPTH FORCE (1355, $2.95)
by Irving A. Greenfield

Built in secrecy and manned by a phantom crew, the *Shark* is America's unique high technology submarine whose mission is to stop the Russians from dominating the seas. If in danger of capture the *Shark* must self-destruct—meaning there's only victory or death!

DEPTH FORCE #2: DEATH DIVE (1472, $2.50)
by Irving A. Greenfield

The *Shark*, racing toward an incalculable fortune in gold from an ancient wreck, has a bloody confrontation with a Soviet killer sub. Just when victory seems assured, a traitor threatens the survival of every man aboard—and endangers national security!

THE WARLORD (1189, $3.50)
by Jason Frost

The world's gone mad with disruption. Isolated from help, the survivors face a state in which law is a memory and violence is the rule. Only one man is fit to lead the people, a man raised among the Indians and trained by the Marines. He is Erik Ravensmith, THE WARLORD—a deadly adversary and a hero of our times.

THE WARLORD #2: THE CUTTHROAT (1308, $2.50)
by Jason Frost

Though death sails the Sea of Los Angeles, there is only one man who will fight to save what is left of California's ravaged paradise. His name is THE WARLORD—and he won't stop until the job is done!

THE WARLORD #3: BADLAND (1437, $2.50)
by Jason Frost

His son has been kidnapped by his worst enemy and THE WARLORD must fight a pack of killers to free him. Getting close enough to grab the boy will be nearly impossible—but then so is living in this tortured world!

Available wherever paperbacks are sold, or order direct from the Publisher. Send cover price plus 50¢ per copy for mailing and handling to Zebra Books, 475 Park Avenue South, New York, N.Y. 10016. DO NOT SEND CASH.

THE BEST IN ADVENTURES FROM ZEBRA